Kizuna: Fiction for Japan

Edited and published by Brent Millis

Kizuna: Fiction for Japan
© 2011, Respective authors and translators

ISBN: 978-1466223172

Book Interior design by The Mad Formatter
http://www.TheMadFormatter.com

Cover Design and Related
Christian Krank (front/back cover) @ http://facebook.com/deadearthcomic
Jason Wuchenich (webpage buttons & banners)
David Naughton-Shires (Back/spine design & Facebook icons) [first pages]

All stories, excerpts, and translations are copyright to the respective authors and translators. Reproduction of any kind, without permission of copyright holders, is expressly prohibited. All rights reserved.

Names, characters, places and incidents, are the products of the authors' imagination or used fictitiously. Any resemblance to actual events, locales, or persons, living or dead, is entirely coincidental.

To the people of Japan.

Table of Contents

Introduction
A Quick Note
From Tokyo : Katherine Govier ...10
Downtown Pharmacy : Ken Asamatsu ...12
E-mail to Mother : Lee Pletzers ...15
Small Ocean After Solar : Joseph S. Pulver, Sr. ...18
A Cure for the World : S.A. Gambino ...22
100 Fingers and the Tree : Michael Allen Rose ...25
Ploughman : Nickolas Furr ...28
Orpheus in the Underwear : Garrett Cook ...31
Pocket : Touya Tachihara ...34
The Norwegian Makes Lemonade : Jess Gulbranson ...37
Breakwater : Alvin Pang ...39
HO(locaust) Scale : Robert M. Price ...42
Inconceivable : Kevin Lovelace ...45
Memories of Ken : Junichi Ashikawa ...47
Kamiya Bar : Dan Ryan ...49
Whispers : Adam Joffrain ...54
Jackie Ω Has Gone Too Far : Moxie Mezcal ...56
Throat Wad : Andersen Prunty ...59
The Push of Man : L. Christopher Bird ...61
The Old Man and Honey : Minoru Inaba ...63
Sharan Gali : Richard Wright ...68
Island Swarm : Kirk Marshall ...71
Kopy Cats : Davide Mana ...74
Why Wear Red? : Show Tomono ...78
Thrones & Powers : Jon Courtenay Grimwood ...80
Yara-ma-yha-who : Christene Britton-Jones ...84
Billie_Goat_Gruff_2056 : Philip Overby ...87
Cherry Guard : Yuusuke Tokita ...90
Eternal Case of the Mondays : David Agranoff ...94
The Game : Bradley Sands ...97
Initiation : Naohiko Kitahara ...100
The Ice-Flock Storks of Sørøya : Michael John Grist ...103

Pepperroach : Edmund Colell ...106
Nothingness Dust : Trent Zelazny ...112
Five short Twitter novels : Riri Shimada ...114
Conservation Hero Blues : Made in DNA ...116
Dissolution : Glynn Barrass ...119
Dead and Breakfast : Fulvio Gatti ...121
Quelling the Troll : Nirnara ...125
Plum Blossom : Melissa J White ...128
The Flower : Fumihiko Iino ...131
A Tale of Smoke and Ash : Curt Seubert ...133
Back Beyond The Hedgerow : Elizabeth Black ...136
Sherlock Holmes and the Case of the Giant Rat of Sumatra : John F. Rice ...138
A Summer's Melody : Hiroshi Yamamoto ...141
Humanitas Ex : Volker Baetz ...143
Tarma's Song : Andrew Freudenberg ...147
The Power of Perspective : Terrie Czechowski ...149
Legends : Lucía González Lavado ...152
If Only Flowers : Mie Takase ...155
Dial Tone : Stephen A. North ...157
The Starlet and the Fishman : Ran Cartwright ...159
Recollections : Ukyou Kodachi ...162
The Loft in the Sky : Danilo Arona ...164
Last Embrace : David Naughton-Shires ...167
The Girl with Eyes in the Back of Her Head : John Shirley ...169
Heart of an Angel : Jonathan Moon ...172
The Music Box : Tadashi Ohta ...174
Not Alone in the Dark : Richard Salter ...176
Natsumi's Diary : Midori Tateyama ...179
Sweet Hearts : Grant Wamack ...181
Appointment at the Oji Inari Shrine : Massimo Soumaré ...183
The Story without a Key : Yufuko Senoh ...186
The Feast of the Fly : Berry Sizemore ...188
A Second Metamorphosis : Ash Lomen ...191
Homecoming : Adam Breckenridge ...194
Mom, Dad and Hiro : Yasumi Kobayashi ...197
The Bubbling Road of Self-Loathing : Jason Wuchenich ...200

That Day… : Ryuto Hijiri …203
The Dream-colored Morning : Vittorio Catani …205
The End of the Royal Palace and the Kingdom : Joji Hayashi …209
The X-ray : Kevin David Anderson …211
The Mermaid Princess' Love, Curse and… : Tamao Kanroji …212
Walking the Hog : Michael Moorcock …215
That Long Day : Shinya Gaku …223
Acknowledgments
Contact

Introduction

It was March 11, 2011. I was in a meeting with a client when the earthquake struck. It was jarringly long. My client and I entertained the idea of leaving the building, but nixed the idea pretty quickly. The building didn't come down on top of us, so we figured everything was okay. Much later, we would understand just how lucky we were we were not on the other side of the island.

Earthquakes in Japan are 'no big deal.' As you will learn from Mr. Gaku, one of the Japanese authors in this anthology, everyone expects earthquakes in Japan; what they don't expect is for the earthquake to be so devastating that it claims nearly 20,000 lives when a follow-up tsunami strikes. But this is the reality of the Japan we live in today. It is a lesson I hope none of us soon forgets.

In the days and weeks that followed, overwhelming scenes of complete carnage streamed through the television and into my life, and indeed the lives of the millions (perhaps billions) who watched. I turned to social networking sites to offset the mounting horror and stress of witnessing so much pointless death and destruction. Familiar faces, and new ones too, offered comfort. It helped. And it didn't. It was hard to watch it all happen, and not be able to do something.

But what? I have a family. (At the time, a pregnant wife and two young sons. At the time of writing, I am blessed with a healthy newborn daughter.) Getting up to go and help was not an option. Yet, I was *compelled* to do something, even after our family had given to charity numerous times.

Musicians and artists began donating proceeds from their current shows to organizations like Red Cross. Could I write something? Seemed like a good idea. The problem was, would sales of my ebooks increase enough to make it worthwhile just because I was offering to give the money to charity? I thought not. I'm not a well-known author.

I turned to my friends in the writing community. Would they contribute? Sure they would! Soon I had ten authors. Then twenty. Thirty... Author friends of author friends were submitting. Authors from Spain, Singapore, Japan, Italy, New Zealand, Germany, France, America, the UK, Australia and Canada all stepped forward. I was stunned. Even now, as corny as it sounds, the gratitude I feel at their selfless desire to help makes me very misty-eyed.

Over seventy authors in total have contributed to this anthology. Approximately ninety percent of it is original work written specifically for this anthology. And while you might see it somewhere after, it was here first.

Kizuna: Fiction for Japan is a mixed-genre anthology of short fiction, most of it 1000 words or under. It boasts internationally-known authors like Michael Moorcock, Ken Asamatsu, Jon Courtenay Grimwood, John Shirley, Shinya Gaku, Vittorio Catani, Robert M. Price, Joseph S. Pulver, Sr., and Alvin Pang; genre-authors like Bradley Sands, Jason Wuchenich, Andersen Prunty, and Garrett Cook; and independent authors like Trent Zelazny and Glynn Barrass. One hundred percent of the proceeds will go to helping orphans in the disaster-devastated areas of Miyagi, Iwate and Fukushima via the NPO, Smile Kids Japan.

Please help spread the word of Kizuna, a word that means "bond" in Japanese, and create your own bond with the people of Japan.

Thank you,
Brent Millis, editor/publisher
Niigata Prefecture, Japan
July 20, 2011

From Tokyo
(excerpt from *The Printmaker's Daughter*)
Katherine Govier

From my hotel window on Tokyo Bay I watch a lighted Ferris wheel spin slowly in the dark. I wish its little buckets could raise the dead souls of Edo buried under the rubble of World War II, the ash of earthquakes, fires, the garbage of eras. But they can't.

Strange mission, looking for a woman painter whose name meant "Hey, you!", who almost never signed her work, was briefly famous, and then disappeared – one hundred and fifty years ago. Another country, another language, another century. Am I mad? Hokusai's daughter. Do I think I will see her, walking on the street? In her indigo striped cotton kimono with the red trim wearing her wooden clogs, her head cocked at that extreme angle that said, 'You may think I'm nobody, but don't be so sure"?

Who was she? Flourishing woman, she wrote. Or drunken woman; the characters could mean either. It depends how you read them.

But how funny. On my JR Pass, embossed and in foil, is the Great Wave. Her father's image: straight out of old Japan. And she was there, under the snarling lip of it.

At Asakusa, I walk the long pink aisle under plastic cherry blossoms, passing hawkers of chestnuts and straw sandals. I pass through the Kaminari-mon Gate, five times my height. Between its persimmon pillars a giant lantern is squeezed, red with huge black characters. I love the gaudiness. Inside the temple grounds, incense burns in a large round drum. People scoop the dark smoke over their faces.

And it begins. I can sense it. Maybe it's because there are still trees here, protected by their proximity to the sacred. Or because in their shade I hear the Holy Crows, conducive of long life. There is the drone of the monks, chanting. The clunk of the padded mallets marking time. The old well, with stone bucket; she would have drunk from there.

I leave by the covered market, now clogged with people. They come at me, face after face, an army of the present day. I shift to the right, to the left, cannot walk in a straight line, can't get past, can only shuffle along with everyone else. I try not to lose her. 6.30 train: Ueno Station to Nagano. 8.30: change for Obuse, on a slow commuter. Kids on and off in school uniforms. 9.15: I'm there. Kubota-san is waiting for me under the station roof. We've never met. He looks nervous: I don't blame him, facing the odd arrival of the lady writer, searching for someone long dead. But he told me she was here. "According to collective memory", he wrote. *kolekutibu memori*.

He shows me the letter from Oei. It is in her hand, and probably written in 1843. He reads it to the translator, who repeats it in English. And then her voice comes out of the silence, over that long, long distance: "We have never met," she says, "but I trust that you are well..."

Katherine Govier's fiction and non-fiction appears in the United Kingdom, Canada, the United States, and the Commonwealth. She won Canada's Marian Engel Award for a woman writer in mid-career, and the Toronto Book Award. *Creation* was a New York Times Notable book of 2006. She has published 9 novels and 3 short story collections, and edited two collections of travel essays. *Three Views of Crystal Water* and *The Ghost Brush* are set in Japan. The latter appears in the US in November 2011 as *The Printmaker's Daughter*. Katherine has lived in Washington D.C., and London, England and now lives in Toronto. Her web address is http://www.govier.com.

Downtown Pharmacy
Ken Asamatsu
Translated by James A. Smith

It was during my first year at university that a friend of mine suffered a broken heart. This was more than merely a case of severe heartbreak – he had been betrayed. So in despair, he decided to kill himself. Pondering over the method with which he would put an end to it all, he decided upon suicide by poisoning. However, he was a guy of somewhat weak resolve. He did not feel that he could go through with it while sober. Which is why he decided to hit the bottle, drink himself to the verge of oblivion, purchase some over-the-counter drugs, and die under the momentum of his inebriation. With this in mind, he contacted a well-meaning friend and invited him out for a drink.

That well-meaning friend was me. We started drinking in the early evening. I provided him with a shoulder to cry on and listened to him curse the girl at whose hands he had met with betrayal, all the while draining cup after cup of alcohol and wiling away the time in anticipation of his sob story coming to an end. We left the bar at 11 o'clock. We started walking through the outskirts of the downtown area, but at that time the last vestiges of the energy crisis meant that the stores all closed early. There weren't even many drinking establishments that were open. We continued walking through the forlorn and sombre district which did not resemble downtown Sapporo at all.

After a while, we came upon a dirty side street called *Susukino Hanakoji*. It was lined with drinking establishments. Turning down the street, a sign appeared ahead of us.

Thinking back now, I understand that it was rather a peculiar sign. It consisted solely of the word 'medicine' in red on a white background. The meandering characters looked as if they had been written with a shaky hand. However, we were drunk and didn't give it much thought.

We burst into the pharmacy. Inside was a man in a white coat. I remember his strangely clean face; it seemed as if he had just taken a bath.

"I need something to help me sleep," said my friend, his speech somewhat slurred.

"I have just the thing. You will have a good night's sleep with these," laughed the man as he produced a box of medicine. It cost one thousand yen. My friend bought the box and we got on the subway at Susuki Station. On the train, my friend opened the box. Inside was a glass bottle containing pills of a garish colour that, for some reason, hurt my eyes to look at.

Allowing the box to fall to the floor, my friend eyed the label and muttered, "There are sixty pills. Right, if I take all of these in one go, I will no longer have to breathe the same air as that girl." He got off the train at Sumikawa Station.

A few days later, I heard from a second friend that my friend had failed in his bid to commit suicide. "As he took the sleeping pills after all that alcohol, they had no effect. But from what I hear he was in a lot of pain," said my friend with what appeared to be a smirk.

According to him, my friend did not die but was taken to hospital in an ambulance, where, after having had his stomach pumped and receiving an enema, he had his contaminated blood drained and was given a transfusion. The story up until this point is fine. My friend got what he deserved and, at any rate, had known what he was getting into. I had no sympathy for him whatsoever. However, what made me frown was something the friend who told me this subsequently let slip.

"You know, it's strange. It seems that the medicine he took was an extremely potent sleeping pill of the sort which shouldn't be obtainable without a prescription. If he had been found any later he would have died."

"Don't be ridiculous! That medicine was over-the-counter..." I was about to say, but held my tongue as I did not want him to find out that I was with our mutual friend when he bought the medicine. I thought what he said was improbable. The medicine had been purchased over the counter and had come in a labeled bottle, after all. It is said that criminals always return to the scene of the crime, and at this point I was feeling a bit like a criminal. But I just couldn't let this go. Thus I made my way back to that drinking establishment from the night before. I had a drink at the same time as on the evening of the incident, and went to the area called *Susukino Hanakoji*. However, the pharmacy was nowhere to be seen. Nor was there a sign with the word 'medicine' written in red on white in meandering characters that looked as if they had been written with a shaky hand. All that remained was the neon of the bars and cabarets. Then it struck me. The kind of pharmacy where a couple of drunks could go in and ask for sleeping pills, and after having been assured of being able to get "a good night's sleep", obtain said sleeping pills of the kind of strength that would necessitate a prescription, does not exist in Japan. If it did, then one thing is certain: it would be operated by Death himself.

Almost forty years have passed since that day. Susukino has changed beyond recognition. There are no vestiges of the past. Even so, when I return to Sapporo and go for a drink with old friends, inevitably I always return to that place where *Susukino Hanakoji* was located. I have to make sure... that that sign with the word 'medicine' written in meandering characters is no longer there.

Ken Asamatsu was born in Sapporo, Hokkaido in 1956. He graduated Toyo University and started work at Kokusho Kankokai, famous in Japan as the publisher of Lovecraft and many other works of horror and fantasy. His debut work as an author was *Makyo no Gen'ei* (*Echoes of Ancient Cults*), in 1986. He continues to write extensively in the weird historical and horror genres. While remaining extremely interested in the Cthulhu Mythos, lately he has been concentrating on weird historicals set in the Muromachi period (1333-1573) http://homepage3.nifty.com/uncle-dagon/

E-mail to Mother
Lee Pletzers

Hi Mum,

Sorry I haven't written in a long time, I've been really busy. I found a place to stay at last, it's not great like home, but it's a start. I'm sharing with three others and one's a girl. Brandon, Josh and Sarah. I think she likes me. We were watching a movie last night and she fell asleep against my shoulder. I didn't mind.

I know what you are thinking. Girls are a distraction to my studies, but she's not. Really. I study every night. I know what is required of me.

Thank dad for the introduction to his parent company. I have an interview there tomorrow.

I know this is short, but I promise to write again tomorrow.

Your loving son

~

Hi Mum

See, I said I'd write today.

I went to the interview this afternoon. It was at 1pm, and man was I nervous. I didn't think I would be, you know, Dad works for them as well. I know I'm heading in a different direction, I hope he understands why.

They asked some difficult questions, especially about astronomy. Unfortunately I have to admit I struggled to find the answers they wanted to hear. They asked about timing, star alignment, and dimensional doorways. They seemed pleased with my answers but I have a bad feeling I didn't do very well, despite their smiles.

I have to cut this short Mum, I have a date tonight. Remember the girl I told you about, well she wants to take me to a seafood restaurant to celebrate my interview. I know you don't approve of human girls but I am quite drawn to her.

Sorry Mum, I have to follow my heart on this one.

Your loving son

~

Dear Mum

I am in love. Sarah is beautiful and kind and last night at the restaurant she asked me to go steady with her. I know! It sounds so old fashioned but coming from her, it was refreshing. We dined and walked the shoreline hand in hand. The stars glowed brightly, the moon was full. The cosmos smiled upon us.

Ha! I just read what I wrote and I sound like a fool. But I won't delete it. Oh, I have a second interview next week. They want me to meet with some other people before making a decision. It sounds like a panel interview. They make me nervous. I'm sweating just thinking of it.

I promise to study until the information slides out of my ears. And I will brush up on Astral-Dimensional Travel as I have a feeling that will be the theme.

I better get to it.

Talk to you next week Mum.

Your loving son

~

Dear Mum

I hate humans! I caught Sarah in bed with Josh yesterday. We had a big argument and she said something about having a free spirit and that my self esteem must be very low if I couldn't handle her being with Josh as well. She asked me to go steady, so I don't understand this.

I'm fuming with rage, Mum, and I don't know what to do. The bumps on my lip quiver and thoughts of destruction fill my head. My hands are often clenched fists.

Will this pass? I don't like this pain. Emotion sucks.

Argh! I'm so damn angry. But I must calm down for the interview tomorrow. Wish me luck.

Your loving son

~

Dear Mum

I got the job! They knew I was the right choice. There were several higher ups in the interview and as expected they wanted to question me on Astral-Dimensional Travel. I answered all the questions with confidence and without pause.

Then they threw me a question out of left field. They wanted to know what my driving desire was and how I would put that into practice. I think I knew what they wanted to hear. And if I had been asked this a couple of days ago or at the first interview my answer would have been different.

You see, Mum. My interaction with Sarah taught me a lot about the human race and their inadequacies as a species. I know why we must hunt them and why all of us are born with human masks until we reach awakening.

I await that time with eagerness, mother. I swear I do. I wish it were now. The anger has turned to hatred, even after slaying Sarah and Josh, I do not feel sated. You will be happy to know I used my hands, tore her skin apart and ripped out her lying, cheating heart. Her cry for help fell on deaf ears as my heart was ice towards her. Josh just stood there, splattered in Sarah's blood. Shock had a hold of him. He muttered something as I approached but I know not what he said. Nor, Mother, did I care. I don't blame him for bedding Sarah. She was a luscious woman and felt so nice, irresistible. Her skin was soft and tender to the touch. It tore easily. Josh could not control himself, so I assign him no blame. I still crushed his face with the television. If Brandon was here I would destroy him as well, but he is away for the weekend.

The company is coming to pick me up tomorrow for a location transfer for training. Tell Dad, I'm off to R'lyeh. The mysteries of the universe await me and I am eager to study them. I am told there will be a period of sleep before I can return to Earth. This worries me not. For when I return I vow to bring all the Elders with me and lay waste to this land and the hairless monkeys that walk it.

I will destroy them all.

This is my last email, mother. I promise I will study hard. I will master the magic and the secrets of the cosmos. And I will bring the Old Ones, the Elders, back home.

Your loving son
Cthulhu

Lee Pletzers is the author of three novels. He currently resides in Japan. http://kobefiction.we.bs

Small Ocean After Solar
Joseph S. Pulver, Sr.
(for AM)

"Angelis."
    Very first thing that seized you was her eyes. Like galaxies across the room, they could fold joy around the contradictory twitching of your attempts at penance. Purge afflicted from the afflicted too.
    Stared, guess it was more like taking cutlery to dessert, my glee and hunger was massive. Dreamed, climbed the stash of her *Forever is the easiest thing to do.* They drew me—another poet trying to translate desire.
    Then the shoulders. Dune-soft bedspreads of mercy. More dreams lit my drift.
    Longings.
    Then she spoke. The poetry of birds opening delightful weather. I ascended into air.
    As women so often do, Angelis didn't turn away when I nodded my simple hello.
    Smiled in fact.
    The stars brightened, gutted my bleakness. My blood liked the velvet air.
    Another, "Hi." Another smile. The words of night *andante amoroso*; reborn in the hands that found me.
    Hearing was kiss.
    Her smile became a laugh. A wave. Jobim was playing. I felt like a monk—*Vespers,* My soul doth magnify—
    Her good was enormous, all feathers and sky and red ribbons—the sweetness of poppies.
    Screwed my courage up enough to ask.
    She said, "Yes."
    We danced, her hand, a pastry so tempting you could not turn away from the perfection of its language, on the small of my back, mine on hers. Swans without tears. The song was a street of lilies. And her shoes were off.
    I was swimming in joy and flames.
    The hair on the back of my neck spent a lot of time on what will be. I let it ride and prayed. Could have sworn her smile said plenty of time. To a drowning man not even close.
    Her scent was in my hands. My landscape could taste the magnitude of her forget me nots.
    Jobim's "Wave" swayed back out to the moonlit-guarded deeps. We drifted into a booth. A corner and a candle. Jacob Young, "Blue" "Evening Air", subtle. Spacious, the quiet fire of a sparrow's song. The guitar and the trumpet suited her.

Sat. No schemes.

I was so nervous I forgot to smoke. Was glad I didn't have to write and spell anything. Had I, *just now* and *a little more* would have been Homeric undertakings.

Weightless, I hung on the just now. And if.

She was the perfect countervoice to the places where my swelling tongue of belief lay out. Forgot my blues as she exorcised ghosts. Began leaning on never ending.

Too many stars in my ears, I didn't see the emergency. Didn't drift in, no one counted it down, came right out of the nightwoods. Nimble as a fist spitting nuclear. Spread out grim. 4th degree burn engraving the space your clothes occupy fucked unaware hard.

Shots fired. Screams going to hell in the splash.

Blood, 3 race run. Dying blooming.

Jumped. The whole room.

A broken glass that wouldn't be hefted again.

"What?" Eyes without a wishing well for their pennies.

"*He's*.... Dead."

No one dialed the hospital to sing. Wouldn't be no charts or pills. No tending by steady hands.

"*Dead?*"

Collapsed would stay collapsed.

Calendars split. Gasps jumping out of their affluent illusions. Faces in fantasies of hurry. Flood and tongues blindly rolling out the doors, trying to.

A dozen hunkered down under tables.

Panic at ground level for me too. My face 6 inches from Angelis' knee. My broad scurry of thoughts are scraping, "Robbery?"

And she's sitting there, could have been waiting for the waitress to drop by with a glass to cure appetite or for the next song to crackle. I'm under the damn table, my blood aggrieved thunder, and she's just sitting there. Neon-lit. Hard, and soft.

High noon and she has not inched.

I'd turn to go if I could; rabbit-lightning in my heels wants to.

Black boots. Heels, long dark-road worn.

Had the idea there might be a knife or terminal on the serving plate. Had to look.

Silver cross lapel pins. Cleric's collar. Soul of holy bells and bloody plan locked. Loaded all the way to go. Witch hunter. Hand of the Cross, white and straight, crusader-lean. Eyes that had never prayed for cash or upstream. Wrath ready to swoop fury and happy to sing flush.

An old chase as conclusion. Guns ready to grunt and judge.

"Soul-robber. I bring you the wind of cemetery." Terms articulated.

Tattoos of weight and hate don't touch her slow and soft.

Angelis grazed him with a rock smile. "Migrations." Sounded like a shrug. "Finish it here."

"It is time for your sin to become ashes."

"Time for something, yes." Smile that would have made permafrost shiver.

Zero hold-the-amnesia drove up and parked.

Figured hardcore was about to rev-up way over wild side and I was going to be standing in a pit fight without an umbrella or a wet suit. Didn't hear anything crank up or an alarm go off. The balletic grace I'd danced with became a panther. Iron hands. Something not challenged by human limitations skipped, ambled, and went for the jugular.

No shots fired. No struggle.

Blood.

One more down. Dying blooming.

Looked at the fortress delivered to worse, just a carcass on the floor. Wondered what the ring of fire counterfeiters in Hell would make of the one-man kill posse whose Icarus wings didn't get him to Heaven's door.

Hand after violence offered. I reached up. Accepted it.

Letting her guide me up; her hand, velvet to my fear.

She sat back down. Looked at my chair.

Invitation accepted.

I sat.

The current her smile offered hadn't changed directions. Velvet moon soft, its ripples lingered on my dreams, offered a pillow.

Angelis.

"Devil or Angel" on the jukebox. She laughed. Something playful was crisp in her eyes.

Empty joint. Chairs that couldn't stay on their feet.

Nothing in the shadows.

Confessions of vodka on the floor. Bar without an addiction or elbow on it.

Her. Not a soft hair out of place.

Me, eyes never leaving her face.

Face to face. Hers holy, glowing.

Very first thing with Angelis was her eyes. Like galaxies, every ounce bell, book, and candle. Glued to them. They drew my let it be me.

Then the shoulders. Skin's a keeper you want to sip.

Then she spoke. "I can show you the tiger inside." Held out her hand. "Let this be medicine for your solitude."

Let my washed-up roll back out to sea. Took it.

Hayat's Small Ocean after solar. Some things got deleted when I left my lonely winds to be confirmed by some other motion.

Didn't stop to wave bye-bye to horizon getting ready to cough its garish sun.

I slipped quietly into the seat of a new universe. Caught never before. The sound of water. A moonlight drive on a road by the aquarium ocean, its arrows not distracting me. Didn't need to slip into are we there yet, there were whispers of resolution in her eyes.

Far from the coiled blocks and the instant storms spraying full-blown Hitler-tongue over next of kin and the coffee shops and the bland neighborhoods that fool their hands with attention spans renting space in whiskey glasses. Little place in the foothills by the sea. The curiosity of summer insects pushing through the grass, their thirst excited enough to come right up to the terrace.

Angelis has a double-wide coffin. White lining pale and soft as her naked shoulder. Her lips on my lips, between them, a poem taking stars from each other. A conversation that ends summer; a kiss from a rose.

Two drops of blood on my neck.

Two on hers.

The taste of her voice in my veins.

Interlaced fingers.

Lid closed. The boat of being really alive, awash in satin darkness and a world of closer. Her eyes—shores of Now uncovered—are chalices.

Angelis kisses my cheek. "We'll pick flowers and drain the sugar tonight."

[a wave of various Jobim, Jacob Young, Anat Fort, and Pat Metheny songs]

Joseph S. Pulver, Sr., is the author of the Lovecraftian novel *Nightmare's Disciple*, and he has written many short stories that have appeared in magazines and anthologies, including Ellen Datlow's *Year's Best Horror* and S. T. Joshi's *Black Wings* and many anthologies edited by Robert M. Price. His highly–acclaimed collections, *Blood Will Have Its Season* and *SIN & Ashes* were published by Hippocampus Press. His new novel, *The Orphan Palace* will be released by Chomu Press in 2011. His work has been praised by Thomas Ligotti, Ellen Datlow, Laird Barron, S.T. Joshi, and many other notable writers and editors. http://thisyellowmadness.blogspot.com/

A Cure for the World
S.A. Gambino

I removed the needle from my arm and sighed, relieved that I'd finally developed the right serum. For too long I had locked myself away in my homemade lab searching for it.

Those idiots at Biotropy had fired me for not following company procedures. They had other plans for my research, but I had my own agenda. They said I was self-destructive and walked me out. What did they know? Everyone in the world would see what I had created, and understand what I'd accomplished.

I smiled and blotted the blood off of my arm with a cotton ball, certain that everything would be fine. I had really done it this time – the lab rats had reacted favorably to the final tests.

Stupid assholes at Biotropy had no idea I had snuck several samples out from under their noses. But what did it matter? This was *my* creation. I'd use it how I had originally intended.

I sat down feeling the warmth of the liquid coursing through my body. *Just relax and let it do the job. You've discovered the cure for mankind.* I couldn't wait to share it with the world.

Suddenly my blood began to boil. Sweat poured down my face. I screamed in agony, dropped to the floor and convulsed.

"Take the pain; this is for the good of mankind," I moaned out loud and then passed out.

When I woke, my body screamed with aches. I pulled myself up off the floor. Fever had set in. My legs wobbled as I walked. Looking up at my wall clock, I noticed that I'd been passed out for the entire evening. Hints of sunlight beamed though the curtains. I smacked my lips. They were dry; I needed something to drink.

In my weakened state, it took me a while to shamble up the basement stairs. I poured myself a glass of water from the kitchen tap and greedily consumed it.

My hand was covered in red splotches. In the bathroom mirror, they covered my body. *Already. That was fast*, I thought.

My body was afire. I splashed cool water over my face to cool myself. My long black hair only worked to intensify the heat. I pulled it back into a ponytail. Reddish lines shot through my retinas. Strange, this was not a symptom I had noticed before. I changed out of my sweat-drenched clothes.

The time had come to show the world my discovery...

I drove as fast as possible, but my eyesight was blurring on me. I pulled the car over and got out. I'd made it downtown. Good enough. There were great number of people walking; the sidewalk was packed. I joined them, brushing up against the denizens of the city – letting my hands graze theirs.

Some gave me strange looks. Perhaps they'd noticed the splotches on my hands. They had gotten worse. Surely my face was a disturbing sign.

Filled with mucus, my throat burned, and an incessant cough infected the air. More folks took notice. This was happening a little faster than I had anticipated. It was important I made it to Biotropy.

I blundered through the crowds turning it into a game of human bumper cars. Giggling, I wiped away mucus as it dripped from my nose. Coughs exploded from my chest like biohazardous bombshells. A gentleman in a suit and tie gave me a disgusted look. I reached out for him. He backed away in haste.

My vision was impaired now from the watering itch that had invaded it. I was going to need help to get to the lab. But who would do so?

From my left, a male voice spoke to me. "Do you need some help?"

"Yes, please. I'm trying to make it to Biotropy labs. Can you take me there?" I asked.

He took my hand and guided me. He spoke as I stumbled along after him, but his words were lost to me until he pressed with a repeated question, "Is this the place?"

I could barely see the front of the building. My legs went numb. I fell to the ground. The stranger asked if I was OK. I could feel the wedding ring on his hand.

"Yes, thank you. Go home to your wife and kiss her," I said. He released my hand, and I smiled as he disappeared.

Then, a familiar voice. "Ms. Smith, are you OK? It's Hal from the front desk. I saw you as I was walking into the building."

I hacked all over him as Hal tried to help me up. Someone yelled "Dial nine-one-one!"

I blacked out.

I woke up in a hospital bed. Somewhere close people were chattering. I gathered that they had no idea what was wrong with me. With great effort, I lifted my head – blurry images of other patients around me in the ER. My cough returned. The taste of blood filled my throat. I moaned. The pain was so bad I could hardly take it anymore. The nurse put a needle in my arm, and I started to feel numb. I was glad; the pain was getting to be too much.

Trying to remember … Did I make it to the lab? A memory of Hal helping me returned. He took my arm and walked back into the lab. *Good*, I thought.

My research there had led to my release from contract; a virus that had driven an entire monkey species to the edge of extinction. With the exception of those with a natural immunity, it was 100% lethal. My co-workers discovered I was working on a strain that would infect humans. It would give the human race a fresh start. It would cleanse this wretched world.

The folks I had infected today would be the key to a world pandemic. I laughed. Blood rose into my throat. I choked on it.

As death pillowed my weary body, she leaned in to comfort me with words, "You'll be alright dear."

Yes. In fact, soon the whole world would be.

———

S.A Gambino works as a full-time sales manager and part-time horror writer. Current publications include: *Lilith's Revenge and Stories of Femme Fatale,* a novel by Panic Press; *Vicious Verses and Reanimated Rhymes,* by Coscom Entertainment; *End of Days 2, Love is Dead,* and *Book Of The Dead 3* by Living Dead Press; and *Zombonauts* and *Letters of the Dead,* by Library of the Living Dead. Several other horror short stories are due out through Library of the Living Dead in 2011. When not writing, she enjoys photography, reading, and playing with her three dogs. She currently resides in Kansas City, Missouri.

http://www.amazon.com/S.A-Gambino/e/B003RQHAW0/

100 Fingers and the Tree
Michael Allen Rose

Once, there was a man with one-hundred fingers; on each finger he wore a different adornment, and one day this man – Queue was his name – came across an unusual plum tree growing from a crack out in front of his house.

Queue was easily distracted, which is why his first finger had a red ribbon tied around it, leading off around his body to parts unknown. It was there to remind him.

The tree had interrupted his daily journey to the mailbox. He stood over the tree in the hot mid-day sun, looking down. It was small, but had somehow forced its way up through the concrete and grew right in the middle of the sidewalk. Queue hated to see such a delicate thing in the path of all those feet.

He carefully dug the tiny plum tree out of the crack, holding as much soil around the roots as he could, and cradled the sapling gently. The moisture dampened the folded scrap of newspaper wrapped around his second finger. He wrapped twelve other fingers around the stalk to protect it, careful not to damage the stem. The metal rings on each of those fingers helped weave an armor around the tree; gold and silver down to tin and brass.

He walked back home with his new cargo. Opening the gate proved difficult, but he managed to brush against the latch with the knuckle of his fifteenth finger, around which a dusty rubber-band was stretched.

"I'm going to plant you right by the fence." Queue smiled down at the tiny tree, and placed it gently on the ground next to the white picket fence outside his house.

A musical voice called out, making Queue's heart skip a beat. "Hello, Queue." His neighbor, Ache, stood on her tip-toes on the other side of the fence, her emerald eyes just able to peek over the top at him. "What do you have there?"

Queue swallowed hard, as he wrung a dozen other fingers together, nervous sweat pooling in his palms. The thimble on finger number twenty-seven caught drops of his perspiration like dew, and the sweatband around finger number thirty lapped it up like a thirsty animal.

"It looked lonely," he said.

Ache's laughter tinkled like an orchestral triangle. "Do trees get lonely?"

He had been in love with Ache since he had met her, which seemed like an eternity ago. He knew however, that it had only been one year, fifteen days, twelve hours and fourteen minutes. He had been keeping careful track using the tiny calendar fastened around his forty-third finger. He glanced down now, unable to speak, as Ache stared down at him with an amused grin. As he simmered with impotent rage at his inability to speak to her, he took a visual inventory of fingers fifty through fifty-nine, all of which held regrets and heartaches marked by tattoos, scars and scrapes in small fractal patterns.

Queue felt the weight of the letter in his pocket. He looked downward again, as his hands automatically continued re-planting the tiny tree. He used the hooked ring on his sixty-first finger as a spade, clearing a space for the plum tree.

"Do you think this is a good spot?" he asked, blushing.

Ache reached over the fence and touched his arm as he planted the tree in the hole he'd made. He felt himself grow warm as her fingertip traced the width of his shoulder. "It's perfect." Queue glanced up at Ache as the woven straw ring around finger number seventy swept the soil back into the hole around the little tree. He could just see the top of Ache's head from where he crouched, but even the way her hair cascaded around her eyes made him want to weep with joy. "See you, Queue" she said, smiling, as she receded from view behind the fence.

Queue stood up and peered over the fence. He watched Ache walk to her little house and disappear through the front door. A faint trail of barely perceptible ribbons floated in her wake that only he could see, and each one made his one hundred fingers ache with want. Glancing down at the mood ring he wore on his seventy-third finger, he saw a pink that was gradually fading to a deep blue, and pondered its meaning.

He stared down at the diamond ring on his eighty-second finger. A flaw glinted in the heart-shaped diamond, a crack in the perfect facade that only he knew was there. He reached into his pocket and pulled out the letter. It had been written one year, fifteen days, one hour and sixteen minutes ago. Updating it was unnecessary: everything he felt for Ache poured into the letter like blood without need for pen and ink.

He gazed down at the plant and saw that during his absence from it, a ripe, juicy plum had appeared. Reaching down with deft fingers, he picked it up and took a bite. Something caught between his teeth, and he used the nettled wooden splinters fastened around finger number ninety-four to pick it out. It was a length of red ribbon, which he followed down and around his body, around the tree, back and forth over the fence, stretching from his first finger all through the puzzle pieces of his life. As he approached the end of the trail, expecting to see the ribbon tied around his one-hundredth finger, a paean to his cyclical nature, he was surprised to find that the digit in question was missing. Ninety-nine was there, with its green plastic ring from a cereal box, but finger one-hundred was a ghost. The last few inches of ribbon wound their way into the envelope that he held in his hand, and now he noticed the bulk and the weight of his hopes and his passions along with one finger-shaped lump.

He strode to the mailbox without stopping, dropped the letter into the box and walked back home, whistling a sweet and obscure melody, harmonizing with the sun.

———

Michael A Rose is a writer, performance artist, producer and musician living in Chicago with a cat named Dandelion. Originally from the frozen wastes of North Dakota, Michael's plays have been produced in New York, Chicago, Portland, Denver and several other major cities. He is founder and artistic director of RoShamBo Theatre, and releases industrial and experimental music under the pseudonym Flood Damage. His debut novel entitled *Party Wolves in My Skull* will be published by Eraserhead Press at the end of 2011. He is honored to be part of this amazing anthology.
http://www.partywolves.com/

Ploughman
Nickolas Furr

Somewhere overhead, flies buzzed and a hawk called. Tall grass swayed in the breeze, tickling his face and arms. He breathed raggedly, open-mouthed, the only human sound around. Beyond the smell of blood and death, the scent of wheat still lingered, drifting to his nose, his mind. The smell of good earth and green grass; it was the smell of life to a ploughman.

He touched again the blade that pinned him to the earth. Slick with oil and his own blood, it had resisted his attempts to pull it from his belly. He'd lacerated his fingers trying; now he was too weak to do anything but try to push it away.

He had never meant to be a soldier. He'd never wanted to wear the leather for his king, never wanted to go into battle with an axe in hand. An axe was meant for trees and stumps. It wasn't meant to be used on another. His axe was steel and oak, and lay just out of reach. He had always planned to use it until the grave, never knowing how close that would be.

His king had called him, and he, a man of the plough, had come.

The king was not a bad man. He taxed his subjects at the same rate. It was steep, but it was fair. The taxes paid for the wardens who patrolled the lands, the roads that carried the goods, the priests in the city, the walls of the stronghold, and the men that stood upon them. They paid the price of civilization.

They paid the price of protection.

Never before had the king called on his subjects to stand and fight, to pay the price. He had called them all – ploughmen, smiths, tinkers, greengrocers. They had come. He had left his plough sitting in the field, his mules standing in the stalls.

His son, Jed, could reach the plough handles, but he was still too small to control it. Sharlotte would have to hire a man to work the fields that he had worked since he was a boy. She would do so, even though she would grieve the loss of her husband in battle. She would never know that he waited for an army that did not come. She would never know that he had fallen, not to the soldiers of an invading army, but to something worse.

She would never know that his life was taken by heroes.

He lifted his head, trying to find his axe. He reached for it, unable to touch the wooden haft. Stretching, yearning, his fingers fell short again and again. Exhausted, his head fell back to the earth. Coughing, he spat blood from his mouth. It fell on his chin and neck, joining that which was already there.

A tyrant, one of his fellows had said. From over the horizon, an army rode toward us, and they believed our king to be a tyrant. Taxing his people wrongly, imprisoning his people in the gaols below the stronghold; our king was a tyrant whose reign needed to end.

Yes, there were men and women in the gaols – people who deserved to be there. Bandits and thieves, murderers and drunkards; these sorts were held to task for their crimes. Had he been king, had he been born to rule and not to plough, he would have done the same.

Yet he was no tyrant.

He lay still, wishing he had brought his cutting knife with him to the battle that had never come. A knife in his hand would have ended the pain quicker than the sword that was doing it.

This blade would be his epitaph. No words would be spoken over it.

No one made any noise, save for the insects and the birds. The others had died during the night. Those few that had lasted until morning had coughed, cried, and prayed, but all were silent before the sun rose to noon.

The ones who survived, those few had run. He would have run, had he been able to. But he had fallen early to a man in mail, a man who drove him to the ground and left his blade inside him. Heroes fought not for king or country or coin, but for an idea. That their king should die and so should all who tried to stop the heroes – that was an idea.

He and the others had arranged themselves in ragged lines, watching the horizon, waiting for the army to come from the north. None of them knew who would sit on the throne if the king were gone, but all of them would fight to keep him there. They were not warriors, but they were men of honor, men of the earth, their king's men.

As boys, they often dreamt of fighting for honor and king. Jed did, with his friends. Holding sticks like swords and axes, they played at war, but it was only play. Like his father, Jed's hands would callous from the plough handles, not from weapons he would choose not to wield. He would never be a warrior. He would never be a hero.

The heroes had come, seemingly, from nowhere. At one moment, it was only the king's men, watching and waiting. A moment later, a dozen or so men appeared, cutting into them, opening chests and bellies, taking heads from shoulders. The heroes bristled with weapons – swords and poleaxes, bows and crossbows, some things he had never seen. The man in mail who had left him pinned to the ground had drawn another blade from off his back and cut open the neck of the smith who had spoken of tyrants.

It was over as quickly as it had started. Those that couldn't run lied on the grass and joined their fellows in death. Cursed or blessed with a few more hours of life, he had sweated through the night, weighed down by the leather, unable to free himself. He didn't sweat now, now that he was cold.

He raised his chin, straining to look back over his head at the sun. It was descending to the west. Nightfall would soon arrive, and like all ploughmen he would close his eyes with the coming darkness.

For a moment, sunlight glinted off his axe's unstained blade. He smiled and reached once more. Turning his body, forcing the sword deeper into him, he stretched and found the handle. He wrapped his calloused fingers around it, pulling it to him.

Strength gone, he sank back to the earth, gripping the axe, but unable to lift it. Cold and exhausted, he closed his eyes.

This is not a weapon. It is the tool of a ploughman. In a just world, this would become my son's.

He pulled the axe as close to his chest as he could, pressing the oak and steel against him.

Sharlotte, my wife, I should never have left. I should never have taken the leather and left the plough in the field. I should never have left you my widow, or my son without a father. I will pass with your face in my gaze.

I dream of a place where we see each other again, where we can watch our son play. I dream of a place where an axe is only a tool, where the earth is rich and moist, where the grass is green and sweet, and the harvest is bountiful.

I dream of a place with no heroes…

Somewhere overhead, flies buzzed and a hawk called.

―――

Nickolas Furr is a freelance writer, part-time journalist, occasional pundit, and extremely non-traditional student. He has written for newspapers and magazines; typed and polished scripts; scribbled copy for print ads, television commercials, and radio spots; ran a political election blog; and launched enough press releases to sink a moderately-sized ship. Originally from the American South, he now resides in Imperial Beach, California, with his girlfriend, Liza, and their dog, Adam.
http://www.thewriterswashroom.blogspot.com/

Orpheus in the Underwear
Garrett Cook

Thwack. Crack. Splat. The poetry of head hitting bat. Hard to ignore it. The fourth of these guys he'd had to kill today. He'd gotten used to it. He'd been in the store for a week and it wasn't getting any less dangerous. He kept moving, through aisles where multitudes of waterbra'ed mannequins in inhuman poses taunted him with their plastic assets. He wondered how long it would be before he broke down and tried to do something to one of them. Wouldn't be too long. He didn't recognize the waterbras. Fuck. He was more lost than ever. He felt a gun at the back of his head. Another goddamn gangster.

He'd gotten used to this. He ducked, turned, smashed a kneecap. The pinstriped hooligan let out a yelp. Let out a louder one when he gets walloped in the balls. The gangster held his aching testicles. Bent over in pain. Big mistake. He cracked the gangster on the head. It was like a videogame. Same rhythm. Same sounds. *Thwack. Crack. Splat.* The gangster became just another headless mess on the floor. So much crime in this lingerie shop. He found a spot obscured by mannequins and drawers of bras and sat there for awhile. When he felt safe as he ever would, he slept.

He dreamt about wandering the lingerie shop killing gangsters with an aluminum bat. He very well might have been awake, wandering past lacy monotony, skewed human shapes. Semi-tasteful colors. In his dreams, the mannequins became less human as he descends deeper into the store. They have the heads of fish, bulls, camels, lions, sharks, like a pantheon of weird half-naked Egyptian goddesses. He wondered if they were where the babies came from or the gangsters. Is this a room he has been to or a room he needed to go to? Did they know where his wife was, or would they be like the little mushroom fellow in Super Mario Brothers and simply reveal that she was in another castle? Or was this just a dream?

When he awoke, a salesgirl was standing over him, a Mexican lady in her mid forties, dressed in a black bra, pink panties with "OUTRAGEOUS!" printed all over them, stockings, garters and lime green flip flops. Three children ago she might have looked sort of alright in such a getup. She looked alright to him, although he knew that she could not really have looked that great.

"There something I can do for you?" she asked him.

Out of the corner of his eye, he saw some of the babies crawling around the mannequins. Always babies in the morning. Why were there always babies in the morning?

"Yes," he replied, "I'd like to know why this shop is infinitely large and full of babies and gangsters."

"I am new here," she said and took her leave of him. He tried to pursue her, but babies began clinging to his legs, weighing him down. They let go, crawling off only when she was out of sight and thus were unable to help him. He returned to mechanically wandering the store, telling himself that he would find something, a telephone, his wife, the exit. He had to be at least partially certain this was so, or else he would commit suicide – create a rope out of thongs and hang himself, or cut his wrists with underwire from the bras. He felt he was making some sort of progress as he entered the blue and orange bra room, filled with glass mannequins wearing bras that were blue, orange or blue and orange.

"I'm going to have to ask you to leave," said a voice behind him.

He turned around to see a teenage girl wrapped in a yellow towel on which the word "Fierce" was printed. She was beautiful, delicate, with a well formed nose and big pouty lips. There was a big black bruise around her left eye.

"I would love to," he said, "I've been here for days."

"Then why don't you?" She pulled off the towel to reveal that she was wearing a bikini covered with Warhol Elvises.

"Because…"

Before he could finish his sentence, she was gone. She was hiding something. They were all hiding something. He hanged his head as he made his way through the blue and orange room, feeling as if he had somehow come closer. He had. For the past few days, he had not encountered any salesgirls, only babies and gangsters. If he was getting "help", then he was surely closer to the entrance and the register. Right? *Right?*

Upon leaving the blue and orange room, he traversed a cavern of perfume bottles, each bearing the name of some superlative quality. Fierce. Outrageous. Spectacular. Seductive. Temptastic. He cried, feeling that he was none of these things, particularly Temptastic because that was not a word.

The familiar feeling of a gun at the back of his head alerted him that it was night time. As he prepared to dispatch the gangster behind him, he was surprised to find that three other pinstriped gentlemen bearing tommyguns had entered the room and were pointing them at him. He held up his arms in surrender.

"Finally," said the gangster behind him, "you're willing to cooperate. Good."

The gangsters led him into a room which was completely empty save a creature that had the head and torso of Bettie Page, the wings of an eagle and the hindquarters of a lion.

"What has four legs in the morning, two legs in the evening and three legs at dawn?" the Bettie Page sphinx asked. It made no small talk, gave no explanation. It was an old riddle, but he did not remember the answer.

"I don't know."

The sphinx shook her lovely brunette head.

"That was an easy one."

"I'm sorry."

The gangsters led him out of the room…to the register. A salesclerk was ringing his wife up. Although he had found her again, although he had made it out, he was still overcome by a deep, inexplicable sense of failure.

―――

Garrett Cook is an author of horror and Bizarro fiction. His books *Murderland part 1:h8*, *Murderland 2: Life During Wartime* and *Archelon Ranch* are available at Amazon.com. His work has appeared in Exquisite Corpse, The Magazine of Bizarro Fiction and *The Bizarro Starter Kit: Purple*. He is grateful to the good people at Hayakawa publishing for reprinting his story *Mr. Plush, Detective* in Hayakawa Mystery Magazine, allowing Japanese readers to check out his work.
http://www.chainsawnoir.wordpress.com

Pocket
Touya Tachihara
Translated by Matthew Sanchez

One morning, I woke up and there was a pocket in my tummy.

Did my belly button get bigger? Or is this some strange sickness?

I didn't tell my daddy, mommy or little sister. After all, Daddy can only talk about work, money and his job. I'm pretty sure he's turned into a robot. Mommy only pays attention to my newborn sister. She doesn't care about me anymore. Now, all she can say are things like, "Hurry up!" or "You're a big brother now." My little sister is just a little squirmbug. She just cries all the time. It's so annoying!

I decided to solve the mystery of my pocket all by myself.

I went to the only place I know where no one else can see me – the bathroom. I rolled up my shirt and felt my shiny new pocket with my fingers. It was so soft and tickled to touch. When I pulled on it, it stretched a little, but it wasn't any different than the rest of my skin. I was just like one of those robots in a science fiction comic or cartoon. Would I be able to pull something out? I slowly put my hand inside, but felt nothing except an outbound breeze.

I was overcome with a feeling of disappointment when I heard my mother screech, "Son! What are you doing in there?"

Why did she always have to yell? I wish she'd just disappear. Hey, maybe I could fit her in my pocket! Leaving the bathroom, I walked up and stood behind my mother while she changed my sister's diaper. "Mommy," I called. She turned around... and her eyes went wide. I grabbed her hand and pushed her into the pocket in my tummy. Whoosh – the pocket made a sucking sound, and my mother was sucked inside.

Ah, it was finally quiet. Now I can sleep in and nobody will scold me.

Much to my dismay, my little sister started bawling. She's always so noisy. I put her right into the pocket, too.

Ah, I thought, now I can have all the candy I want, and can leave my toys around and nobody can get mad at me. This was going to be great.

It was dark outside when Dad's blustering voice woke me. "Why aren't the lights on? Just who do you think supports this damn family?" I dislike Dad the most when he smells like booze. He hits Mommy and kicks me when I'm in his way. I made sure to put him in my pocket before he had a chance to kick me again. That took care of that.

In the morning, I'll put the neighbor's dog in the pocket. It's always barking and Mommy grumbles about it. Mommy... I wonder how she's doing. I put my hand in my pocket to find her, but no matter how hard I tried, I couldn't find her. Or my daddy. Or my little sister.

After a while, a strange man and lady came to my house and took me to a strange place. I tried to tell them about my pocket, but they didn't believe me. They told me I didn't have anything like a pocket in my tummy. They told me that the shock of being abandoned and left all alone had made my head funny, or something.

Well, that's just fine. Anything and anybody I don't like – *anything* that annoys me – can go right into my pocket. It'll be my secret that nobody cares or knows about. It'll be *my* pocket. My world.

Throw him in! Throw her in! Throw it in! Throw everything in! *Throw everyone in!*

It's so dark. Is it because I put the moon, the sun, the lights, the candles, the fireflies, and everything else in my pocket?

Is everyone gone? Because they're all in my pocket?

Hey. Can anyone hear me?

I yelled as loud as I could, but nobody's there. Nothing is there at all.

I'm all alone now, just standing around.

What should I do?

Mommy, Daddy, my little sister, all the men and women I don't know.

Dogs and cats and crows and *everrryone*! They're all right here in my pocket.

When I put my hand in, I can't pull anything out.

Yet, I can't climb in either.

What to do now?… I'm all alone.

"Waaah! Waaah!"

I hear someone crying. It's my little sister. It's coming from inside my pocket. It's a good, strong voice.

I can tell.

Any minute now, I'm sure my little sister is going to be born from my pocket. My mommy and daddy, too. So will the dogs, and the cats, and the man and the lady I don't know, and everyone. *Eeeverrryone!*

It'll be a happy, new life.

Oh my, the pocket has burst open.

Hello there.

In 1991, Touya Tachihara won Shueisha's readership award with her novel *Cobalt*. As a fantasy and horror author, she has written over thirty books. She also translates Chinese science fiction into Japanese. Currently working as an associate professor of writing, specializing in Chinese literature.

The Norwegian Makes Lemonade
Jess Gulbranson

"Popcorn, get your red-hot popcorn!"

"Sno-cones, get your red-hot sno-cones!"

The street vendors could say anything, really, or nothing. The streets were empty except for a fishy reek, like broad arteries clogged with frigid menhaden oil. Still, the vendors hawked their wares in raucous voices over the dinging of buoys and distant resonant foghorns. Their trays were slung in front of them, hanging on leathern shoulder straps, weighted down with food and gewgaws as if they were counterweights preventing these doomed men from simply falling over backwards under the weight of their own futility.

"Cotton candy, get your red-hot cotton candy!"

They flogged this mercantile impotence day in and day out because they have just been granted the royal seal of sponsorship. The king was as distant as the inconstant moon behind those gray, piscine clouds – and his whims were as inconstant as the distant tidal forces from that same sister moon that drove the ebb and flow in the harbor and canals, going from oily fragrant flood to desolate parched drought, when the canals and harbor and all their secret terrible treasures laid bare in the stinking mud. The moral of the story was, when the royal sponsorship was offered you, you took it. And they did.

There were a thousand delectable treats out on the market, but the flavorless and almost weightless crackers made by Thomson Limited were the ones people bought, because of the royal seal the crackerboxes bore – reproduced poorly though they were. That little seal could have been anything: a moon, a sun, a face, a hand-basket, a naked lady rendered hideous by low resolution. It was what it was.

"Roasted hedgehog! Extra spiny!"

The charter specified a certain part of the waterfront that was their territory, and though it wasn't Bell Street, or Book Street, or Candle Avenue, it would do. The waterfront was east of South Charnel District, west of the fields, north by northwest, and south of heaven.

It was so crowded, nobody went there anymore.

But that didn't stop them. They knew what was good for them.

The mayor had signed off on the royal charters, and the mayor was as close to the king or God herself as you could want. That, and he was there, now, making sure that the vendors took advantage of their good fortune, even if it killed them. Even if *he* killed them.

He was a lean old man with long gray hair, in a white linen suit. He looked seventy but was probably seven-hundred and seventy. The mayor stalked everywhere like the ghost of an ex-girlfriend's dad, or the shoebox of a childhood goldfish. He walked silently – the only clue to his approach was his cologne, a macabre blend of sandalwood and murder.

"Peanuts, get your red-hot peanuts!"

The peanut vendor experienced a moment of pants-wetting terror as the mayor walked up to him. In those ageless eyes was the look of a man who had just grabbed a wolf by its collar and beltloops, and thrown it down the stairs. The mayor reached out with one long stiletto of a lacquered index fingernail, skewering a red-hot peanut. He popped it in his mouth with a ghoulish grin. He chewed. The vendor held his breath.

"KEEP UP THE GOOD WORK."

The vendor sighed in relief, shivering as if Satan had just goose-stepped over his grave. The vendor blinked, and the mayor had disappeared. His cologne lingered, though, so he could still be anywhere. It didn't pay to relax. Out over the water, a foghorn complained. The vendor walked on.

"Lemonade, get your red-hot lemonade!"

―――

Jess Gulbranson is a renaissance jerk from Portland, OR. His fiction, art, and poetry have all been anthologized. Also a music critic and interviewer, he performs and records as Coeur Machant and DJFalsifier, and is the author of *MEL*, *Antipaladin Blues*, and *10 A BOOT STOMPING 20 A HUMAN FACE 30 GOTO 10*. http://about.me/jessgulbranson

Breakwater
Alvin Pang

Having lost her vada to the sea, she kept watch every dawn on the beach where she had last caught sight of him, adrift in his skoyak midway between shore and horizon. Every morning at the third ori, before the sun called the world to its labours, she would make her way to the ancient breakwater that the villagers called davada meral, grandfather of the coast, clutching her breakfast of dried kan and rice phut as she clambered over the slippery rock to the narrow but sturdy plateau.

She would eat with both hands, scanning the horizon for signs of life, quickly spotting then looking past the lurelights of the sotokan boats and the dim red glow of the jhimcatchers. On occasion a uluabird skimming the surface of the water would take the shape of a distant boat, its one raised wing like a soksail unfurled to catch the shorebound wind. The flipper of a passing bhaphaun would appear for a moment to be a human arm, waving in greeting or distress. It never seemed to rain while she was keeping watch, or of if it did she took no notice, her feet firmly lodged in the crevices of the elder breakwater. Before long the sun would pry the horizon open with golden fingers and the sea would begin to gleam the colour of wet jade. Climbing down from the breakwaters, she would fold her nalal leaf into a little skoyak, leave inside it one last bite of kan and rice, set it afloat where the tug of the waves was gentle but steady, and walk away from the makeshift boat without looking back, as she returned home to her chores, the villagers giving her knowing looks as she passed.

When she was sixteen a dark-haired erbo came to her, adorned with the seaglass bracelets, earrings and leather skirts of a Mayar's erlin from the neighbouring Johrikanti. Without asking for her leave, he sat down crossed-legged next to her.

You are indeed very pretty, said the princeling, who had come to the island to negotiate passage and trade. *The villagers spoke of a mysterious beauty who appears every dawn on this rock, and now I see they spoke truly.*

She had never thought of herself as beautiful. Big-boned and ample like her vada, her cheeks were flat, her lips thin, her hair a tangled pukk of dirty straw, her arms grown stout from years of pulling at the nets. Still, her eyes were clear and bright, and she cut a comely figure in the pre-dawn gloom. So she remained silent, and watched the sea.

He kissed her and pressed her against the sea-moist granite as the tide surged against the breakwater. When she came to her senses, he was gone, having left a large pearl in the loosened folds of her tunic. The sun had risen a handwidth into the sky, the skraws had begun their first hunt, and the davada rock was stained with her blood.

The next night, she armed herself with her vada's old kantoo, which over the years she had kept sharp enough to scale and gut a kan without leaving the visible line of a wound. But the Johribo did not come. Her vigil, for the first time, felt lonesome, and she clutched the blade for assurance. When dawn arrived, she let fall two fresh drops of her blood onto the little skoyak offering and watched the tide carry it out beyond sight, before turning at last towards home.

Her discovery that she was pregnant did not deter her from her daily ritual. Hours after giving birth to her erlin, she made her way to the shore with him at her breast, tucked away from the night chill, and dabbed his dark forelocks with saltwater before taking up her watch. Before long she would prepare two portions of breakfast and craft two nanal skoyaks, as her erlin scratched and tossed about in the nearby sand in the darkness, nameless and unafraid.

One afternoon she heard that the Johribo, who had now become Mayar, had visited her home, having heard of her child and assuming it to be his. He would call again to fetch both nibu and erlin home with him, to be formally installed as part of his extended household.

That day she took her finest illukan, which spends its time in the depths and never sees daylight but has the sweetest flesh, and cleaned it fit for a Mayar's table. Into one of its large eye sockets she inserted the pearl he had given her, its lustre matching perfectly the illu's intact deep-seeking eye. Into its gullet she placed her erlin's pacid, carefully preserved in bohoil since his birth. Then she seasoned and wrapped the dish in nanal, and asked for it to be given to the Joharibo when he came, before leaving the house to tend to her nets with her erlin in tow. The gift was received, a small token was left behind in acknowledgement, and the Johri Mayar never again returned to village, sending envoys instead whenever there was business to be conducted.

In time she became dabu, and later tydabu, but she was never too frail to climb the breakwater every dawn; and if the effort required the assistance of a walking cik and a few willing erlins, none thought to speak against it. Kancatchers and meribos, as they headed out to sea or returned from a night's hunt, would try to spot her silhouette for good luck, and the sight of her would steady them, even if the waters happened to be troubled that dawn. After her passing, the villagers placed a driftwood monument on the old breakwater, shaped like a sitting nuebo, her arms outstretched and watching the sea. For years, although no one in the village had pledged to do so, a kanlam would be kept lit at the monument, from the 3rd ori until dawn, always visible midway between the horizon and the shore.

―――

Alvin Pang is a poet, writer and editor who has been featured in major festivals, anthologies and journals across Asia, Australia, Europe and

America. A Fellow of the University of Iowa's International Writing Program, his many publications include *City of Rain* (Ethos Books) and *Tumasik: Contemporary Writing from Singapore* (Autumn Hill Books, USA). His work has been translated into over a dozen languages. He was named Singapore's Young Artist of the Year for Literature in 2005 and received the Singapore Youth Award in 2007 for Arts and Culture.
http://twitter.com/#!/alfpang

HO(locaust) Scale
Robert M. Price

Ben Fischer had worked as a plumber and electrician in the old neighborhood for... could it really be whole decades? He was, he thought with a chuckle, the last doctor who made house calls. He had visited a good number of the crumbling but often revamped houses over the years, only to find that the dwellers had changed since the last time. Elderly folks died or moved to the Sun Belt to be replaced by young professionals with a yearning for some permanence. Living in an old home was like living in a past age when things were not always in a hurricane of bewildering change. As these new householders welcomed him in to rejuvenate the pipes and the wires, he felt almost that he was the host and they the guests.

Here he was again, outside number 32 Faison Street in the oldest section of town. Good to see the place again. The bolt clicked, the door opened, and a new face met him with not much of a smile, no doubt preoccupied by the water problems the house was prone to. The fellow's name was Something Reinhart. He did not shake hands but indicated the direction, down the hall, he wanted the elderly plumber to go. Tight-lipped, this man. Uptight, too, as his crew cut suggested and his conservative clothing confirmed. There was some kind of black T shirt just visible above the buttoned shirt collar.

Past the television room they hastened, but not fast enough to prevent Ben from noticing the surprising number of Hitler and World War Two documentaries on the shelf. "History buff?"

"Ah, you might say so. The blockage is worst in the upstairs bathroom." The two men climbed the stairs, and Ben put his "medical bag" on the cracking tiled floor. He started to ask more detailed questions about the "symptoms", but Reinhart evidently felt he had told the old man enough.

"Look, I have somewhere to go. I forgot when I called you. I'll most likely be back before you finish, but if I'm not, just leave the bill."

The plumber nodded and went to work.

First he took some towels from the closet and piled them on the floor in case the bowl should overflow. Then he flushed. The thing seemed to want to bubble, like someone with gas who wants to burp but can't quite do it. The sink faucets worked a bit better, drooling out modest trickles. Bathtub: same thing again. Neither hot nor cold was completely off, and the force in each fixture seemed to vary without any regular rhythm as he let them run. It was a puzzle. He would have to start taking pipes apart and exploring.

Then something occurred to him. The problem might stem from another point in the house's system. He thought he recalled this old pile hiding a secondary bathroom down the hall. He'd try that before going downstairs.

He stepped into a large bedroom, which the current resident had converted: the length and breadth of it was filled with a vast tabletop railway set! Such spectacles had charmed him since boyhood, but his family, who had gotten out of Nazi Germany by the skin of their teeth (or by the tip of their foreskins, some mocked), could never think of providing such a treat for him and his brothers.

Ben did not dare find the switch so as to watch the train chug its way around its eternal loop. But nothing was preventing a good, long look. The scene was somewhere in war-time Germany or Eastern Europe. There were exquisitely detailed buildings whose architecture suggested Prague, Vienna, or Berlin. The cathedral looked handmade from scratch, no mere model kit. Tiny plastic figures simulated the busy inhabitants of the city. As his old eyes made their lingering way further along, he saw that German tanks had entered the city to make their ineluctable way to the city square. Even these had small electrical strips under them, so they, too, could be switched on and caused to move.

But on to the powder room. He passed through a smaller bedroom, probably once a child's. The modeler had extended a neck of his train table into this room as well, though one had to sweep aside curtains that hid the contents. This new scene, set apart from the city, showed a fenced-in camp of some sort, and a length of track fed into it through the break in the drapes. The semicircle of letters over the entrance gate read: ARBEIT MACHT FREI. Tiny human figures were filing out of the train and through the gates, frozen forever in a scene of infamy.

He felt a sense of alarm, like a fever slowly rising within him, as he squinted to see into a couple of the larger camp structures. The detail here was truly incredible. The sculptor, presumably the crew-cut Mr. Reinhart, must have used a microscope and the finest surgical instruments, like those people who assemble tiny ships inside bottles. But Reinhart's imagination was far more arcane than that: the scenes depicted were those of laboratories of supervised rape and torture, involving miniature doctors and soldiers and naked scarecrow-men and even animals whose strange clustering suggested the unspeakable.

Just before he clicked off the light, Ben noticed the sole piece of furniture in the room, an old sofa against the wall. When he saw what kind of leather covered it, he lost all interest in the plumbing problem.

But he did have a solution in mind, a final solution.

He returned to his truck for some chemicals.

The neo-Nazi Reinhart was later than he had expected to be. He had worked up quite a sweat and looked forward to a nice, hot shower. That old Jew had better have fixed the damned water!

Imagine the young man's surprise when he turned the knob for hot water and something else came out of the nozzle.

—

Robert M. Price is an American theologian and writer. He is professor at the Coleman Theological Seminary and at the Center for Inquiry Institute, and the author of a number of books on theology and the historicity of Jesus, including *Deconstructing Jesus, The Reason Driven Life, Jesus is Dead,* and *Inerrant the Wind: The Evangelical Crisis in Biblical Authority.* He has also written about the Cthulhu Mythos, created by the writer H. P. Lovecraft, as well as "Horror, Sword-&-Sorcery, hero pulps, Tolkien, and old time Science Fiction".
http://www.robertmprice.mindvendor.com/

Inconceivable
Kevin Lovelace

Thanks for coming, Susan. I know things have been a bit awkward since... well. Anyway, have a seat.

Oh, I keep the lights low these days, does that bother you? I've found that the lights hurt my eyes a little, lately. We can turn them on later, if you'd like. Just... Listen, I know you're uncomfortable here after we broke up, so I'll just say my piece, okay?

I kept having those urges, even after we broke up. They just kept getting worse. I know you tried your best, and you were really a saint about the whole thing. You put up with the games and the costumes and the weird role-playing and the strap-ons. You were so understanding; it was me who needed something that you couldn't give. Nothing we did could fill that void, you know?

I was pretty depressed after you left. I felt like I was sick or lost or something. Like I was a bad person just because I... Well, you remember what I wanted? What I needed?

No, please let me finish before you turn the lights on, okay? I... I just don't want you looking at me right now.

You don't know what it's like to know with cold, clear, rational certainty that you were born incomplete – that you were born missing something that you didn't even have the language for. I've always known deep down that I needed them – the Greys, the Space Angels, the Shining Ones – to make me whole with their science. It's like those people who come into this world knowing that they never should have been born with legs and arms and stuff. So they find black-market surgeons to amputate them or they stage "accidents" with power tools.

Well, a few months after you left, I found some folks on the Internet who also knew what it was like. I'm not alone anymore. There are hundreds of people like me all over the world who wake up in the middle of the night feeling... empty.

I started talking to a guy named Marty on the Facebook group. He told me about an article he read in an Argentine newspaper. Marty told me that the article mentioned a possible solution. So I looked around on the Net and found the guy he was talking about. You see, there's this doctor in Argentina who understands and is trying to help people like us. So I saved up some money, the last of it, and sent it to him. It took over a month to hear back from him. The doctor sent me the cure and a sheet of instructions use.

It came in a jar, he never told me where it came from, and I really don't want to know, but there it was. It was kind of moist and had all sorts of sharp edges, like a wad of bones, teeth and old meat. And Jesus Christ, the smell! It smelled like rubber and gasoline and roadkill. I was scared at first, but his instructions said I could do it if I really wanted to be whole.

Don't get up. Don't. Susan, I've got a gun.

That's right Susan, just sit there. I promise I won't hurt you. I just want to finish my story, okay?

So, I got some painkillers and followed his instructions. I had to slit my belly open right here. Oh, that's right, you can't see. Well, just wait a moment. Anyway, I slit myself open; I thought I was going to pass out from all the blood. But I followed his instructions and I slid it into the cut and then sewed myself up. I did pass out for a bit, but it was okay.

Yeah, for a long time I was shocked. I couldn't believe what I'd done. I thought that maybe I'd been wrong. What if I was just some guy who had just put a rock or something in his belly? What if there was something wrong with me? I thought about that for a while, actually. I'd press down and feel the lump sealed in here and sometimes it would be rock hard and sometimes soft like a blister. I'd look down at where things looked kind of putrid and bloated, like it'd gone bad with gangrene, and just cry. I would dream that it was rotting in me. I'd dream that I'd done something bad to myself, and maybe I needed help... Or that maybe I was just going to die with my guts gone black. I was thinking about that last night when I was in the bathtub. I was about to drop the radio in with me when it happened.

It kicked.

I was lying about the gun, Susan. I just wanted you to hear me out. So you know where this came from, why it's special, why *we're* special. It's going to want a mother, Susan.

Turn the lights on.

———

Kevin Lovelace is a freelance writer and mad doktor-about-town. He is currently hard at work on his first novel and is one of the founders of Grinding. He is in love with comics, body horror, prosthetics, sex, and different systems of knowing. When not writing or attempting to punch the future in its smug face, he can be found lurking in the back alleys of the San Francisco Bay Area, fighting crime and playing with his cat.
http://grinding.be & http://www.twitter.com/moonandserpent

Memories of Ken
Junichi Ashikawa
Translated by Dan Luffey

This is a story from a time when Tokyo still had vast open fields.

When I was in third grade, my friend Masato, who was sort of like the leader of our class, invited me to join the baseball team he was putting together. I had never played a game of baseball before, just catch, but he assured me that skill didn't matter, so I decided to join.

After class, we were out practicing in the fields when a young man named Ken came along and asked us if he could be our coach. We discussed this among ourselves, and decided that a coach would be a good addition to the team.

Ken was a small-built man, ten years older than us nine-year olds. We had no idea what his job was or where he lived. He was great at complimenting every player, though. At first, I was hitting nothing but air, and couldn't even catch a cold in the outfield. After a month of getting complimented whenever I did something even remotely well, however, I became much better. I was even moved from left field to second base, and I climbed up from ninth batter in the lineup to fifth. My goal was to improve, to become third or fourth batter, and to play shortstop.

Ken also set up games for us with other teams on Sundays. Almost all the teams we played against had their own uniforms, while Ken and our team had nothing but our street clothes. We always lost, but Ken never got angry.

"You did well. If you practice harder, you'll be able to beat them someday," he'd say, encouraging us. It was a lot of fun for everyone on the team. No one ever skipped practice.

When we became fourth graders, we had to change homeroom classes, so Masato and I were separated. There weren't many kids from the team in my new class. I figured we'd still keep practicing and playing games even though we were in different classes, but Masato had a different idea.

"Now that we're in different classes, we have to break up the team," he announced.

I was shocked at how nonchalantly he stated it. "What does Ken have to say?"

"Nothing. I didn't bother asking him. You don't need to either. We never won any games, so it's not like he did anything worthwhile for us."

"But everyone's getting better. I'm sure we'll be able to win some time soon. Come on..."

But as Masato ran off, I don't think he heard me.

Soon came the day our next practice. When I went out to the field, only Ken was there waiting.

"Everyone else sure is late." Ken was apparently under the impression everyone was going to come as usual.

Stammering, I informed Ken of the situation.

"Oh. Well, I understand."

I thought Ken would be angry, but he was surprisingly calm. "Thank you very much for training us," I said sadly.

"Don't mention it." Ken smiled and waved goodbye.

Ken seemed dejected as he walked off. I was terribly sorry for what had become of things, and I felt like I had lost someone very important.

Afterwards, Masato joined a bigger team, and the rest of our teammates spread out to yet others. I played baseball for a new team too, but the coach did nothing but yell at me. Baseball with Ken had been fun, but I was never able to experience that joy again. So I never really got any better.

I'm an adult now, but I still think back to Ken now and then. He was an amazing coach... at least to me. And I'm proud that I was able to properly thank him when the time to say goodbye came.

Born in Tokyo in 1953, Junichi Ashikawa is a graduate of of the School of Letters, Arts and Sciences I of Waseda University. After working for a publishing house, he made his debut in 1990 in the genre of young adult literature. Currently Mr. Ashikawa makes his living writing mostly period literature. Major series of works include: *Nizuraeshi Jikenchou, Utsukeyoriki Jikenchou, Kyokugiri Jinkurou, Kenshiro Kagebataraki, Goinkyo Yojimbo, Yojimobo Kirinosuke Ninjo Otasukekagyou.* http://ashishi.exblog.jp/

Kamiya Bar
Dan Ryan

The old timers had been going there for over one hundred years, and I was finally back after more than twenty.

It was Kamiya Bar, in the Asakusa district of Tokyo, and it was the oldest western-style bar in the city. Western as in high ceilings, with wood-veneer wall panels, chrome light fixtures and those patterned tin ceiling tiles you see in old saloons in Tombstone, Arizona or Virginia City, Nevada.

But I don't mean it also had brass spittoons and buffalo horns on the walls. Kamiya Bar is western in contrast to the small, pub-like *izakaya* and tatami-mat sake parlors scattered all throughout Tokyo. The main drinking room is more like a European beer hall, with elongated tables often shared by strangers. Condiment stations and menu holders are placed on the tables the way they would be in a typical American diner. Everyone wears Western clothing, and foreigners are not only a common sight, the Japanese welcome them quite warmly.

Sometimes in unexpected ways.

I had been dreaming of returning to Tokyo for many years. I was a bachelor here, fresh out of university, working for an American company for two years. During the course of our relationship, I had told my wife many stories of the happiness and wonder I had found here. So we had decided, six months before this day, to pool our resources and use her frequent-flier miles to take a grand 11-day trip to Tokyo and my old haunts. Which included, of course, Kamiya Bar.

And, actually, this was our second visit to the place. We had come to Asakusa a few days before to see the temple and do some shopping. My wife was utterly charmed with Asakusa and its more traditional appearance and overall feel. Before leaving Asakusa that day, I wanted to show her Kamiya Bar, where we had many drinks and several plates of excellent fried potatoes. Most of the food in the drinking rooms is western-style. Most of the drinks are large mugs of Asahi Beer and *denki bran*, a luscious, fragrant brandy made and served exclusively by the bar.

On our first visit, my wife and I had a smaller table to ourselves along the wall of the main drinking room. This visit, I wanted to go to the bar before she was done with her shopping. When I got there, the place was very crowded and I ended up sitting at a table in the smaller front drinking room with an elderly Japanese man. Our table touched another where a middle-aged Japanese couple were seated.

At first I thought all three of them were together, from the way they were talking and being friendly to each other. Empty food plates on the seam between the two tables made it look like these had been shared. Because of my perception, I used my poor Japanese to defer to the elderly man when asking if I could sit at his table with all three people.

It turned out the middle-aged couple spoke some English. So while the old man waved me to a chair without batting an eye, he spoke through the middle-aged lady who told me I was welcome to sit with them. There were many empty beer mugs and *denki bran* glasses on the tables, and I have often wondered since how much of a factor they played in the wonderful hour which was to come.

When you first enter Kamiya Bar, you have to buy drink tickets at the front counter before taking a seat. In addition to the shopping bags which were now tucked behind my chair, I had tickets for two large beers and two *denki bran*, which I placed on the table in front of me. That's how it works: the waitress comes by, takes the tickets you've put out, and then comes back with your drinks. For subsequent rounds, you just put your cash yen on the table, and the waitress replaces the drinks you've had with fresh ones.

I had just gotten my beer and brandy when the middle-aged couple asked me some of the standard questions. Where was I from? How did I like Japan? I told them that I used to come to Kamiya Bar when I was a young man many years ago, and this made them delightfully surprised. The old man asked the lady what I had said, and when she told him he nodded approvingly at me and raised his glass to the one I had just picked up. When out glasses clinked, we drank and he nodded again. Then he put another bite of fried potato and croquette into his mouth.

For the next few minutes, the middle-aged couple and I talked, with the lady translating for the old man and I when we had questions for each other. Although far better than my Japanese, her English was not that great, but here is what I learned:

The couple were married, but lived separately during most of the month because he had to stay in a company dorm for his job in Tokyo. The lady and their children stayed at the family home far outside the city. The couple and the old man did not know each other, had only met that very afternoon at the tables we now occupied. I had thought the old man was a father or elderly uncle, but the lady said no. And the old man was a veteran of World War II, had served the emperor.

By this time my wife had arrived, and I tucked her packages and shopping bags behind my chair with mine. In busted English and broken Japanese, my wife, the married couple and the old man managed to introduce themselves. The lady and I further summarized for my wife the conversation she had missed before arriving. My wife was very taken by the fact that the old man had served in the war.

She asked the lady what the old man had done in the war, something she and I both wanted to know. The lady asked the old man, but he apparently wanted to dodge the question. I watched him as he spoke, and he didn't show any shame or embarrassment that I could see. He acted like a man who had happier things on his mind and didn't want anything but light-hearted talk to carry our little drinking session forward. Through the lady he said, while smiling, that he preferred not to say. That settled it for me.

Then the waitress happened by and the old man ordered another round of beer and brandy for our group. The drinks arrived a minute later, and he pushed his pile of cash yen towards the waitress. I motioned for my cash, to place it with the old man's, but he gently patted my hand down and away from his money. He was buying, and that settled that for us.

As we reached for our drinks, my wife asked the lady to tell the old man that her father had served in the U.S. Army during the war. It hadn't occurred to me to mention that, but it did not surprise me that my wife did. After the lady spoke to the old man, he looked at my wife and seemed to beam at her. A very warm look. He then touched glasses with my wife as he had with me earlier, and toasted the rest of the table. He noticed that I was looking at his fried potato and croquette and offered me his plate. I was so full of beer by then I had no room for his kind offer. He smiled at this after the lady passed it on to him.

And as we had asked him, the old man asked my wife what her father had done in the war. Through the lady, my wife said her father had been an airplane mechanic but that he really didn't like to talk about his role in the war very much either. The old man nodded and smiled at this. And perhaps it was the beer, but I suddenly noticed, except for the almond eyes and the lack of a mustache, my wife and I could have been sitting at this table with her father. Both men were the same age, about the same build, and favored long-sleeved dress shirts with sweater vests. At least that is what our Japanese old man was wearing, along with a grey wool driving cap.

And again maybe it was the beer and brandy but for the rest of our little drinking session I could sense real warmth between my wife and the old man. He bought another round of drinks for the table, and another plate of croquette which I agreed to share with him. He seemed pleased that no one had to suggest I put *tonkatsu* sauce on my food. Upon noticing, I asked the lady to tell the old man that all properly-trained foreigner know the value of *tonkatsu* sauce on croquette. The lady, her husband and the old man got a chuckle out of this. It made me happy to make them happy.

By this time about an hour had passed, and the old man announced that he had to go home and get some sleep. He had to spend the day with his grandchildren tomorrow. It was only six in the evening, but he got up and reached for the grey suit coat on the back of his chair. He had one arm into one sleeve, and seemed to be struggling with the rest of the process, when my wife quickly reached up and helped him into the suit coat. When the old man reached for his overcoat, my wife stood and helped him on with that.

For her help, the old man bowed to my wife and reached his hands to shake hers. My wife took the old man's hands into both of hers and kissed them as the old man bowed a little extra bow to her. The kiss ended quickly, and my wife looked up smiling at the old man. He in turn was smiling at me as we reached out with single hands and shook. He had one of the most confident grips I have ever felt.

The drinking session had ended.

The middle-aged couple said they had to go as well. My wife and I were bone-tired and a bit tipsy. We decided to leave Kamiya Bar and head back to our vacation rental across town in Nakano to regroup before planning the rest of our evening. We ended up staying in, having a snack dinner from the local convenience store and good beer and sake from a store called Life. We didn't regret staying in, for we still had a few nights left in Tokyo. And one night out in Tokyo can often be worth two or three in any major western city.

But we didn't go back to Kamiya Bar, though we talked about it. Even if we had, there probably would have been little chance of seeing the old man or the middle-aged couple again. I did give the couple our address and phone number with instructions to call us and stay with us if they travel to the States. But it has been almost two years now and my wife and I have not heard from them. That's okay. We are already talking about going back to Tokyo next year, this time with a promise from me that we will make proper plans in advance to take an overnight trip to a *ryokan* in Kyoto. I intend to make good on that promise.

But I have thought often about the old man since we returned from that trip, and I think of the bond he and my wife seemed instantly to share. I found it beautiful, but still don't quite understand it. But I have never been a daughter, or the child of a war veteran, so perhaps real comprehension of this will always elude me.

But from my point of view it doesn't matter, because I know this:

I don't care what the old man did in the war, if he was a medic, a cook, a commando, or a pilot who strafed Pearl Harbor. For a short time he was our benefactor and our friend. And he was Japanese and we were Americans and it was Kamiya Bar.

———

Dan Ryan earned BA in Journalism from Lehigh University in 1987, but is only now attempting to get into the serious writing game. He has been a private investigator, a market research journalist, and a public school teacher. Most recently, he served as an editor for the Japan disaster-relief book project *2:46: Aftershocks* (http://quakebook.org/), and he currently writes for Giant Robot Magazine (http://www.giantrobot.com/). Dan has had an abiding love of Japan since living in Tokyo for two years in the late '80s. He currently lives in Brisbane, California with his wife and two cats. His text and picture stories can be found at http://brisbanegraphicartsmuseum.com/smallstories/

Whispers
Adam Joffrain
Translated by Kirsten Alene

It started with a light breath through her hair.

The air was filled with the soft scent of mimosa.

Clarisse lay stretched out for a long time. She couldn't sleep. She had a stomachache, which made the hours when she was lying down seem like an eternity. This was because time had the terrible power of contracting when someone was having fun, and dilating when someone couldn't sleep.

The murmuring in the hollow of her ears didn't help.

Clarisse wasn't really paying that much attention. But at the exact moment she became aware that something abnormal was happening, she concentrated completely on this breath, this song, which was like a soft breeze.

Finally, all her senses alert, she looked around for the origin of the sound.

It was coming from her dresser. No, from under the bed. Or out the window. From nowhere, from everywhere. Or from elsewhere. Then, gradually, the whisper became a sort of call. Yes, each recess of her white room called her now: "Clarisse... Clarisse."

The child sat in her bed, her eyes sweeping the room, searching for the least little glimmer of light that would tell her who or what was calling her.

There! There, hadn't she seen a light flickering? Moving? And there, again! And here also, and again there... Everywhere, little fires came to light. Blues, reds, yellows... a ballet of multicolored fairies, as if all the fairies in the world had gathered together in her bedroom at the same time!

A little confused, and a little afraid as well, Clarisse finally felt the dancing sparks surround her. They were there, in front of her, for her, dancing; each shape, each movement more beautiful than the last. And her ears resounded with the song, smooth and languorous, so delicious it made her heart shiver. She rose and without thinking, her tiny feet began to tap on the cold floor, slowly. Then, at last, joining the fairies, she danced with all the delicacy and grace of a princess.

Soon she thought she could hear laughter, little whispers of amusement. And that call, she could hear, growing more distinct, "Clarisse!... Clarisse!"

Thousands of sparks filled the space around her. They shadowed every movement. She lifted her little arm, making them turn in swirls of bright colors. Millions of tiny fireflies turned around her, kissing her little legs.

It felt good. She was happy. She laughed.

What did it matter if, in the adjacent bedrooms, the other children were woken by the noise?

She didn't have to be quiet now. She felt light, finally removed from the intense and unbearable pains which had confined her to her bed. She had been crippled by sickness for so long.

She had never been able to get used to it. How are you supposed get used to pain, anyway?

But tonight she wasn't even thinking about the pain. She was completely diverted: she was at a party. She was cured. Cured by the fairies who had come to save her and who kept calling: "Clarisse! Clarisse!"

One last twirl, one final spin. A last glance toward the bed, a goodbye. A last little wink at the heavy and cumbersome body which she had left under the covers, farewell to the yoke of pain and suffering. A final, radiant smile before she raised a foot, no longer touching the ground.

A tremendous laugh shot out from her throat, and there, finally, she exploded into a billion little lights, mixing into the billions of little lights that guided her.

She was happy.

She was free...

It was in Chinon, the French city of wine, that Adam Joffrain came into the world in 1972. Employed by the post office (to pay invoices), he is a father to two. In the evenings, he writes fiction. He has published games in various children's magazines (featuring famous characters such as Mickey Mouse and Bugs Bunny), and his homage to Lovecraft was published in *HPL 2007*. These days, he loses his hair, cultivates to his beer belly, and continues to write when his (lazy) muse remembers him. http://www.joffrain.net

Jackie Ω Has Gone Too Far
Moxie Mezcal

The six-foot-six hermaphrodite laid her immaculately sculpted body across the polar bear skin rug, turned her head to gaze seductively into the camera, and batted her five inch long glowing fiber optic eyelashes. Then she parted her lips, which were coated in a liquid crystal lipstick that shimmered and sparkled mercurially under the camera lights, and spoke:
"Let me break it down for you like this.

"One day, eons ago, back before the concepts of days or eons had even been invented, a being found herself alone in the infinite darkness of the cosmos. For lack of a better term, let's call her God.

"So God was feeling a little bored, and a little lonely, and so she started imaging what it would be like to have someone else to talk to. She closed her eyes and pictured what he would look like, down to every last detail, every tiny hair on his body, every pore in his skin, every cell in his blood. And through her imagining, she made him real.

"She called him Adam. In order to make the conversation interesting, she made Adam believe that he wasn't God, that he existed somehow apart from her. That way, it wasn't just like talking to herself, you see?"

A clubfooted eunuch wearing a crotchless jester's costume entered the frame and knelt between the hermaphrodite's legs in supplication before lifting a large, multi-pronged stainless steel sex toy and introducing it to the hermaphrodite's many-splendored genitalia.

"What the fuck are you watching?" I asked, looking over my receptionist's shoulder at the bank of nine video screens. Each were a different shape and size, displaying the same scene from different angles.

"Jackie Ω," he replied without taking his eyes off the monitors.

Jackie Ω (pronounced Jackie Ohm, though hardly anyone alive today would get the reference) was an Internet celebrity and counterculture icon. Part porn star, part punk poetess, part modern-day oracle, she had a weekly webcast in which she'd expound on topics of political, philosophical, or social importance whist performing sexual acts that usually went far beyond society's generally accepted standards of healthy exploration.

In the bottom left corner of each screen, nine synchronized timers counted down from twenty-three minutes. Jackie Ω's shows always lasted exactly twenty-three minutes, which was the precise amount of time that it took the authorities to untangle her elaborate web of proxies and decoys to pinpoint the location of where she was filming. As soon as they got a fix on her, she pulled the plug and bolted. The next week, she'd be back at a new location broadcasting to a new set of feed addresses. (Usually pages hidden on some major corporate or government site) Somehow her core audience always knew where to find her, like my receptionist, Chrys. He spent hours scouring forums and blogs, sifting through speculation and misinformation to somehow prognosticate where she'll pop up next. All this was done on my dime, mind you, but I usually didn't bother complaining. It wasn't like I had a lot of legitimate work for him to do anyway.

On screen, Jackie continued to writhe in pleasure, with the rhythm of her sensual gyrations matching the slow, seductive drum beat that pulsated on the soundtrack.

Soon, however, God grew just as bored with Adam as she had been of being alone. He was too predictable, too repetitive; she knew his every thought and reaction before he even expressed it. The problem was that even though he had forgotten that the two of them were actually one, she still knew the truth.

"God is. God says The Word. God hears The Word.

"So she imagined that instead of God, she was someone else. Let's call her Eve now. And Eve believed that she was a wholly different person from Adam. She convinced herself that she couldn't see into his soul, just as he was convinced that he couldn't see into hers. Therefore, she had to wait for him to say what he was thinking before she could let herself know it. And whenever he did something she would pretend to be surprised, as if she hadn't been the one who made him do it. This kept the game interesting, and with practice, she got better and better at deceiving herself.

"Eventually Adam and Eve had children. In order to keep the game going, each child also believed that he or she was a unique person, not just different aspects of the same being. They kept the game going with their grandchildren, and then their great-grandchildren, and so on across the millennia, until eventually we had gotten so good at playing the game, we completely forgot that we had ever been God at all.

"This is the forbidden knowledge, the serpent lurking in the garden."

Jackie suddenly arched her back and jerked her head, spilling the platinum blonde tresses off her shoulders as the jester brought her to orgasm. The video morphed and flexed, like ripples across water's surface, warping the image with fish-eyed perspective. Meanwhile, she erupted into a flurry of exaggerated moans and obscenities, overloading the audio with a piercing shriek of feedback like an air raid siren, which mixed hypnotically with the mechanized whirring of the sex toy's motor and the throbbing, incessant drum beat.

"She's really gone too far this time."

He was right, of course. Pornography was one thing, but Homeland Security was never going to let this kind of religious sedition slide.

The timers on the screen counted down to zero, and simultaneously, all the displays went dead.

Moxie Mezcal is the author of the postmodern pulp novel, *Concrete Underground*, as well as the upcoming sci-fi noir novella, *Invisible Kingdom*. Moxie lives under an assumed name in San Jose, California.
http://moxiemezcal.com

Throat Wad
Andersen Prunty

I awake with a wad in my throat. I turn to the prostitute sleeping beside me and viciously nudge her jailhouse-tattooed shoulder. Frantically, I try to tell her about the wad in my throat but everything comes out all garbled.

"I can't fucking understand you, you little creep!" She's very abusive. Has been ever since I paid her. When did they start staying over anyway?

I jump up on the bed, bashing my head into the ceiling, pointing at my throat and spouting jumbled gibberish.

"You need a doctor, honey!" Why does she talk so loud?

I flip on the light but can't find the phone. I hold my hand to my ear in the universal phone gesture.

"Yeah yeah. Hold your horses. I'm gettin' to it."

She rolls out of bed and squats down. The phone tumbles from her vagina. I vaguely recall the antics from earlier that evening before I went into the haze.

"I'm takin' off. You make it impossible for a girl to sleep."

She pulls on some stained underwear and a white snowsuit before heading outside.

I dial emergency. A woman answers. She sounds tired. "Yeah?"

I growl and gurgle into the phone.

"Hold on," the operator says. I hear a feverishly whispered conversation followed by a burst of laughter.

An authoritative male voice comes on the line. "What seems to be the problem?"

I growl and hiss.

"Sounds to me like you have a nice-sized throat wad."

That sounds about right.

"We'll send somebody out."

I turn on all the lights in the house so I don't feel so alone. Two hours later, just before dawn, the prostitute barges through the front door. She now has a dripping red cross painted onto the front of her snowsuit. She smells gamey and glistens with sweat.

"I had to run all the way back here. They sent me to take care of your throat wad."

I nod and point to my throat.

She crosses the room and straddles me in a way familiar to the lap dance she gave me earlier.

"Open up," she says. "I'm the only one who can do this on account of my small hands."

She holds her right hand in front of my face, flexing it. It is ridiculously small.

I open my mouth and she reaches down into my throat. She pulls out a screaming newborn. I try to talk—to express dismay, utter thanks, anything—but I'm still choked up.

She plops the baby, male, onto the floor and says, "Twins?"

She reaches in again.

She pulls out another baby and places it next to the first one.

This goes on for the next several minutes. I lose count after twenty-one.

Finally, she says, "All clear."

Now, looking at the squirming mass of babies, I'm too astonished to talk. The prostitute heads toward the door and says, "I'll be back in a couple hours. You're gonna need a babysitter."

She's absolutely right. I don't know what to do with all these babies. I strip off my clothes, collapse to the ground and pretend to be one of them.

———

Andersen Prunty lives in Dayton, Ohio. He is the author of *Morning is Dead*, *Zerostrata*, and *The Sorrow King*, among others. Visit him on the web at http://www.andersenprunty.com.

The Push of Man
L. Christopher Bird

So here I am wearing skins, working the earth, my bare chest glistening with sweat under the sun. This is not like the Garden at all, if I wanna eat, I have to make it happen. No free rides anymore. You'd think I would be bitter, but this work is in its own way more rewarding than picking any fruit I want. Well not *any* fruit actually, that's how I found myself in this situation ya know. Nose to the ground and mind on my work I hear a familiar voice behind me.

"Hello Adam."

Well by the serpent's tongue, its dear old Dad. "Don't you have some other pottery project you can bother?" I'm sitting there waiting for a response, but the Lord just stands behind me. I sigh and straighten up, turning to face him. Its like looking in a mirror, only he's smiling. I wish I could say that it's a smug, condescending smile, but its warm, and loving. And something about his eyes make me resign not to hate him forever like I had planned. I close my eyes and remind myself that I'm still mad at him.

"Something on your mind, Son?"

I glare at him, wondering whether to say anything or not, then find myself talking before I know it, with such emotion it surprises me, "This really ain't fair you know. You really set Eve and me up. I mean you give us a rule, a simple little rule not to eat of the tree of knowledge. But what knowledge was contained in that fruit I ask? Good and evil. Knowing the difference between right and wrong. So we ate the damn fruit, you know why? *We didn't know any better!* We didn't know right from wrong, naked from clothed, we didn't know that breaking your rule was wrong. We were ignorant, remember?"

"Actually, I would use the word 'innocent' to describe you and Eve. Blissfully unaware."

"Ignorance is Bliss."

"You should write that one down, Son. But remember ignorance is only bliss, because the ignorant don't know any better. Of course I knew you would eat the fruit, and believe me, you are better off for it."

"Better off?! Better off! You think working my ass off to feed the wife and myself is better off? I work this dust… the mother from which I sprang, and to 'which I will return' as you so eloquently said that fateful day, thank you very much. And you say I'm better off?"

"I won't argue with you that the life you lead is harder than the one in the Garden, but there is no going back now. Nor do I think you would want to. When you bit into the fruit of knowledge, it was the first real decision you ever made. You no longer were a creature that would eternally follow my will, you took your destiny into your own hands. You now make your own fate, not I, *you!* I shaped a garden for you, but now you have a world to shape for yourself. It will be *your* world. What happens to it will be the result of your own hands. The world doesn't need me to tend to it, that's your job now."

"But I can't make the rains fall, or the sun rise, only you can do those things!"

"Those things will take care of themselves, Son. I've set things up so that they will run pretty smoothly. The rain will fall, the sun will rise, don't you fear. I've given you everything you will need, you just have to find it for yourself, within and without."

"So if I'm in charge here, what will you be doing?"

"Oh well, I have another 'pottery project' that needs a little work over by Vega, but don't worry, I'll be checking up on you from time to time. But remember, its your show now kid, so don't expect any miracles. You'll see, someday they will talk about the Fall of Man to be the best thing that ever happened to the species."

And with a flash of fire, he was gone, leaving me to my work. 'Fall of Man' he said. If you ask me, I was pushed.

———

L. Christopher Bird has written free-prose poetry, haiku, senryu, and short stories under a variety of pseudonyms. Most recently poetry as Tadhg Christopher Bird. However he also writes under his Second Life Username, ZenMondo Wormser.
https://plus.google.com/u/0/116417560883731706834/about

The Old Man and Honey
Minoru Inaba
Translated by Ken Kusuki

From the converted gymnasium being used as a shelter, it is about two kilometers to the hill. On the steep path, Shuhei Abe climbs very slowly, watching his steps carefully. Surrounded by small woods of pines and oaks, he hears the wind blowing and rustling the leaves around him. Every few steps, Shuhei pauses on the path, looks up at the high noon sun, and wipes sweat on his forehead with the back of his hand.

Spending complete days in the shelter has been distressing. No one has privacy there. People around him often cry and grieve aloud. They talk about nothing except about who survived and who was rescued. Everyone in the shelter hates the disaster, loathes what has happened to them. They stand on the edge of desperation. Once Shuhei complained that the meals portions at the shelter were too small, and he was told that he shouldn't complain about something so trivial after the misfortune they had all survived. Shuhei kept his complaints about the meals to himself after that.

He arrives at the top of the hill and takes some deep breaths to calm his heart. He is in his late sixties so the path to the hilltop is rather challenging, but for him, this is the best place to bring himself to calm and reflect upon his life. However, even on the hill, his thoughts are always flooded with the terrifying images of the disaster.

When he is able to breathe normally again, he takes in a deep breath. The scent of the ocean is unfortunately faint. He sighs and casts his eyes upon the distance. Sunlight reflects off the surface of blue ocean. There used to be any number of fishing boats out there before the disaster. Now, he can only see part of a naval fleet and a police patrol boat cruising along, their wakes trailing behind them. He cannot see any fishing boats at all.

He looks inland. The view, although he has seen it many times, overwhelms him. Anger and resentment fill him, but he tries to calm himself – his lips pressed fast and his teeth clenched. He sees everything – ships, cars – broken and useless. A wrecked ship far from the water. A trailer overturned. A car broken and crushed. Buildings and houses have been destroyed – disintegrated. In many ways it is a cemetery. A mountain of death and trash.

It is a horrible thing. Offensive. They are the only words he can use to describe the view, because it seems beyond description. He wonders why God allowed these terrible things to happen – if God really exists. Shuhei is not a religious man, but he has been trying to believe in God. The closer he gets to the end of his life, the more he becomes aware of God. He ponders redemption, which he never found in youth.

Lately, he feels he's lost all faith in God.

The little town of fishermen, once peaceful and tranquil, has been completely destroyed. The wind does not bring him the scent of the sea. Instead, it smells like a mixture of something rotten and dusty. It reminds him of the smell of the dead.

He clenches his fist and intently looks over the ruins. His eyes become bloodshot with anger. There was a road there. A cigarette shop was on that corner there. His new house, which he used a long-term mortgage to build, is totally destroyed and is now covered in wreckage somewhere. He can only guess at the location where his house was.

Before the earthquakes and tsunami struck the town, he enjoyed the flowers. Usually, this time of year plum tree blossoms were beginning to fall and the flowers of white magnolia would cheer his heart. Migrating birds would have been returning, tweeting happily here and there. The town would be peaceful. Walking down the street, you would always meet someone with a smile and a greeting upon their lips. There were jokes and laughter.

However, they are gone now. Shuhei sighs again and again. He feels helplessly sad and resentful, but he resists the desire to burst into tears.

The earthquakes destroyed the town. And then the tsunami came and swept everything away. It is not only the town that was damaged but also the hearts of the people in the town that were incurably injured. There are countless people who saw their parents or children lost in the disaster. He knows a child whose entire family was killed. He also knows a parent who is the sole survivor of the family.

Compared to them, he is certainly fortunate because everyone in his family is alive. Nevertheless, his heart is burdened.

He will never forget what happened on that day. The tsunami warning got on his nerves. "Emergency! Evacuate to a safe place. Evacuate immediately to higher ground." The speakers repeated the warning and everyone in town was taken aback and moved around in confusion. No one expected such an enormous tsunami to come. The onslaught of the wave was sudden. His family understood the danger, got out of the house immediately, and called to Shuhei who was still lingering inside. Here and there, he heard people shouting and crying. Perhaps these disturbing sounds urged him to get out of the house. He got into the car where his son was waiting in the driver's seat. But the moment he was seated, he remembered his beloved dog – still chained alone to the doghouse.

"Honey is still chained to her house. I must get her!" he said.

Shuhei tried to get out of the car, but his daughter-in-law wouldn't let him leave, holding him back with a strength he had never expected of her. As he resisted her, the car started off. Shuhei shouted to his son to stop, but the younger man did not listen. Instead, he shouted back, "Stop shouting, Father, if you don't want to die."

Shuhei looked back at his house, his face pressed to the window. Honey was there. She was barking. He did not know why she was barking. Perhaps because she noticed Shuhei going or heard the family car leaving. Shuhei's eyes met Honey's. She looked sorrowful. Her eyes full of despair. She looked as if she were asking him why he did not take her with them.

But he could not save Honey. Before long, she was out of his tear-blurred sight. In the far distance, the enormous wave of the tsunami was approaching.

It was in that way that he and his dog were parted. It still dismayed him to think that he had done nothing to save her.

He cannot forget the appeal that had been in Honey's eyes. Standing on the hilltop, he says silently, "Honey, please forgive me."

Shuhei thinks back to the misfortune Honey has suffered since birth. She was discarded by her previous owner when she was still just a stumbling pup. On the verge of starving to death, she was found and brought to a center where she was put in line for euthanasia. As if she had been born to die.

Fortunately, a dog-loving volunteer decided to adopt her, saving Honey's life at the last moment. Shuhei came to know the volunteer, and he agreed to look after Honey though he had never given thought to keeping a dog.

His granddaughter came up with the name Honey. Shuhei liked the name, and the dog became a member of the family. Honey was brought up affectionately and got on well with the rest of the family. She was a beautiful dog and quickly learned to play tricks like "shake hands", "sit", and "wait".

But the earthquakes and tsunami tore Honey from the family. Never again will he forget Honey's baleful eyes as they drove off. He often remembers their departure and prays she survived the disaster. But as time goes on, he becomes aware that his prayers might not be answered.

It has been two weeks since the disaster. Every day, he hears news of the missing found dead. In the shelter, there are many people who have lost their wives, husbands, or children. Shuhei wants to talk about the missing dog, but he doesn't dare to do it because he knows it would be inappropriate given the circumstances. Only once did he talk about Honey.

"You're talking about a dog. I've lost two children!" one said.

The reply had been cold and disapproving. But he had expected it.

With a final glance upon the ruins of the town, he sighs and starts down the path of the hill. The sky darkens slightly as a cloud blocks the sun.

Three days later, Shuhei and his family move to his relative's house in a neighboring prefecture. Although difficult to make himself at home, it is far better than living in the shelter because he doesn't need to worry about aftershocks, and he can enjoy good meals, take a bath regularly and watch TV. He feels as if some bit of normality has returned to his life after such a long interval. At the same time, he knows he cannot live in this house forever; it will depend on his relatives. His son goes to the unemployment office every day and examines the classified ads in the newspaper to find a job to support the family.

Shuhei is retired and can't find work. He is too old to be hired. He is entirely dependent upon his pension. But he thinks he can live without difficulty if he is careful about his spending. The problem is that he has no house to live in. As he knows his son is trying to resolve that problem, he decides to stay quiet about it.

The news come three weeks after the disaster.

It is the evening and his granddaughter is watching TV. Suddenly she shouts, "It's Honey!" Shuhei, who is seated on the floor reading a newspaper, looks over at his granddaughter in surprise.

"Grandpa, look! It's Honey. That's Honey!"

His granddaughter shouts, pointing at the TV. Shuhei all but crawls to the TV, staring intently at the screen. The news segment ends almost immediately and the anchor person begins relating a different story. Throughout the evening, the story of a dog rescued from the ocean by the Japan Coast Guard's special rescue team, is run over and over. Shuhei is astonished to see the dog on TV. It is brown and white. There is no mistake – he recognizes Honey. Honey has survived for three weeks! And she looks relatively well in the arms of the rescue team member holding her.

He calls every office he can and asks to where the dog has been taken and how he can get her back. It is the police that finally help him. The officer who receives his inquiry informs him to call him back later and, after an hour, he is told that he can pick up his dog at the Japan Coast Guard office in Kamaishi.

The next morning, he borrows a small truck from his relatives and hurries to Kamaishi. While he is driving, all he is capable of thinking of is Honey. Every happy image he has of his past includes Honey. But he also remembers the sad expression that Honey had when he left her at the house.

He is afraid that Honey may not be as happy as she once was. He fears that she might reject him because he discarded her. But even if that's true, he can accept it, and he decides to love the dog more than before.

As the roads and bridges are damaged, it takes half a day for him to arrive at the Japan Coast Guard's Kamaishi office. But he isn't tired from all the driving. At the reception desk, he tells the clerk that he is Honey's owner, and the clerk tells him that the dog is in the parking lot behind the office. He hurries to the door, and as he enters the parking lot, he finds Honey sitting in the warm sunshine.

"Honey..." he says.

As Shuhei approaches, Honey looks up at him and whines softly. Shuhei calls to her again. She seems to be unsure. But then, her eyes light up. Happy to see her master, she wags her tail frantically, begins barking over and over, and stands on her rear legs.

Shuhei realizes that she remembers him and has not discarded him. Her loyalty fills his heart with a warm joy. A deep affection for the dog overwhelms him.

"Honey!"

Shuhei runs over to hold his dog, and Honey leaps into his arms.

———

Minoru Inaba is an accomplished Japanese novelist with a mountain of scriptwriting and TV credit to his name. Born in Kumamoto Prefecture, he made his debut in 1994. He has a large volume of original samurai period shorts as well as popular anime and manga fictionizations such as *Yamato*, *City Hunter 2*, *Stray Dogs*, and more. http://mutyudo.exblog.jp/

Sharan Gali
Richard Wright

The streets refused to feed him.

The day was a drought, driving him from one end of New Delhi to the other. Hot sun whacked the canvas roof of his auto-rickshaw. Only by moving, encouraging a breeze to blow through the open sides of the tiny three-wheeler, could he generate air to breathe. Ashish had heard of places in the world where the sun was worshipped. Perhaps it was kinder to the people there.

There had been fares – rupees here and there – all from countrymen who stared religiously at his meter during short journeys. They had bought another day of food for his daughters, but no more a future than that.

Dispirited, he turned onto Shanti Path, into Chanakyapuri. Behind stretches of verdant green grass hid the eyes of the world. This was where embassies clustered, chunks of other nations cut adrift from their homelands and transplanted into India. Some he knew of. The United Kingdom. America. Australia. Countries that drew his countrymen with dreams of gold and riches. Passing these places made his small life somehow larger.

Sometimes, there were rich fares to be had, from foreigners with no idea of the value of the rupees they waved about.

Near Norway's gates, a tall, muscled white man with a shock of red hair scanned the traffic. His grey suit was pressed and expensive. Ashish pulled in with expectant eyes. Mr. Red climbed into the back seat, and the auto sank a little beneath him. Ashish eyed his enormous passenger in the rear view mirror. "Where?"

"Sharan Gali."

"No."

Asylum Alley. He would take no man there.

"Yes. Name your price."

Ashish scanned his vocabulary for the words to explain. Some drivers had taken foreigners into that black hell. They came back alone, rumours of abduction and dark rites at their heels, forever meeting questions with cold silence and haunted eyes.

There was one certain way to end the discussion, and he touched the image of Ganesh in favour of that reason. "Twenty thousand rupees."

"Fine." Mr. Red nodded despite the ridiculous price, settling back in his seat and sealing their fates. Stunned, his moral principles slapped down by the sum offered, Ashish eased into the evening traffic, switching on his single headlamp.

The sun collapsed beneath the horizon, as though fearful of what was to come.

Mr. Red's bulk flattened the auto's inadequate suspension, and they jolted awkwardly along Delhi's hidden by-ways. Ashish did not wish to be seen on this shameful journey.

The entrance to Sharan Gali was a narrow gap between two collapsing tin huts. The darkness beyond was blacker than Kali's darkest dreams. Ashish slowed, making a final plea. "Is not safe."

Mr. Red, a bulky shadow, shifted, rocking the auto. "You are a good man. Drive on, please."

As they entered the alley, the light from his single bulb seemed to recoil.

The first people Ashish saw were dead, though they drifted in mournful circles around a man whose face might once have been imperious, but was now wasted with despair. He sat on the edge of the dirt track, huddled beneath a faded black robe. Ghosts beseeched him with imploring eyes, as if entreating him to majesty.

Back rigid with awe, Ashish glanced at his mirror.

"Drive on," said his passenger. "There is a place prepared for me."

As the sad man and his ghosts receded into the darkness, the auto's light picked up an upturned wooden boat. Perhaps drawn by the noise of the engine, the occupant leaned out, his naked torso too powerful a frame for the withered muscles that clung to it.

A human neck struggled to support the oversized head of a kite.

Ashish swallowed bile.

The creature reached out a hand in supplication, wet ebony eyes latching not on the wealthy passenger, but on Ashish himself.

"Drive on," came the backseat rumble. "Many here hunger for what you can provide."

Following a curve in the road, they passed a shallow dip in the ground. The muddy, drying remains of a forgotten rainfall slouched at the centre of the dip. Sitting in the viscous mud, another emaciated giant – his tangled auburn beard reaching down his naked chest and pooling in his lap to protect his modesty. Scooping mud into his shovelled hands, he smeared it across his mighty torso, weeping openly, his grief and longing piteous. Half buried in the dirt at his side was the snapped, rusting upper portion of a massive trident.

"Drive on," said the passenger.

The lamp shined on a dwelling of corroded, corrugated iron. Half buried in the dirt at the dwelling's entrance, a mighty hammer. Two emaciated goats lay panting on their sides, insects scurrying through their matted fur.

"Stop," said the passenger, climbing out.

Ashish watched the man strip out of his suit and shirt, wanting to flee, but desperate for the monies promised. The passenger wrapped a fur cloak around his shoulders, throwing his discarded clothes in the back of the auto. "You will find my wallet in the jacket pocket. Sell the suit, if you wish."

Ashish stared, and the stranger settled to the ground. Looking up, his outstretched hand absently patting the bony flank of a goat, he sighed. "Old ideas."

Ashish shook his head.

"Dead beliefs, decayed concepts, forgotten gods. Dried up memories of divinity."

"Here?"

"We have claimed asylum." He looked wistful. "So many gods here. Such capacity for belief. We bathe in ripples they cannot absorb. Your deities tolerate us because they fear us. We are their future."

Glancing at Ganesh's image, Ashish revved his motor, letting it voice his desire to leave.

The old god held him by the eyes. "Promise you will return. Lie to me that you will bring me a cup of your belief and let me sip."

"I promise."

"I understand, friend. Drive safe."

―――

Richard Wright is an author of strange, dark fictions, currently living in India with his wife and daughter. He is the author of the novel *Cuckoo*, the novella *Hiram Grange and the Nymphs of Krakow*, and the play 'Black Hearts'. His short stories have been widely published in the United Kingdom and America for over a decade, and include entries in the canons of Doctor Who and Iris Wildthyme, as well as appearances in recent anthologies such as *Dark Faith*, *Withersin*, and *Dark Wisdom*. If you enjoyed "Sharan Gali", drop by his manor at http://www.richardwright.org, and say hello.

Island Swarm
Kirk Marshall

The man with the sun-upholstered feet gazed out toward the sea's lazy marine warmth as it presented a constellation of fruiting blue paddocks to the fascinated, haunted human eye and he was again overwhelmed by the sensation that exile was desperately similar to abandonment.

He couldn't discern or quantify exactly how long he'd been hunching, with heat-parched mouth and burn-mottled forehead, on the strand while a pleiades of terns converged and dissolved above the waterline or a skulk of crabs veered into the shallow assault of the ocean whenever he snapped an eye open to observe their orderly coastal reconnaissance. He may have been here for months.

Time was a privilege here, an unnecessary luxury, because the ocean's implacable modulation and randomised locomotion would not allow for a clock's chronology in the same way you could not chalk numbers on its inconstant surface. It was like applying the laws of gravity to interstellar flight. He'd once tried to exchange handshakes with the rippling element but it had warped beneath his touch, adhering to subterfuge lest the man know its static identity and so proceed to tame, to master it.

The man did not expect intimacy or companionship or disclosure from the sea.

It existed to thwart proximity, it prevailed to perpetuate distance: it was definitionally opposed to being possessed, being owned, it disavowed transparent interaction as a human imperfection. So the man came to know things about the sea which betrayed its transformative character, anyway: it would not tolerate friendship, it continuously changed its parameters for play, it resented the man's arrogance and fragility, it was frivolous and forever consummating bursts of passion with itself, it was furtive and lacking in imagination, it was crippled by a boisterous and basic sense of humour which failed to apprehend the intricacies of a nimble wit. But it was troublingly alike, also: like man, the sea was given to funks of introspective brooding, it was frequently violent or vituperative, it strived in vain to exercise control over free and untamed agents, it was incapable of fraternity and therefore forever lonely.

So the man with the yielding pink palms was consoling himself with deep, demotic ruminations on the plight of his extraordinary exile, one whose existence was enriched by the spectre of misery, when he saw a human figure about twenty yards distant emerge from the suck of the sea, before the apparition set himself upon the descending bank of the fourth island, his arms spreadeagled and his tongue grappling for air.

There were about five islands in the man's beleaguered domain, and they described a hemispherical cluster which resembled a haphazard frown or an inelegant smile depending on the direction you viewed the arrangement.

Each island was separated from the last by a channel of water which extended to twenty yards, but there were occasions in which the moon dangled, fat with superluminal fire, just low enough for the ocean to retreat and the man might, after three weeks of nautical enclosure, relish the opportunity to navigate a landbridge brokered from salt deposits to the next island and make occupation there. Each island was different (the second island, clockwise from the man's current post, was abundant with bananas and plantains that littered its shore, whilst the fourth island, on which the stranger now sprawled, benefited from the shade of a pandanus canopy), but each island shared identical dimensions.

They were six feet wide and eight feet long, just snugly configured to suffice in accommodating a man's sleeping body if he were to splay himself lengthways. But it was an ideologically threatening development for the man with the sun-mutated complexion to welcome the new arrival. He was an intruder, after all, encroaching on a marooned individual's pleasant, if abandoned, island monopoly.

There was little that the man with the rash-harassed shoulder blades could do to assume an immediate authority of this uninhabited cove of tiny assorted sandbars, particularly since all the conch-shell trumpets and cuttlefish blades remained scattered over the surface of the third island, so he resolved this dilemma of dominion by whistling on his fingers, and waving aggressively, with a pump of the forearm, just militantly enough to display his meaning. Parrots cavorted in the foliage of the pandanus behind the stranger, so all noise tripped across the trough of the tropics in a distorted incarnation, too muddled by the undercurrents and assailed by the winds for the man with the summer-boiled face to interpret what the rasping newcomer had howled in response.

The words came again – "Why are you waving to me? I don't know you" – but at this point the gulls were performing synchronised plunges into the water dividing the two men, to skiff the current with their sun-glanced bills, and there was far too much screaming for the man with the island-charted smile to make much sense out of the stranger's repeated dismissals.

The man kept waving and the stranger continued snarling, and between them the sea tried its damndest to maintain the heaving distance separating the islands, to ensure the new friendship didn't result in blood being purged in ugly Cyrillic across its smug and pretty face. There was something about the social appurtenances of company that a lonely thing like the sea would never understand.

———

Kirk Marshall is an emerging Brisbane-born, Melbourne-based writer. He has written for more than sixty publications, both in Australia and overseas, including "Award Winning Australian Writing", "Wet Ink", "Going Down Swinging", "Voiceworks", "Verandah", "fourW", "Mascara Literary Review", "Word Riot" (U.S.A.), "3:AM" Magazine (Paris), "(Short) Fiction Collective" (U.S.A.) and "The Seahorse Rodeo Folk Review" (U.S.A.). He edits "Red Leaves", the English-language / Japanese bi-lingual literary journal. Kirk's début short-story collection, "Carnivalesque, And: Other Stories", will be published by Black Rider Press in October, 2011. http://fun-with-kites.livejournal.com

Kopy Cats
Davide Mana

It started the night his trophy girlfriend dumped him.

He sat outside on the patio of the hottest lounge club in town. Her firm, Gap-furbished ass and high heels walking away from him, but all he could do was stare at the bill.

There was an extra zero.

He snapped his fingers in the air, calling the waiter.

"There's a mistake," he said, handing back the bill.

The waiter looked at it without touching it.

"I see no mistake," he stage-whispered.

"Whaddyamean?" he said, a little too loud. "I ordered two coffees!"

People around started staring.

The waiter smiled. "And two coffees it is," he said. "Sir."

Never talk money. That was the rule; only the poor talk money.

But it had been a hard night. "You can't be serious," he said, ignoring the stares and the whispers. "One hundred and thirty euro?"

"You might have noticed," the waiter said, "that this is not the sort of two-bit Starbucks place you are used to. This is a luxury spot, and we offer our patrons the best of the best."

The whole place was suddenly very quiet.

Everybody was staring at him. The waiter, leering. The other punters, shocked. People were walking by amused. Even the fake mariaci were doing their rounds of the square, trying to raise some cash by playing "Deguello".

"We," the waiter went on, "serve the best certified Sumatran Copi Luwak, an exclusive product, for which a retail price of sixty-five euro per cup is very reasonable, and nobody," and here he stressed the words, "has *ever* complained."

He felt like the whole plaza, the whole neighborhood, the whole town was staring at him. Smile frozen, he pulled out his credit card.

"Cash, sir, if you don't mind."

With dead fingers, he fumbled three fifties out from his wallet, dropping them on the table.

"Keep the change," he croaked.

And he staggered away, the people's murmurs following him to the car.

Back home, he googled around.

And believe it or not, the damn waiter had not been lying. It really was called Kopi Luwak, and it really was the most expensive coffee around.

The Wikipedia entry stated, it was named after the Luwak, some kind of Sumatran rat-monkey that ate coffee grains and shitted them whole.

Some sicko got the idea of collecting 'em, baking 'em, and brewing 'em. Horrid.

Two hundred and thirty kilograms produced per year.

Not much, but it went for five-hundred to fifteen-hundred quids per kilo, and the brew was pushed on filthy rich connoisseurs at over sixty quids per cup.

Big money.

He found a photo, of the constipated rat-monkey, which did not look so much like a rat, monkey, or marsupial civet, but was rather similar to a stray cat.

That was it.

In two days he secured a storage locker in suburbia, put fifty rabbit cages inside it, bought a truckload of cheap coffee from a supermarket, and found ten kids that would make two euro for each stray cat they brought him.

By the next weekend, his first ten kilos of coffee grains shat by stray cats were ready.

He put down two euros and fifty on craft paper bags, and ten more for a quick print job of a logo.

Then he did the rounds of some pretty exclusive eateries and digs.

He mentioned travels abroad, political friendships, exotic locales.

Then he pulled his paper bags out.

Fifty euro for a one hundred grams bag.

As it takes six grams to brew a cup, it was reasonable.

His clients' avidity was satisfied.

And his, too.

Money started pouring in.

The cages became one hundred, one hundred and fifty, a warren of wire boxes filled with mangy cats, force-fed an obscene mix of Tender Vittles and coffee grains, the high-protein content of the fodder causing a drug-like dependence.

Granted, there were losses. The protein surplus messed up the cats' kidneys, and a few dropped dead each week. But replacements were easy to get.

The kilos per week became thirty, then fifty.

Kopi Luwak, or a reasonable copy thereof, flooded the market.

The media picked up on the new trend, running pieces about the new fad.

The brew was what everybody wanted.

Within six months he had a new car, a new girl, tables reserved in the best spots in town – where he stuck to bottled Perrier, anyway.

He was a winner.

He was young and rich.

Even if "rich" was the wrong word, his new friends (who were rich) knew he was just a lucky climber, a sleazy busybody in the money.

Most of them thought he was into something bad, but socially acceptable. Like selling cocaine, or pimping for his fiancée.

Maybe he was blackmailing some politician.

He was ok.

At the top of the furor, a charity event was held in which assorted glitterati put down one hundred and fifty euro each for a guided appreciation of what came down to, when all was said and done, cheap coffee shat by highly-strung nephrotic cats.

It was a success.

His only problem was the neighbors complaining of the racket made by the two hundred caffeine-addicted cats in his sixteen square meters of coffee plantation.

A racket made even more disquieting by the fact that no cats could be seen roaming the neighborhood.

He had to grease a few wheels.

He started toying with the idea of using illegal immigrants instead. They would be biologically closer to the Sumatran thing, produce higher volumes of coffee, and keep mum.

Then, one night, it was all over.

He vanished.

Most thought he had done a runner, cashed in his assets, dumped the girl, and moved to some exotic tax paradise.

Sumatra, maybe.

Sure, he knew a lot of things about Sumatra.

The cynics guessed a fall-out with his friends (the Mafia, the Russians, the Colombians) and pictured him pushing daisies in some empty lot.

The smart ones pointed to the Chinese Triads. He had been renting a storage space where illegal Chinese immigrants sewed clothes for Dolce & Gabbana.

Or something.

They found the body after the neighbors complained. About the smell, this time.

He had been ripped to shreds, his remains buried under a pile of broken cages.

His Porsche was parked nearby.

The CSI guys had little doubt about the dynamics of the killing.

"The fucker kept two panthers in his garage," said the crime scene guy, pulling off his latex gloves.

They filed it under 'domestic accident.'

The story of the two panthers got some media coverage. But nobody ever saw them around, and it slipped into oblivion within days.

Nobody ever connected his death with the horde of rampaging stray cats that swept through the city like furies. They assaulted coffee bars and restaurants, raided supermarkets, and one was even found stuck and rabid inside a coin-op coffee machine in the railway station.

Two firemen were badly injured freeing it.

Davide Mana (Torino, Italy, 1967) is leading a double life. By day, he is a paleontologist specializing in environmental data analysis, working on his belated PhD at the Università degli Studi "Carlo Bo", Urbino. By night he is a science fiction & fantasy writer; his stories have been published in Italy, UK and Japan. He is one of the editors of the *ALIA* international anthologies of fantasy fiction, and a regular contributor to independent literary magazine *LN-LibriNuovi* and *L'Indice dei Libri del Mese* (the Italian edition of the *New York Review of Books*). His other interests include photography, jazz music and Zen philosophy.
http://strategieevolutive.wordpress.com/

Why Wear Red?
Show Tomono
Translated by Yuli K. Bethe

On the train heading home from work, I encountered a group of Santa Clauses.

It was the middle of summer!

Three young girls, dressed in miniskirt versions of Santa costumes, had just walked into the compartment. Their bare, white thighs drew my eyes.

"What do you think of them?!" I asked one of my coworkers, a younger man who had started at the company after I did and who happened to be sitting right next to me.

"Gorgeous. I like the one on the right. The long-haired one."

I had expected him to say something like that. My coworker's so direct, that it actually charms the women.

"I didn't ask which girl you fancied. I was asking why the heck you think they're wearing Santa costumes in the middle of summer."

"Who cares? Miniskirts and sleeveless tops, they look nice and cool."

"I can see that, idiot."

"You might not want to stare so hard. People will think you are ogling."

"Shut up!"

I already happened to be aware of that fact. I'm slightly near sighted, but don't wear glasses. When I want to see something clearly, I squint. The wrinkles that form around my eyes when I do that, make me appear to be leering.

Still, something kept nagging me, and I could not help but peek at the girls from time to time. Then, my eyes met with the short-haired girl. She looked away. Too bad.

"I told you so!" My coworker said with a chuckle. I smacked him upside the back of his head.

"Shut up, or I'll hit you."

"But you've already hit me!"

"Why are they dressed as Santa Claus in the middle of summer?"

"You seem strangely obsessed. It may have been a costume party, or perhaps it's some kind of bar uniform. Nothing special. Though, that outfit would be mighty cold in winter. What's your problem with them?"

True. It didn't seem like a big deal. And yet, why was I so concerned?

I looked back at the girls, this time openly. The short-haired girl glared back at me, but I didn't look away. What was it that was nagging me? Was it their good looks, or was it the out-of-place feeling of summer Santas? That said, the southern hemisphere always enjoys Christmas in the summer.

I continued staring. The train jolted to a stop. The conductor's voice echoed through the compartment.

"There has been an accident at the railway crossing ahead, and we have come to an emergency stop. Please try to relax, and we will inform you of the details as soon as we have them."

That jolt gave me the answer.

"Hey, I got it." I said to my coworker.

"Got what?" He answered, never lifting his eyes off the thighs of the long-haired girl.

"It wasn't the girls that was bothering me."

"Then what?"

"It's the contents of their sacks."

Dressed as Santa, naturally the girls would be carrying large white sacks. Yet they carried their bulging loads with such ease that I had first thought them to be full of air. From the way they moved during the emergency stop though, I realized they must be stuffed with something.

Something, probably human-shaped. About the size of a child.

The short-haired girl noticed my gaze was on their sacks. She whispered something to the other two.

All three of them looked at me, and grinned. A glimpse of surprisingly long canine teeth showed from between their blood red lips.

Ahh, I thought. The red of the Santa costumes would hide any blood spilled on them.

A red glow began emanating from their eyes, paralyzing my ability to think. Clearly, tonight is going to be my last summer night ever, was my last flickering thought.

―――

Born in Osaka in 1964, Show Tomono is a member of the game designer group SNE and a novelist who graduated from Osaka Prefecture University. He has worked on a variety of projects such as GURPS Runal; a comedy fantasy RPG; a Chinese mythos RPG; and *The Damned Stalkers*, a story of demons living in the modern world, with Hiroshi Yamamoto. http://www.groupsne.co.jp/.

Thrones & Powers
(excerpts from a crime novel set in Heaven, Hell and Mexico City)
Jon Courtenay Grimwood

The two men met in a café near St Peter's, because meeting there amused the first, and the second needed his help enough to accept a location he regarded as provocative. He was also unhappy about his companion's choice of costume. Although finding someone dressed as a cardinal in a Vatican café was not usual. Certainly, it raised few eyebrows among the tourists, faithful and staff from the Holy Office, who drifted in and out buying iced lattes.

'Highness,' he said. 'You could have worn something else.'

'Possibly. But I am allowed the sash and biretta.' This was true. The prince had been a cardinal once and no pope stripped him of that rank.

So, technically, he still was.

The *clip-clop* of horses came through an open window. But the only sound either heard was the silence between them. They had been sitting at their table for at least fifteen minutes. In that time they had said sixteen words. Those being the comments about the first man's robes.

'So,' said the prince, adding a seventeenth to the mix.

'Indeed.'

A waiter came to offer more coffee. As the original cups stood cold and untouched in front of them, he took their grunts as proof that these were men who wished to be left alone.

'This is difficult.'

The prince nodded. 'Your choice…'

'Is unacceptable?' This didn't surprise the man wearing a suit. 'Equally,' he said. 'Your suggestion…'

His Highness smiled ruefully.

They sat for another five minutes. Both took the fact the other had agreed to meet as proof that a compromise was possible. Unfortunately, neither could work out what the compromise should be. 'It's true?' the prince said. 'You wear formal dress only on special occasions these days?'

The suited man wasn't listening. 'How about Abdiel?' he said suddenly.

'He's gone native.'

'You suggest someone then.'

Reaching for a menu, the prince flipped it over and produced a silver pen from inside his robes. His companion expected him to scrawl a name. Instead, he sketched a crude shield and then a smaller shield inside that. The border between shields he filled with a dozen hastily drawn fleurs-de-lis. It was a blazon not seen in battle for nearly seven hundred years.

'Think about it,' he said. 'Who saved the King of Spain's treasure from Jacques de Sores in 1555, solved the murder of that Florentine sculptor, and got back Marie Antoinette's necklace?'

'He'd never do it.'

'Why not?' said Lucifer, shooting the cuffs on his robes to check an ostentatious Breitling Bentley chronograph. 'He has the instinct and the hunger. Besides, you have Jeanne. What card is stronger?'

'Do you know where he is?'

'Of course,' said Lucifer. 'He moved from Tokyo to the Upper East Side and from the Upper East Side to Mexico City. Doing my work under the mistaken impression he was doing yours.'

'And there I was,' San Gabriel said. 'Thinking it was the other way round. Do you know if he still has that cat?'

'What cat?' asked Lucifer.

It was the archangel's turn to smile.

***

Compared with this climb, Don Gil's flight from New York to Tokyo had been simplicity itself. He'd sat under a blanket, tipped back his seat and fastened his seat belt on the outside, pushed his feet into the complimentary slippers and fastened his eyeshade. He took it for granted the cabin crew would know he didn't want to be woken up for meals or anything else, and he was right.

From the airport at Narita, he took the limousine bus to Haneda, and bought himself an internal flight to Sapporo. A coach carried him from Sapporo to Iwamizawa, using the new six-lane expressway. It was only then he ran into problems. None of the taxi-drivers in Iwamizawa would take him where he wanted to go.

Having caught the local bus Don Gil understood why. The village he needed was a good day's ride on roads that were largely ruts and gravel, around bends with sheer sides and across wooden bridges that rocked under his bus's wheels, small though it was.

Wind rippled the wild grass and shook the firs. Waterfalls lit with rainbows that vanished if looked at too closely. A deer froze on the edge of a forest until they passed. At least he thought it was a deer, although its swept-back horns looked as if they belonged on a more primitive animal.

After a long afternoon, a student across the aisle offered him sushi from a little plastic box. She did so with a small bow.

'Please,' she said. 'I've eaten enough.'

She smiled widely to show that she meant it and Don Gil bowed in his turn. He used the disposable chopsticks she'd been using, but turned them upside-down first. This seemed politer than picking up the left-over balls of rice and raw tuna with his fingers.

After a while, she asked if he minded her listening to her radio. He thought she meant a Discman or iPod or something like that. But she meant a radio. A small one, with a long antenna she had to keep moving to catch the music. They listened to several tracks from *There Is No Emoticon Available To Express My Suffering*, a Japanese group seemingly singing English songs composed of lines randomly borrowed from other songs.

Although he suspected he was missing something.

'You're visiting?' she asked later.

'I think so.'

'You think so?'

Don Gil nodded. 'Maybe I'm just running away. Sometimes I think that's all I ever do. All those planes, all those cities, all those houses. All that hiding in the gaps between one place and another.'

'You're a poet?'

'Yes,' Don Gil said. 'Sometimes.'

The young woman smiled, obviously deciding that this explained whatever it was that this explained, and went on to translate into English a short poem about sex, barley and a starving cat. 'Beautiful,' he said.

'Basho.'

Her smile faltered a little when he took her face in his hand and peered deep into her eyes. 'Just checking,' Don Gil said.

'For what?'

'That you're not someone else.'

She got off at the next stop. But she was getting off at the next stop anyway, and she left Don Gil her bottle of water, what remained of the bento box and a copy of that day's paper. He had another hour at least, she said. Perhaps more.

He watched her go. A young woman in jeans and a tee-shirt, with her hair cut short to her shoulders and almost no make up. The only out of the ordinary thing about her was her earring, which had been made from a feather.

Wintermute? he wondered.

No, the feather would have been too obvious. She wasn't the angel he was hunting. Unless it was the angel who was hunting him. Just a young woman smelling of soap and shampoo, who liked poetry and was kind enough to talk to a foreigner on the bus.

She was right about the distance. An hour passed, and began to creep towards two. Time felt elastic and sticky and his head began to slip forward as the warmth from a heater tipped him into sleep. When he woke the bus had stopped and he was the only one on it apart from the driver, who was standing in the aisle, looking at him doubtfully.

'We've arrived,' the driver said.

'Where?'

'Here. I turn round here.' A tight loop in the dirt did indeed come back to where they had stopped. It was just large enough for a bus, provided the bus was small.

'I'd better get off.'

'Onegaishimasu.'

They bowed to each other and Don Gil watched the bus leave. After a few minutes, he decided to start climbing. He wasn't sure what would be waiting. But he knew something would.

Jon Courtenay Grimwood was born in Malta and christened in the upturned bell of a ship. He grew up in the Far East, Britain and Scandinavia. Apart from novels he writes for magazines and newspapers such as *The Times, The Telegraph* and *The Independent*. His novels include *redRobe, reMix, Falaheen, Effendi, Stamping Butterflies, Pashazade, End of the World Blues, 9tail Fox, The Fallen Blade,* and *Arabesk.* http://www.j-cg.co.uk/

Yara-ma-yha-who
Christene Britton-Jones

"Bloody Hell! Life doesn't get any better than this!"

I'm a writer.

Yeah, well, I try to be. Always got my publisher and agent tugging my work this way and that. Wanting something outta me. Some damned deadline. But how the hell anyone expects me to write in this god forsaken Brisbane is beyond me. The damned city is a rat race…hell, the damned noise sounds like a mob of Old Man Roos thumping over hard ground. I need to get out in the countryside, out there under those tall trees beside a stream so peaceful that I can finally hear myself think. Sure, the stream makes noises too, but not like the city. Trouble is it's so damned peaceful that I usually doze off and I don't get nothing done.

Maybe the grub has something to do with it.

The grub's always the same great tasting stuff you know; Rosella Fruit Chutney and Coon Cheddar on crusty bread, washed down with Robert Channon 2008 Reserve 05. Red.

Just makes me want to lie back under that big ol' Morton Bay Fig and listen to the stream babbling past.

That's about when I start nodding off. The head gets heavy; eyes sink deeper into my skull, eyelids flutter. And I kinda slip down onto the ground for a snooze.

"Yeah, s'truth Mate, I'm a goner." Yeah okay, I talk to myself.

Then, I'm out like a light.

That's about the time I start having this nightmare. The same damned nightmare. Every time. Right out there under the tree. I just get to feeling like something really heavy is weighing down on me. I can't breathe; my arms and legs get real heavy; I feel like I'm all tied up.

Yeah, trussed up tighter than a pig on a barbie.

Or like a mob of Roos all sitting on me. But it ain't no Roos.

I open my eyes and there's this lil' red thing-a-me-bobbie sitting there on my chest, sucking out my blood through suckers on his fingertips and toes. The air's stinking hot 'n fetid, with thick globs of hot slime oozing down on me.

Now this little red bastard, he ain't very big, but hey, it's got the biggest mouth I ever seen. S'truth it just opens that mouth and swallows me whole, head first. Right down into its slime stinking gullet. Then it pewks me back out again; whole. Then the lil' bastard runs off right up to the top of that tree, and there I am, covered all over in spit and drool, smelling like sour vomit, my skin bleached white, and these little red sucker marks all over me.

Man I'm in deep shit; no other word for it.

Yeah, right funny, ain't it mate?

Well, it's a bloody nightmare. Could just be a combo of the cheese and the wine.

Of course, on hindsight it doesn't explain me waking up with bleached skin, red sucker marks, covered in drool, and smelling like sour vomit. No, that's real. Four times that was real. And be bloody damned if I ain't getting shorter too! Shrinking up!

Every time I sit under that tree, thinking I'm going to write something, that lil' red bastard pounces on me, it's tiny toes and fingers latching on to me with those suckers, sucking on my blood. Then that lil' vampire bastard swallows me, n' spits me back up. Bleached skin and red sucker marks, drool all over me, and me smelling like pewk.

And shrinking, did I mention that I'm shrinking?

I'll end up being a bloody midget at this rate. Bloody Hell, that thing's damn near as big as me now. Or I'm damn near as small as it…eh!

Okay, you think I'm crazy, don't cha?

Well, I ain't.

You see, I went off to the library, hunted me down a computer and started looking into this thing. Found out those lil' monsters are called Yara-ma-yha-who, and they're an Aboriginal legend straight out of Dreamtime. Gave me a top idea for a story. A Yara-ma-yha-who story. Took myself back out to my favorite spot under that big Morton Bay Fig with pen, pad, Rosella Fruit Chutney, Coon Cheese, a bottle of the good ol' Robert Channon 2008, and stared at the blank page.

Waiting for that story to form up.

It just wouldn't come.

About that time something fell on me 'n knocked me out cold.

The next thing I know I'm seeing through a red haze, my vision all kinda fuzzy. Four beady eyes are looking back at me. Two of those big mouthed, big headed, red furry Yara things sitting side by side up on a tree branch staring right back at me.

Yeah, two of those lil bastards!

One moves his tiny legs and arms, flinging a twig at me. The picture broke up crazy-like into a myriad of ripples as the twig broke the water. I stared in…what the fu…?! It's a reflection. I'm looking at a bloody reflection in the stream!

"We're both Yara-ma-yha-who," came the words clearly in my mind.

I rub my eyes to clear away the foggy red mist and find myself staring at the back of my hands. Tiny hands, red with red fur, fingers tipped with suckers like a little octopus. Well yeah, it did say in the library that if those things swallow you enough times, and shrink you down to their size, you end up being one of them.

Crazy? Maybe? Might just be interesting too.

On second thought, could damn well be a whole lotta fun…
"Bloody Hell! Life doesn't get any better than this."

Christene Britton-Jones is an expatriate Aussie gal who encamped to the distant shores of the USA in 2006. It didn't take long for her to settle into a big rambling old house circa 1860 in the wilds of Pennsylvania with an assortment of weird wild 'beasties'. Her days and nights are spent either reading or writing Historical Fiction, Lovecraft, Horror/SF, Prose, the occasional film script or a bluesy ballad etc. She also loves riding her Harley, 'Valkyrie's Ride' out through the highways and byways of this picturesque land with her hubby Ran, also a writer. http://rancartwright.com

Billie_Goat_Gruff_2056
Philip Overby

"your mothers a stupid ugly whore, lol." banana_hammock2005 posted August 23rd, 2:32 am.

John Toombs, a.k.a. banana_hammock2005, would be the first victim of Billie Wing, self-proclaimed "Troll Hunter." He changed his screen name from "Wing_2056" to "Billie_Goat_Gruff_2056." Toombs was found dead, sitting at his computer, multiple axe wounds to his face. All of his fingers had also been removed. Crumbs of potato chips and streaks of lotion covered his jean shorts. banana_hammock2005 was only forty-five years old.

Billie found it bothersome that he could not post a picture of his mother online without someone making a crude comment. Then it happened again.

"dude, your mom's face looks like a pig uterus" Skies_R_Falling posted August 25th, 3:49 am.

Billie failed to see the resemblance of his mother's face to the reproductive organs of a swine. Yet the insult was once again quarrelsome.

When Billie commented, "Why do you say such horrible things about my mother?"

Skies_R_Falling replied, "STFU asshole"

After a quick internet search, Billie found the meaning to be "shut the fuck up." Now this faceless internet spectre had insulted both his mother and had rudely told him to be silent. So Billie traced some IPs, did some research and found his next troll to hunt.

Gary Washington, 1843 Oak Street, Apt. 39C, Pittsburgh, PA, United States of America. Credit Score 230. Works at the skating rink "Good Times Roll." Owns a parrot.

Home of Skies_R_Falling. Run-down beige apartment, swarmed with cats. Black curtains and pictures of glittering, waifish vampires. Billie found the skeletal frame of Skies_R_Falling resting in a coffin-shaped bed. He caved in his head with a bowling ball.

The parrot squawked, "OMG! OMG!"

Later, more comments appeared on his publicly posted picture of his dear mother.

"looks like that skank that lives down by the train tracks. is that her? roflcopter" AmericanHardAss99 posted August 28th, 6:03 am.

Billie was unaware of what "roflcopter" was. He assumed it was a helicopter of some sort. Perhaps AmericanHardAss99 was a helicopter pilot. His mother had nothing to do with helicopters of any sort.

Nonetheless, Billie knew that referring to his mother as a hobo prostitute helicopter was rather uncalled for. Another trace, and he found AmericanHardAss99 in a basement in Queens, New York. Watching online streaming pornography and American football simultaneously. He put up some semblance of a fight. Managed to scratch Billie's face with his orange-hued, cheesy smelling fingernails. Ultimately, he failed. Billie crushed his throat with a big block of ice.

Soon more remarks flooded in. Racist ones. Dirty ones. Religious ones. Political ones. Ones that made no rational sense such as:

"looks like a dingleberry tree" xXSlayerDeathCrossXx posted August 29th, 1:32 am.

"i tap dat" closedfist333 posted August 29th, 2:22 am.

"gross" Glamor_Hammer2012 posted August 29th, 2:40 am.

"dislike" Butter_Scrumlicious81 posted August 29th, 5:32 am.

"Must be part of Obamacare." Rush_Fan22 posted August 30th, 2:32 pm.

"I found the love of my life at Delaware_Singles.com. You wouldn't believe how fast!" Delaware_Hottie2011 posted August 30th, 2:59 pm and once again August 30th, 3:02 pm.

xXSlayerDeathCrossXx was found in his trailer park home, his lower jaw missing. His dog was eating his nose.

closedfist333 was stabbed in the neck with a pair of scissors.

Glamor_Hammer2012 was beaten with a vanity mirror.

Butter_Scrumlicious81 was scattered all over the city of Philadelphia. In at least fifty-six pieces.

Rush_Fan22 had both his arms severed. He survived but later killed himself by jumping off a bridge.

Delaware_Hottie2011 was never found.

Billie didn't understand these postings. Why would these strangers continue to mock his mother? She may not have been the most attractive woman, but she was a strong and kind one.

She had taught Billie how to swing an axe, to wield the ceremonial dagger of the Djarium Cyclops. Taught him the daemon conjuring rituals of Bath-Garmakk-Dulgalath. Helped deliver the Goat Babes from the abyssal wombs of the Burning Yew of the Forgotten Wood. Shown him the ancient path of the Black Octopus, Star-Traveler, Eldritch Destroyer of Worlds and Avenger Against the Unbelievers.

She even drove Billie to the store so he could buy bread. A good, honest woman.

After hunting down and killing twenty-six people, Billie Wing was finally arrested. Killing four in one home. Although the killings were quickly overshadowed by other discoveries at the crime scene.

When the police investigated, green blood coated the walls, the ceiling, everywhere. The house was in disarray. Goat meat was found stashed in the refrigerator. Bone weapons, bloody furs, and books made of skin littered the living room. No bodies were found, only pools of acid burnt into the carpet.

One severed head was found impaled in the front lawn. The head had shaggy black hair, a green warty-face, and tusks.

Other than those, all of Billie's victims lived with their mothers and were over the age of forty.

None of their mothers had been harmed.

The mysterious troll hunter had finally been caught. The scum of the internet could finally rest. Finally breathe. And resume their endless Scorched Earth policy of flaming the entire inter-web.

The severed green head was quickly covered up by the FBI. They claimed it to be a Halloween mask.

Before he was arrested, Billie Wing added one more caption to the picture of his mother.

"Darla Wing, 1950-2056 RIP"

One final comment was left on the picture after that:

"WTF" Joe_Blow1992 posted on October 24th, 2010.

―――

Philip Overby is an ex-independent pro wrestler, chicken factory worker, plumber's assistant, and salesman. In the past, he served as an intern for Raw Dog Screaming Press and also helped edit *The New Absurdist Anthologies 2 and 3*. He worked disaster management in two of the worst disasters in US history, Hurricane Katrina and the Deepwater Horizon oil spill. His poems appear in the *Hurricane Blues* anthology as well as "The Southern Quarterly." He teaches English in Japan and lives in Yamato City, Kanagawa with his wife Kumi. His first teaching job was in Fukushima.

http://philipoverby1.blogspot.com/

Cherry Guard
Yuusuke Tokita
Translated by Takeo Konno

Light pink petals danced in the night wind. In the moonlight, I stood in the forest of cherry trees, listening to the distant din of people.

At the foot of the mountain, revelers were partying under the cherry-blossom trees. They wouldn't come this far up though; the area belonged to the shrine. They were forbidden to enter. So I was alone.

"How do you feel?" A woman's voice from the shadows of a cherry tree.

"Great," I answered. "It's a wonderful view. I have all these beautiful blossoms to myself. I'm happy to be back in Japan."

I had given up my studies in university, and spent half a year wandering around Japan, Asia, and even the United States. Then my father fell ill. So, I returned to this place.

It was spring. On an evening like this, able to take in the fully-bloomed cherry blossoms, I truly felt at home.

"This is your father's workplace," the voice spoke again.

My father was a landscape gardener in town. He took care of the many plants, flowers, and trees in both parks and personal residences in the area. He also maintained the memorial trees at the town hall and the tree-lined roads of the riverside park.

But I had had my heart set on another occupation: becoming an author. After all, I had an elder brother who would take up my father's profession, and my parents thought writing would suit me – my brother had inherited our father's strength, but I was a weak, delicate, and dreamy boy.

"Go your own way and do your best. If you don't succeed, you can always come back home. I will prepare another job for you – as the Cherry Guard," my father said, and sent me off to university in Tokyo.

Cherry Guard. That was my father's other job.

As Cherry Guard, he worked to maintain the cherry trees on the mountain of Misasagi. Misasagi – also called Goryou-san due to an alternate reading of the Kanji – was located behind Rokusho Shrine, and was famous for its beautiful cherry trees. It was forbidden to set foot on the land though, as it was also the mausoleum of several royal families.

Within Rokusho Shrine, there were six gods – Ise-oo-kami, Iwashimizu-oo-kami Kamo-oo-kami, Matsuo-oo-kami, Inari-oo-kami and Kasuga-oo-kami. Our family has visited Misasagi and maintained the cherry trees there for generations.

Maintaining cherry trees was hard work and took a great amount of time, so there was a cabin for the Cherry Guard on Misasagi. The cabin was a simple one-storey house, similar to a small shrine. Within it had an earthen space for cooking and a six-mat room. My uncle had once lived in this cabin, when he worked as the Cherry Guard.

Cherry trees live a lot longer than humans, and our family has raised and maintained cherry trees for generations. How long must it have taken for the cherry tree forest to grow as large as it had?

So, I went to the cabin per my bedridden father's order. He had said nothing but "Go to Misasagi." He hadn't asked me why I gave up university, or why I had gone abroad.

My brother took me halfway to Misasagi in his small truck. I sat staring out the window, silent the entire trip. The cherry blossoms were in bloom, and both the town and the mountain were awash in a beautiful deep pink, but that's not why I was silent. I just felt ill at ease. Aware of my feelings, my brother respected my silence.

Eventually, after a long, winding slope, we had arrived near the crest of the mountain.

"You should stay at the cabin tonight. I'll come get you tomorrow," my brother said, handing me a bag full of snacks and drinks. "Do you know the way?"

"Sure." I answered. I had climbed Misasagi many times, and had stayed at the cabin before, as well. Besides, it was a full moon. As long as there was moonlight, I wouldn't get lost.

"Aren't you afraid?" he asked.

"No, I'm okay." I answered.

"You always say that." He smiled a lonely smile. His face, darkly tanned from the job he inherited, looked so much like our father's. His posture, his mannerisms, his reserved speech, all so much like our father's.

"So now you have become the Cherry Guard."

"Sorry," I mumbled. My brother should have been the one to become the Cherry Guard. He should have inherited this from our father along with the other work. But instead his lazy, little brother had returned, and the job was mine now.

I felt ashamed. I felt like crying.

I had entered university to become a writer, but all I succeeded in learning was that I lacked talent. There were geniuses in my class all right, original thinkers who could come up with amazing pieces of writing, while others devoted themselves in a continuous effort to cultivate their talent.

I can't succeed in life like this, I had thought.

I had desperately searched for a way to establish myself. I studied foreign languages, and tried to become the pupil of a famous novelist, but none of my efforts bore fruit. I had neither the patience nor the courage.

I had even considered taking the examination to become a civil servant, living a steady and stable life. But the idea of it was utterly disagreeable.

Finally I had gone abroad, in an attempt to find an original path, but I succumbed to laziness and found nothing.

"Don't worry about it." My brother tapped me lightly on the shoulder. "I don't."

I tried to speak, but the right words wouldn't come. It was one of my failings. I was never nearly as good at talking to people as I thought.

"Talk to the cherry trees," he said, and then drove off in his truck.

I started walking to the cabin as the evening drew in. Cherry petals blew in the wind like a snowstorm. Left alone on the mountain, for the first time, I felt myself calm somewhat. Maybe I...

"Welcome home," said a woman's voice, from somewhere. There was no one in sight. But I had the feeling she had been here for a long time.

"I'm back," I said at length.

I had always been able to hear her voice. The voice of the Misasagi cherry trees.

"The voice of the cherry trees," my father said. "You can hear the voice of the cherry trees."

I think I have known since I was a child. And it had scared me. I was always destined to return to the cherry tree forest of Misasagi, but I was afraid if I did, I would turn into something else. Perhaps that was why I ran away.

While studying literature, I had discovered that "misasagi" not only meant "the tomb of noble families", but it's alternate reading "goryou" meant "the spirits of the dead". It has startled me ever since. In the Heian period, noble men or royal families who were defeated in political strife were exiled to remote regions, where they died – hatred in their hearts – only to become evil, vengeful spirits. Angry at the government and fearing these evil spirits, locals made them gods which they called "Mitama" and enshrined them. Rokushou Shrine is one such shrine. The six mitama enshrined there had been forcibly so.

I had heard her voice when I was in university, too.

"Come back."

Having realized my lack of writing ability, I ran way again, this time overseas.

I couldn't get used to the cramped, squalid towns of Asia. I couldn't escape her voice even in the hustle of New Orleans. It was just when I was thinking of going to Haiti or someplace that my father's letter came.

"Come back."

Something had changed within me. The moment I decided to return home, my heart felt lighter. The Japan I had once hated now seemed nostalgic, and, longing to see it again, I flew back.

So, there I stood amongst the cherry trees.
   Reaching out to touch the trunk of one, I breathed in the air and knew that this was my place.
   A cherry tree whispered to me.
   "This is your place."
   I know, Mother.

———

Yuusuke Tokita is a pen & paper RPG designer, writer, and representative of Suzaku Games. Some of his major works include Shin-en (The Word of Abyss: Dark Fantasy RPG), Shin Megami Tensei TRPG Demon City Tokyo 200X, Blue Rose: Nexus. Psychic City Investigation File: Sin City Shinjuku, and Cthulu Mythology RPG: Hiei Mountain Aflame. He has also worked on translating foreign games into Japanese, such as the fourth edition of Magic: The Gathering and the fourth edition of Shadowrun. He is currently a lecturer at Vantan Game Academy. http://suzakugames.cocolog-nifty.com/

Eternal Case of the Mondays
David Agranoff

Late to work. You chose a world like Ambenix so you don't have to deal with this kind of bullshit. The bodies sped through the city like a thousand archers' arrows towards various tasks. Some towards work, most towards play, but one didn't fly on the freeway unless one was a thrill seeker – or in Luther's case, late to work. Once he spotted the City Planning tower, Luther lifted his body and slowed himself, turning off the freeway. He felt a person zoom past him at a hundred-and-fifty miles an hour.

Gary, his assistant, waited on the landing pad.

"That dude almost clipped you!"

Luther looked up at the bodies speeding past on the freeway.

"Well, you know the saying: the speed limit is in your mind."

Gary handed Luther a pad with City Planning assignments. There were a thousand modifications to oversee during work hours whenever there was construction and development in a city world. Of all the worlds on which humans choose to live, Ambenix was the most urban – known for wild street life and a "lack" of rules. The laws of social behavior, while not meaningless, were different. The same went for the laws of physics, hence a whole slew of special city planning requirements.

That was why, unlike the majority of citizens, Luther had to be at work five days of the week, and when things really got out of hand, seven. Yes, a seven-day week on Ambenix: it made business with Earth easier. As it was, business with home wasn't ideal; Earth was a gritty, unfathomable mess that no one wanted to deal with. The thought of living there was starting to put Luther off. Mentally shivering, he put it out of his mind.

Gary waited as Luther read the pad, and coughed nervously. The list was long, but it was number six that was Luther's problem.

"I see it. Byron is young and doesn't understand the basic laws," said Luther as he walked.

"He built himself a stadium-sized home."

"Yes, but the coding should have prevented that. How was he was able to by-pass it?"

"He didn't call it a home when he submitted the data."

Luther stopped outside his office and grinned.

"Interesting. What did he call it?"

"A gymnasium and sexual retreat center."

Luther gave a pat to his expanding belly.

"I have been saying that I need to spend more time at the gym."

Gary shook his head. Luther put up his hand.

"Alright, I hate messing with sex. Zone the sex centers down to the same space and specs as retail, no grandfather, effective immediately. And Gary..."

Gary had taken a step back toward his desk.

"Expect a backlash."

Byron flew as the wires stabilized his naked body and spun him towards Jeri. She couldn't be called his girlfriend, but she had not left the sex center since it opened. While many pieces of sexual exercise equipment were built for masturbation, he and Jeri kept finding each other. His commitment to fitness was only matched by hers. This was one reason that this planet ruled as far as Byron was concerned.

He was locked and loaded, ready for high-speed boning when the police came. Who knew that the planet known for free love and physics had a squad of flat foots? Byron ordered himself some clothes and demanded to know what was happening.

"You have exceeded city code and by decree of the Office of City Planning, you must evacuate while your space is reformatted to your individual requirements."

Byron grew red-faced.

"Who ordered this?"

Luther leaned back at his desk and watched the traffic outside his window. This wasn't a world for families, but he saw a family fly by, all holding hands. Who would bring children into a place like this? Sometimes he felt like he was the only order left in the whole damned universe. He wondered if Old West sheriffs felt like this.

It had been a long day already, and he had nothing about which to feel guilty. He thought about lunch but he wasn't particularly hungry; it is all mental after all. If he had ordered lunch, he would not have seen the man speeding off the freeway. His arms out in fists, his body armored.

Luther took a dive under his desk just as Byron slammed into the window. Luther signaled security and stood up to give the young man a piece of his mind. Byron was a programmer, had to be. He stood with a comically large pistol pointed at Luther's head.

"Are you the man behind city zoning?"

Luther had not completed his nod when Byron made his head disappear.

Luther gasped for breath as he sat up. The nurses ran to him with the impossibly slow speed of people restricted by gravity.

"We have another deletion from the program," the first nurse said.

He struggled to lift himself out of the bed.

"How long?" a doctor in a white coat screamed.

"Sixty-two years."

The medical team looked at each other. They didn't know what to do. Luther swiped at the cords connected to his head, feeling as if they were holding him down. His body felt old, weak.

"Sir, if you sever the cables we will not be able to re-load into the program."

The doctor pointed to a junction box which was wired to the Ambenix computer core.

"Don't bother, his signal is wiped."

"I can be re-formatted," Luther begged.

The nurses and doctor shared a long look.

"No. Earth's population index and planet zoning rules are strict. One signal carrier per off-world simulation."

"I can't stay on Earth."

"I am sorry sir, but you never really left."

Luther cried in deep waves of sobs as they disconnected each cable.

―――

David Agranoff is the wonderland award nominated (best collection 2010 – *Screams From Dying World*) author of several novels including: the *Vegan Revolution...With Zombies, Hunting The Moon Tribe, Goddamn Killing Machines and Boot Boys* of the Wolfreich. All his novels have been published by various imprints of Erserhead press. He lives in Portland, OR. He likes kung-fu movies, Vegan Straight Edge hardcore, long walks on the beach and vegan junk food. Book reviews and news can be found at his blog. http://davidagranoff.blogspot.com

The Game
Bradley Sands

A Twister mat usually has four rows of colored circles. This mat is unusual. It has seven rows of colored circles. This is to compensate for there being seven players on the mat when the instruction manual only recommends two to four players. The three additional colors are black, white, and cupcake. The mat is very unhappy. It does not like to be crushed by players.

Twister is a game that is manufactured and sold by Milton Bradley. When it first came on the market, Milton Bradley's competitors described it as "sex in a box." This board did not come in a box. It has always been here. So has the void. Beyond the mat lies the void. The mat wishes the void would stop being so lazy. But void cannot help it. The void is not alive.

A referee floats above the mat and players. He is not a gorilla or a free sandwich. He spins the spinner, calls out, "Left foot green." He is not a stripper waiting inside a giant birthday cake.

The players take their left feet off the colored circles in which they are positioned upon and move them to the nearest green circle.

The lights go out. A coop of chickens cackle. The lights come back on. Mr. Boddy's left foot is no longer inside a green circle. Mr. Boddy is dead. The players cannot determine if his left foot vacated the green circle before his death or during it. The referee knows all. He is not a case of salmonella poisoning. A smoking pistol is positioned in a black circle beside Mr. Boddy's left foot. Mrs. Peacock screams.

Mr. Boddy has been murdered!

The referee calls out, "Right hand blue."

Although one of their number has been murdered, the players feel compelled to continue their game. Despite the mashed potatoes seeping out of the hole in the back of Mr. Boddy's head, they all move their right hands to a blue circle, wondering why they cannot fight the urge that compels them to move their right hands to a blue circle. They wonder who they are, how they got here, the name of the game they are playing, what the heck is the deal with the referee, why they like giraffes so much, and what is the nature of reality.

The players eye each other. One amongst the six must be the murderer!

Well, the mat could be the murderer. Although the players do not know this. And the mat suspects the void. But the void is not alive.

Colonel Mustard glares at Professor Plum. The educator looks like a man with murder in his heart. Professor Plum notices Colonel Mustard's staring at his cashmere sweater that is hanging so low the colonel can see inside his chest. He quickly pulls the sweater over his nose.

"Right foot cupcake," says the referee. He is not a she.

The sun explodes, relieving the players of their ability to see in the darkness. An ant roars into the night. The referee puts a new sun back into the sky. All the players' right feet are now on the cupcake circles. Except for Professor Plum's. The educator did not get the same opportunity as the others because someone has decided to change his status to that of a large husk of Swiss cheese with an agonized facial expression. A machine gun lies next to the milk-based cheese product. Colonel Mustard questions his powers of deductive reasoning and feels ashamed.

Mrs. White suspects Colonel Mustard. She also suspects Miss Scarlet, Mr. Green, and Mrs. Peacock, but she suspects Colonel Mustard more than the others. She is a highly distrustful hotel maid. Colonel Mustard is more suspicious than the others because he seemed to feign an exaggerated expression of intensity upon viewing the murder in Professor Plum's heart. Mrs. White believes the colonel tried to frame the professor by putting the murder in his heart while he was not looking.

The players try to remember their lives before the beginning of the game. They fail. The referee calls out, "Right hand red." The players try to move their right hands to the red circles. Everyone except Mrs. Peacock succeeds. Miss Scarlet's body blocks her attempt. Miss Scarlet's body is cruel and unusual. It is unusual because unlike most bodies, it celebrates the failure of its owner's opponent.

Mrs. Peacock's left leg wobbles. She becomes a casualty in the war against gravity. The other players dodge the trajectory of her fall. She lies flat on the mat, astonished. Her body turns to glitter. Her mind turns to religion. She finds this disappointing.

An optometrist borrows the players' eyeballs. A sinister tea kettle whistles. The doctor returns the eyeballs. Mrs. White is dead. A toothpick is lodged in her Achilles' heel. It is a rather large toothpick—the size of a sword—otherwise, the players would have been unable to detect it. Mrs. White's corpse does not suspect that any of the remaining players are the murderer. Unlike Mrs. White, he trusts people, although he does not understand why they do not share the same gender.

Colonel Mustard glares at Miss Scarlet. There are few things that he enjoys more than glaring. Miss Scarlet is the one person stopping him from achieving victory. The referee is not a national holiday. Colonel Mustard wonders if Colonel Mustard is the murderer. After a moment of contemplation, he determines that he cannot be the murderer because he does not recall doing any murdering. Miss Scarlet must be the murderer. She is very attractive, as murderers tend to be. The colonel imagines a scenario where he is not competing against her in a game of Twister, where she does not want to destroy him. He mourns the loss of this opportunity. He is very frightened about being alone on a Twister mat with a murderer. Miss Scarlet is very frightened about being alone on a Twister mat with a murderer. The murderer is disappointed that his potential murder victims lack variety. He tries to choose who to kill, fails. He tries again. It is a very difficult thing to choose who to kill when you are given so few choices. Colonel Mustard and Miss Scarlet await their deaths. The referee spins the spinner. He is not an unconditional act of love.

———

Bradley Sands is the author of *Rico Slade Will Fucking Kill You*, *Sorry I Ruined Your Orgy*, and *My Heart Said No But the Camera Crew Said Yes!* He edits Bust Down the Door and Eat All the Chickens. Visit him at http://www.bradleysands.com.

Initiation
Naohiko Kitahara
Translated by Orie Hiromachi

It is a slightly chilly time of the year and the city is in a melancholic state. A horse-drawn cart rattles along the cobbled stone.

Seated at a desk, his face turned towards the wind-rattled window, the boy observes the scene. In front of him lay his open notebook.

I must say, in all my life I have never met such a strange and yet intelligent boy such as him.

He is always easily distracted, looking outside more often than not, and yet he is still intently listening, answering accurately the questions asked of him. Moreover, he is not just listening, but grasping the fundamentals of the lessons ahead – nay, far ahead even – of my daily lectures. A boy of great insight, even though he is still but ten or so years old.

Even now as I speak he may be listening to my lecture with just half his brain while the other half attentively makes guesses as the occupations of the people passing by in the street.

Are his bright eyes showing me the purity of his soul, or perhaps the depths of his exceptional mind? It is no wonder he did not fit in at a military academy.

If I had not undertaken this private tutelage as requested by his uncle, I would never have met him. Maybe this is what they called fate.

I am pretty confident with the depths and limits of my own intelligence. But I can say with confidence that he will surpass my own intellect in time. It is only natural that he should be the one. That is why I've decided to grant to him the Key.

After finishing illuminating spherical mathematics within the bounds of non-Euclidean geometries on the blackboard, I walked wordlessly towards the bookshelf on the wall and took a book from an eye-level shelf.

His eyes consumed me as I did so; perhaps aware that something unusual was happening.

The book itself opened naturally, landing at that very page I had opened it to many times before.

The roaring fire crackled in the fireplace.

"Are you able to understand this?" I asked.

"Yes, professor." He answered despite the amazed look on his face.

He now understood that the scheme of the universe was not as superficial as he once believed, that in fact, it was really quite profound, exhibiting aspects he had not expected. His reaction is quite understandable.

He was no longer casting his gaze here and there. His eyes rather seemed to be staring at some point in the sky. He must have been trying again and again, at a furious pace, to take in what he had seen in the book.

"That's all for today," I declared.

He gathered his belongs without a word and left. I heard the sound of his small footsteps going down the stairs, and of the front door opening and closing.

I stepped up to the window and overlooked the city of Munich in late fall.

I caught his figure retreating unsteadily home. In his large coat, knee-length pants and deep boots, he was passed by a horse-drawn carriage.

The boy is no longer the same boy he was yesterday. The Key I granted him has been etched into his mind. Though I was only able to find the Key myself, he – Al – should be able to use it to one day open Pandora's box. Not at his age now, of course, not even a lad of his immense potential. However through trial and error, if he keeps the Key in his mind, he will certainly open that box.

And he will indeed be able to obtain the fire of Prometheus.

He is so pure that he will doubtlessly believe his works beneficial to humanity. However, I know the true nature of humanity much better than he does.

I can envision it. A time that will one day be upon us.

I understand very well just what my own true nature is. I believe that initiating the boy was the single greatest act I could ever achieve. Without even realizing it, he will be the successor of my very will. I will die someday, but my intention will echo through history.

I closed the page referencing the relationship between matter and energy, and returned *The Dynamics of an Asteroid* to the bookshelf. I noticed chalk powder on the sleeve of my frock coat and shook it off.

The flames in the fireplace danced, and for a while, I simply watched them.

Naohiko Kitahara was born on December 10, 1962. He is a writer of mystery, science fiction, and horror short stories, and also translates and studies ancient tomes. He has graduated from the Department of Physics and Mathematics of Aoyama Gakuin University. He pens his stories under his real name, and is a member of Mystery Writers of Japan, Inc, the Science Fiction and Fantasy Writers of Japan, and the Japan Sherlock Holmes Club. He is the chairman of the Classic Science Fiction Academy of Japan, which includes Junya Yokota, Yasuo Nagayama, and Shinji Maki as members. He has written essays such as "Hon no Zasshi," regarding classic literature. He is a known collector of books related to Sherlock Holmes, and has translated a number of Sherlock Holmes stories in several anthologies.

http://homepage3.nifty.com/kitahara/

The Ice-Flock Storks of Sørøya
Michael John Grist

Once upon a time in the far-far North, where winters were so cold that Odin's icy breath would at times flash-freeze the ocean waves themselves, there lived a flock of storks on an island called Sørøya.

And they were dying.

In summer, the storks dined well on frogs in the rock-pools of their island, but in winter when the frogs hibernated underground, they starved, and died.

"We must find a new source of food," the patriarch of the Sørøya storks said to his assembled subjects at the onset of one particularly fierce winter. "Or face up to Odin's unforgiving cyclops-eye like the dodo before us."

So, the storks of Sørøya roved their island from beach to beach and tried to eat all the living things they could. Some experimented with beech bark, bashing their beaks blunt to strip it from the tree boles, chewing it for hours, finally swallowing it like lumpy porridge down their gullets. They achieved nothing but stomachaches and diarrhea.

Others sharpened their beaks with conch shells and flung themselves like darts at the larger hibernating animals; winter bears, proud antelope, and ocean-borne whales. Most reached their targets and found themselves trapped like spines on a porcupine, waiting to be torn free and eaten as hibernation snacks.

Still others taught themselves to swim. They plucked away their white feathers and plunge-dove into the ocean depths. Yet they found nothing but eight-tentacled monsters, beasts that promised love but left only burning kisses on their plucked-raw skin.

"It seems we will face Odin's cyclops-eye soon," said the stork patriarch, looking sadly out over his blunted, sharpened, and featherless subjects. His heart sank, and he waded out alone into the rock pools, vowing he would not return until he had found food.

That night Odin's icy breath flash-froze the rock pools, and the stork patriarch was trapped in the ice. He struggled to pull his feet free, but they would not come. He flapped his wings until the black of exhaustion ran before his eyes, but still he could not budge.

At last he called to his subjects for their help. They came in dribs and drabs, all of them painfully thin, their plumage wilting, their spirits broken. They saw his condition, and set weakly to the rescue. The featherless storks lay down their un-insulated bodies to warm the ice, while the blunt-beaked storks pounded cracks into it, and the razor-beaked storks chipped those cracks into chunks.

At last, a moat was cleared around the stork patriarch. He flapped his wings, and flapped some more, and there was a creaking groan from the ice. His subjects gave a lackluster cheer, he flapped with all his might, and at last, with a sucking crack, he flew free. A clod of ice still clung about his feet, weighing him down. Once he was over the beach, he let his weary wings halt, plummeting to the sand.

The heavy ice-clod blasted a divot into the beach. The stork patriarch couldn't have known it, but a turtle was in hibernation there, and the clod cracked its back shell clean open.

"Come, come!" he cried to the others, as blood and meat squirmed beneath him. "Food from the sand!"

The whole tribe ate well that day.

The following night the patriarch directed all but a few of the blunt-beaks, razor-beaks, and featherless ones to gather and wait in one rock-pool. Odin's icy breath flowed through the water, freezing the tribe's feet in place, so that when morning came, the pool was wholly set.

The storks that were not trapped set to freeing their brethren with fresh energy, warming, cracking, and chipping a moat into the ice.

When it was done, the whole tribe flapped their wings, and flapped, and flapped at their utmost.

Crack! There was a sucking grinding, and the ice broke from the rock. Into the air it rose, a giant clod of ice, pale blue as the sky, held aloft by a hundred beating wings.

"Forward, to the bears," cried the patriarch. The tribe struggled to follow his earnest command. At first, they did little more than hover, as each stork faced a different direction and flapped his wings in a bothersome manner in his neighbor's face. However, in time, they adjusted, and each stork learned to flap backwards or sideways, in synchrony with his fellows. Slowly, the giant ice clod began to move forward. To the storks below, it seemed both a beautiful and terrible thing; a moving part of the sky.

It flew ponderously over the beaches and the stripped eucalyptus trees, to hover at last over a bear cave.

"Razor-beaks, in!" cried the patriarch, and the storks with razor beaks stabbed at the darkness in the cave, rousing one of the sleeping bears to pursuit. He chased them from the cave, roaring with a monstrous cry.

Out in the weak winter light he blinked his eyes, glimpsing the hovering island of blue above. His sleepy brain wondered if it was some kind of cloud. It grew larger. And it whistled as it did so.

With an almighty crunch, the giant clod crushed him. The storks cried out in joy. The many that were released by the impact moved to help their fellow storks escape, and then together at the edge of the cave, they dined well on bear.

To this day, the ice-flock storks still hunt on Sørøya. A ferry will take you there from the mainland, and you can see them stalking bear, antelope, and even whale. If you are especially lucky, you may see them bomb their prey in a burst of blood and ice. But beware! Should you see a patch of pale blue sky different from the rest, know that it is not some unusual cloud. It is the Sørøya storks themselves, looking to fill their bellies for the winter, with you as their prey.

Michael John Grist is a British ruins explorer, short fictioner, and novelist who lives in Tokyo, Japan. His ruins photography has been published in a number of magazines (Outdoor Japan, the Guardian), as has his short fiction ("TQR", "Aoiffe's Kiss"). Generally his writings are surreal, dystopic, and uplifting. He is currently writing an epic fantasy novel set in a steam-punkish city torn by mogrification, caste, and civil war, about a boy named Dawn whose mother nearly scarred him to death as a baby. When he's not out exploring ruins or at the Mac writing, he teaches English at university. http://www.michaeljohngrist.com/

Pepperroach
Edmund Colell

Jorge and Eduardo lean close together and bite the opposing ends of a cockroach on a fork. Jorge takes the end with the head, and Eduardo takes the end with the jalapeño shoulders and stem extending out the back. They both wince as the insect and pepper textures grind in their teeth and pile on their tongues. Soon after they swallow, they grab for glasses of water. Eduardo's face reddens and he says, "I know my tongue is peeling right now. It's cooked."

Jorge picks the antennae from his mouth and says, "It was your idea. And, seriously, do you crouch over the shower drain with a fork while I'm sleeping?"

"Yeah."

"I'm never kissing you again."

"It's okay, this got me too. Like I said, my tongue is cooked. That's why I normally don't eat spicy foods."

"Funny. You woke me up saying that the *cucaracha* in front of my face would resolve our eating differences."

"I had to get you to try bugs somehow."

Jorge picks a leg from between his incisors and his lips thin out. "Whatever. Let's just go to the store and get something actually good to eat."

"Fine."

The moment Eduardo twists the doorknob and pushes it aside, a microphone is thrust into his lips. "How did you enjoy our product?" asks a pair of horned-rimmed glasses.

Eduardo looks beyond the glasses to find a thin-haired, grinning woman; cameramen behind her. Trying to pull his lips together, he mumbles, "Not... too bad."

"We have a fan already!" she squeals. She then looks towards Jorge and adds, "Did you get a bite too?"

"Yeah, um, you're not going to try and sell us anything, are you?"

The woman withdraws her mic from Eduardo's mouth and says, "No, we just wanted to try making our first commercial with our first customers. We're not selling you anything because you already had our free sample."

"How do you know that?"

She produces a handheld device from her pocket and says, "We planted a transmitter on the roach." Two rods on the end of the device move towards Jorge's stomach and vibrate. "See? It can even pinpoint where it is."

Jorge's stomach contracts and he moans, "Couldn't you have asked us first?"

"You already ate it. That's enough of a yes for us. Now enough chit-chat, let's get prettied up and ready to shoot!"

Eduardo and Jorge are slammed into opposite walls by a stampede of white-clad people followed by a doorframe-fitting cockroach and a jalapeño that ducks and wriggles on the floor just to get inside.

" 'This will solve our problems,' " Jorge taunts.

Eduardo shrugs. "Hey, we get to be in a commercial at least." His optimism is answered by nurse scrubs being thrown onto him and Jorge.

"What the hell are these for?" Jorge asks.

"You two are going to help deliver. So suit up, let the makeup artists do their jobs, and learn your lines. We begin in ten."

The giant cockroach and jalapeño are arguing in Eduardo and Jorge's kitchen. "Marco," says the roach with an outstretched leg, "come back to me. You know we are meant for each other."

"No, Maria," says the jalapeño. "Your mother, she'll sharpen her machete on my shaft if I spill my seeds with you."

"Ay, Marco, just spill them right here, right now!" Maria then wraps her forelegs around Marco and her mandibles caress the stem. Marco leans in and saliva leaks from the stem, frothing around Maria's antennae. A stork soon swoops into view carrying a writhing bundle of jalapeño-loaded cockroaches.

Eduardo and Jorge scramble into the scene in their uniforms, carrying brown-and-green smiling bags. They shovel the scuttling snacks inside, shouting, "Crave a bunch of the crazy crunch!"

"And cut," says the director, who then shakes hands with them both and adds, "My friend Frank over here has your checks, and that was all we needed from you."

"Can you get this machine out of me, then?" asks Jorge.

"You'll pass it eventually, you know. Anyway, great first take from you both." She then turns to the non-human actors and says, "We're keeping you on standby. We have a promotional soap opera in the works."

Maria grooms her antennae and slaps Marco on his crunchy green rear, scattering a burst of small white seeds from his front.

"Right, awesome," says Jorge, "now please get the hell out of our house."

"Of course!" says the director. "And keep the scrubs and the bags as our gifts to you!"

After all have left and the couple are alone, Eduardo says, "I'd say it was worth it."

Jorge pulls a pepperroach from one of the bags and eats it, saying, "Yeah, I guess they're not that bad, but this is the only bag I'll have. Then I'll pretend I never ate these fucking things." After the second roach, he says, "By the way, where do we keep our laxatives again? I'm not going to sleep tonight unless I shit that transmitter out."

By the end of the week, bleary-eyed Jorge lays the bottle of laxative syrup back in the broken basket of the medicine closet. He imagines Eduardo and the fork behind the shower curtains, swallowing thoughts of Eduardo's growling guts.

Before his hand can withdraw from the bottle, a pale object flashes deeper into the dark. He moves the basket to the side and finds a twitching-nosed, albino rat with raisins for eyes. His hand flexes as he runs through a list of blunt objects to crush it, the list ending with a fat red highlighting of "laxative bottle."

The mouse squeaks as Jorge slams the bottom into the rat several times against the wall. He grunts, "Fuckin'. Mouse. Just. Die!"

Eduardo approaches from the side, naked and slit-eyed. He asks, "Mi amor, what the fuck are you doing?"

Jorge withdraws the bottle from the bleeding, breathing, and twitching rat. "That pepper-assed roach wasn't the only little shit that got into our house. At least I'm glad that you're not waiting for shower treats anymore."

"Whatever, okay? Why are you splattering rat-guts all over the place? You could've just picked it up with a towel or something and thrown it out."

Jorge uses one of the towels to snatch the shattered rat and show the bleeding raisin-eyes. "You see that? Now there are other fuckers trying to advertise to us." He then struts to the living room and grabs the remote. "Now we're gonna watch some Food Network. If I see a commercial for raisin rats or mango maggots or what-the-fuck-ever, I'm going outside with the shotgun."

Eduardo raises his hands and nods his head, making a smile as he says, "Okay, okay, let's watch some T.V."

Within minutes of one show's ending, Eduardo and Jorge are watching themselves play midwives to Maria and Marco. Their part soon crosses into a hyperactive voice-over's cry of "Spicy Cock! ROACHES! Now pepperroaches are confusing your tongue with PEANUT BUTTER STUFFING! A better confusion than your puberty ever was!"

Immediately afterwards, a news anchor defers to a reporter standing next to a gigantic purple rat blinking its raisin eyes. The reporter begins, "So tell me why it is so important to your competitor that your children are sent off to be eaten by customers like us? Most have claimed that you are simply ripping off their formula"

When the mic moves to the rat, he says, "I've been part plant-stuff my whole life, and now someone decides to take jalapeños and cockroaches and make some kind of half-bred snack food out of them? I personally feel attacked from this kind of marketing, and my family is more than willing to sacrifice themselves so that I can get rich."

"Do you fear at all for your public image? Many parent groups are boycotting your business practices and I understand that people have been making artwork and fiction of you, Marco the jalapeño, and Maria the cockroach involved in unsavory situations."

"No telling what I'll do if I see them."

Jorge clicks the T.V. off and rushes in and out of the bedroom with a loaded and shiny shotgun. Eduardo blocks him in the hallway, saying, "Babe, we don't have to start pointing guns at people."

"That wasn't even a fucking person on the T.V.! There's no law against pest control!"

"Put the gun down, Jorge!"

"You want our stuff to be covered by crawling munchies? You going to finally get pissed when a licorice snake jumps out of nowhere and bites your dick?" Jorge then anticipates Eduardo's lips moving and rushes past him, pulling the stock of the gun to his shoulder as he crashes out of the front door. The rat stands outside with a wide grin and arms spread. The arms and grin quickly drop.

"The hell is this?" the rat asks.

Jorge reaffirms his grip on the shotgun and says, "It's four o'clock in the morning and I am done with our house being tracked. That's two pains in my ass. Now if you and your cameras leave right now and never bother us again, I won't have to take care of a third pain in my ass. You."

"Buddy, buddy," the rat says, trying to peel a smile, "you should know that I had no intention of disrupting your night at all. You could've had my kid for breakfast and come outside in the morning if you wanted to. I am a very patient rat."

"The damn thing was ready to chew through our meds. No disrupting my ass."

Eduardo comes running out of the door, a new pair of boxer briefs pulled up over his crotch. "Hon, listen," he says to Jorge, "I just made some calls. We can sort this out more easily than what you're trying to do."

Jorge relaxes a few muscles from his stance and says, "Okay, I'm running on thirty more minutes of patience just for you."

The rat lowers his paws a moment, his breath rattling in the cold air. "Yeah. Listen, I get it. I'm not going to bother you two anymore. Bad business decision on my part. I just hope you can both forgive me."

Twenty minutes later, another car pulls up to the sidewalk. Marco and Maria step out, the former smoking a cigarette out of his stem. "Okay," says Marco, "why do you have to bother our customers and get our asses pulled out for an emergency call?"

Jorge turns towards Eduardo with his jaw dropped. "You didn't call the cops?"

Both raisin eyes pucker in the rat's sockets. In an instant, he leaps onto

Marco and sinks his teeth into Marco's face. Everyone around them freezes. Maria shrieks and throws herself at the rat. His claws rip deep into her underside and she bleeds white goo. In his shock, Jorge finally passes the transmitter.

Eduardo is the first to speak as he says, "What are you doing, Jorge? Shoot!"

"I didn't actually load it!"

"Just do something!"

Jorge's eyes flutter until he shuts them and rushes in with the barrel in his hands and the stock raised above his head. He bludgeons the rat in the head until it bleeds and cracks. Maria bleeds over Marco and tenderly holds him in her forelegs. Eduardo rushes among the camera crews, urging them to turn their cameras off with pepperroach bribes. "Maria," Marco says, "take a bite out of me one last time."

Tears drip down Maria's face as she buries her head in his wound for a minute. She turns to everyone present and says, "Clap, you *cabrónes*! We die to your loving applause!"

The camera crew shrugs and drops their equipment. They, Eduardo, and Jorge clap and cheer as Marco and Maria collapse. Their clapping stops as blaring police cars rush onto the street. The lady with the horned-rimmed glasses bursts out of one and howls on her way to the corpses. Jorge drops the bloodied shotgun and stares.

The officers call for an ambulance as they see the dead Maria and Marco and the twitching rat. Soon the rat coughs up blood and it says, "Wait, wait just one moment…" It then crawls over to Maria and Marco, embracing them both. They soon twitch into life with their limbs gliding over each others' bodies. Soon the rat moves his mouth towards Marco and kisses his stem, then kisses Maria's mandibles. The couple move further, embracing the rat as they roll around kissing and fondling each other.

"Can it be…?" asks the director.

One of the cops pulls off his glasses and says "Yes."

"So that means…"

"Yes." Soon the car door opens and smaller rats with raisin eyes, cockroach undersides, and jalapeño tails scuttle out and call for their fathers and their mother.

The director leaps in front of the camera and says, "We have merged! Now pepperroaches and raisin rats make chimera-crunches!"

The booming-throated voiceover guy crawls out of the microphone and bellows, "Chimera-crunches! When you say 'screw you' to your enemies, point and wink!"

"No," says Jorge. He throws the shotgun to the ground and storms off towards the house. "No. Just no. Fuck you all."

After the door slams shut behind Jorge, Eduardo pauses and looks at the check being held in front of him by the director. He holds his hand out with a grin. "Yes."

———

Edmund Colell is an intern for Lazy Fascist Press and community college writing tutor. His strange works have appeared in or will be appearing in Verbicide, LegumeMan, New Flesh, The New Flesh: Episode 1, Technicolor Tentacles, Christmas on Crack, and Bizarro Central.
http://www.facebook.com/edmundcolell

Nothingness Dust
Trent Zelazny

He had been schlepping himself for years.

He didn't see it, really; all he caught was the sight of its movement. Swift, graceful, and fast, so damned fast. A split-second shadow, not there and then there and then gone again, a camera flash, only backwards.

Then from out of nowhere came a ringing in his ears, and he looked where he had seen the thing go. It rose up. It was there before him, big, black, ragged, translucent like a giant shredded cheap garbage bag hovering in the dusk, torn flaps fluttering in the mid-September breeze like a once proud flag, now rotted from failure and abandonment.

It was twice his size, and as it inched closer, the ringing grew louder. His skin began to warm. The ringing continued up in volume but dropped down in pitch, until it was the sound of his own voice screaming. Wailing in torment and he became so hot that he felt he was burning.

It was slow now, steady, floating like an apparition, the little daylight remaining showing wearily through its paper-thin body. From somewhere in it that he couldn't see, he knew there were eyes, possibly hundreds of them, thousands of them, watching him.

He brought his hands to his ears but the sounds of his own voice didn't muffle. As the daylight went away, from within the thing's center there came a red glow, faint, then brighter, until it filled his eyes with the sight of his own blood. A blood of light that dripped and poured from him, even though he was watching it from a distance.

His screaming voice slowed, quieted down, and stuttered in odd lisps he couldn't understand.

"flesruoy dewolla uoy evah tahw"

And:

"ekil eb ot lla ti detnaw uoy tahw reven si siht"

And so on, in loops, undulating like waves, panning from one ear to the other, sometimes one line in one ear while another chattered away in the other.

His blood was glowing and turning into droplets, spatters floating about and running away from him. Only then did he wonder why he was standing here before this thing. What the hell was it? What the hell was this thing?

"oga gnol pu evag uoy"

"no dleh evah dluohs uoy, timmad, no dleh evah dluohs uoy"

"uoy ta kool won"

As the blood pitter-pattered away, the black thing grew smaller, smaller, shrinking with every lost drop. His skin raced from burning hot to icy cold.

Amidst the sounds and sights of red, a blank came to him.

"no dleh evah dluohs uoy"

His name was gone. He couldn't remember his name—
—But he had to. He had a name. He had to have a name.

He shivered. His bones rattled like ice cubes in a glass. The thing withered to about the size of a pillowcase. The blood dripped away as though rinsed. He saw a familiar face within. When he tilted his head the face tilted as well. When he winked, the face winked, and when the tattered shriveling black thing became the size of a baseball, the face within said: "I am Christopher Dean Marshall. Good luck, and goodbye."

Christopher Dean Marshall?

"tsol era uoy"

How's that?

"tsol reverof"

He reached his hand out to the thing. His arm disappeared into it. He felt around frantically, grasping for what was vanishing into this odd, shrinking, nebulous void. He tried to pry the thing open with his other hand but it was no use. It was shrinking. He had waited too long.

A hand from inside took his briefly. It gave him a hearty shake, then let go.

There came a sucking sound. The thing slithered off his arm. A second later it was gone with nothing to show it had ever been there.

He stood there, blank, unable to grasp, then walked away as darkness grew, wondering what had happened. What had that thing been, what had it done to him, and who was he, anyway?

Then he'd realized he'd had no choice. It would have found him wherever he was.

A large still puddle nearby reflected the moonlight and when he chanced a look at himself, what he saw was a set of old dry bones. Ordinary human bones, indistinguishable from any others. Reaching down, he touched the water, then plunged his hand into it, feeling nothing. No cold. No wet. Nothing.

He continued walking, wanting to go home, but not knowing where in the world home could be.

When next he awoke someone was sweeping him into a trash bag.

Trent Zelazny was born and raised in Santa Fe, New Mexico. He has lived in California, Oregon, Arizona, and Florida. He currently roams throughout the country aimlessly. He is also a basketball fanatic. http://www.trentzelazny.com/

Five short Twitter novels
Riri Shimada
Translated by Mamoru Masuda

Come into Me
It was lonely being a white star. Lonely despite being in a mutual orbit with red and yellow stars. I grew smaller and smaller, collapsing upon myself until I became a small black hole. Spinning in their orbits, other stars closed in. They whipped around and around until they slammed into me. The fixed stars and planets too, they all smashed into me. Very soon, the whole of the universe, will I swallow.

Two Can Play that Game
Our arms come together. Our chests. Our laps. Our lips. Not a molecule of space between us; we are perfectly meshed. The boundaries that are our skins, melt. Every single one of our cells and mitochondria sing a song of joyous of welcome, meiosis occurs, the protoplasm of our bodies flows into each other. And once the Fused-One, diverges, you are no longer you and I am no longer I.

The Shape of Love
Gorging on the poisonous earth, gulping down the acid sea, devouring the methane air. Defecating fertile soil, excreting water, passing oxygen, and moving on, ever on. The two terraforming machines work in from either side of the landmass, in search of their better halves. When they meet, they devour one another. The view from ten kilometers above reveals they have left behind a heart-shaped supercontinent.

Kizuna (bond of fraternity)
"I've just received my afforestation subsidies." Today, her skin is a healthy light green. From this day forward, she will breathe in carbon dioxide, soak in the sunlight, and breathe out oxygen. She lets out a small gasp. "Look, my first flower." A small bud bursting from the skin of her palm blooms in that very moment. "Me too." Opening my hand slowly, to reveal an identical red poppy blossom.

Artifact
His trembling metal claws scrape away the white frost encasing the casket and trace the epitaph in ancient characters: *Here Sleeps My Beloved Daughter Alice.* Tears of lubricant brim in his plastic eyes and slowly run down his cold metal cheeks. He has finally encountered that which ensures he will never again find beauty in any work of art.

Riri Shimada is a Japanese author of Fantasy, SF, and YA novels. She made her debut as a writer with the short story "The Afternoon when the Shadow has a Doze in the Backyard." She graduated Joshibi University of Art and Design, from the department of Fine Art. Visit her English website at http://web.me.com/ririshimada

Conservation Hero Blues
Made in DNA

Shinji cranked the little laptop to get it started.

It yawned awake and auto-opened the file he was currently working on.

No time to waste, he scanned the last two paragraphs, typed in the next character, saved the file, and shutdown the computer.

He smiled as he checked the little machine's fading Saver indicator – Green.

This was Shinji's daily routine. He was an author. Every day he allowed himself to type in one Japanese hiragana character of his short story. On really special occasions, or when necessary, he took the luxury of typing in a kanji character, which usually consisted of one to three converted hiragana characters. Equivalent to several days work. On those days he was particularly careful to watch the indicator.

He worried constantly that it might turn yellow, or worse, red. The guilt of spending so much energy would force him to perform a hot shutdown, losing the day's work.

Since the inception of Conservation Summer – a year-round energy-conservation campaign conceived by the government and endorsed by media outlets – six years ago, he had typed in nearly 1900 hiragana and several hundred kanji characters.

His novella had progressed. At this rate, it should only take another... he calculated the time in his head, and let out a small sigh. Too long.

His wife Kizuna walked into his study.

"Are you finished for the day?"

"Yes," he replied, turning to her.

"Good. There are a few things you can help me with around the house."

Shinji pursed his lips and nodded ruefully.

"You don't want to help me?"

"Oh no. Sorry. I was just... well... lamenting that I can't write another character today."

"You already typed in one character, right?"

"Yes."

Her eyes widened. "Two characters in one day?"

He nodded.

"Pretty extreme. You know we have to suffer for the good of the nation."

"Oh yes, of course. Naturally I am happy to do so," he spat out suddenly, his heart racing.

"What would the neighbors think?" Her expression was one of abject horror.

Shinji began to sweat at the thought of someone finding out he was trying to do more than his allotment. His wife was right. What if someone in his circle of authors found out? Or his editor, or the publisher? He'd become an outcast, shunned by everyone in the business.

"You're a good man. You always do the right thing. That's why I married you during the height of the F-Crisis." She smiled and walked from the room.

He stood and followed her out.

The next morning, he cranked the little machine, studied the previous paragraphs as before and, to his horror, realized that he'd mistyped the character from yesterday! It was '*me*', not '*nu*' as he had intended.

The mistake was understandable as the two looked so much alike. But the damage had been done.

He deleted the character, saved the file, shut down the machine, and left the room. The mistake he'd made yesterday would have to be fully corrected tomorrow.

Over the next two months, the work progressed smoothly, and even took an unexpected turn. The antagonist made her debut six months after that. And eighteen months of more hard work witnessed the start of an electrifying first scene between her and the protagonist.

Shinji put the period on the closing sentence to revealing dialogue between the main characters. He allowed himself a moment to bask in the glow of the scene on the screen before him. It had been just over a decade since he'd begun the novella, and it wouldn't be much longer now. He had come this far, and it was all downhill from here. All the pieces had fallen into place. All that was left was to ride out the story. To let it take him to the finish under the weight of its own momentum.

There was a knock at his door.

His wife stood there, a glass of beer in hand.

"I know you are finishing up that dialogue. Here's a beer to celebrate."

A beer! Oh man how long had it been since his last? Under Conservation Summer's unspoken rules, he had restrained himself from consuming excessive amounts. He had been a beer-a-night drinker before Conservation Summer. Now if he had two a year, he would be considered a lush. Oh, how he craved it. His eyes positively lighted up.

Kizuna set it down on his desk next to the little laptop and left the room.

Shinji reached for it but his shirt sleeve caught the edge of the desk causing his hand to bump the glass.

The entire contents of the beer washed over the machine, down into the depths via the keyboard.

There was a spark, a loud pop, and the smell of fried circuitry as the screen went black...

Made in DNA is an expat American living in Japan with his wife and three small children. He authors extreme fiction, science fiction and occasionally extreme science fiction. "Conservation Hero Blues" is dedicated to his family and all the people of Japan. http://amzn.to/madeindna

Dissolution
Glynn Barrass

Hunger: my first true feeling after an age of self-awareness.

Blind and unmoving, I lay static within the darkness. I wasn't alone however: my future brethren twitched fitfully all around me.

Eventually, something changed. Starved close to madness, my hunger – a painful, overwhelming lust for sustenance – found a victim. Discovering the surface beneath my form amenable, I gorged.

Those around me, squirming in their blindness, joined in. Without questioning our sudden mobility, we transformed our lives into an orgy of feasting.

I ate and ate. The sustenance never ended. Eventually though, I grew so sluggish that the need to consume dissipated.

Stilled through greed, I lay warm and supine, nestled between my trembling companions. During this physical ennui, my body began to change. My skin grew solid, unyielding, a stony case surrounding some occult metamorphosis.

I transformed, my pulpy mass mutating in ways inexplicable.

Multiple chitinous legs sprouted, surrounding a solid scaly form. A pair of folded wings followed.

The shell tightened, restraining my complex new body. Trapped and suffocating, my former skin became my prison cell. Battling my constraints, I fought for life, for continued existence. As the shell surrendered, its shattered form revealed a world of bright liberation.

The light was blinding in its intensity. I had never seen before. Gasping for air I took comfort in its warmth. The light above then sealed and strengthened my flesh.

My fresh new eyes saw clearly now, perceiving a strange new world.

My brothers and sisters were everywhere. Some lay drying like myself, others were only just escaping their cocoons. More still, for we numbered in the hundreds, had taken flight, escaping our former home.

They ascended on beautiful, multicoloured wings.

Longing for their freedom, I focused my all on accompanying my brethren into the light.

I knew patience. As such, I let the warmth do its work.

My wings firmed slowly, gaining power in small increments. Finally they grew strong enough for flight.

I unfurled my wings. Experiencing a slight lift, an overwhelming freedom followed. On flapping gossamer I ascended with giddy abandon.

A master of the air, I whirled upwards, spiralling ever higher towards the beckoning light. I danced in the wind currents my fluttering companions' cast.

The light, my birthright, promised warmth and future joy.

Surprise then horror followed. Pressed against an adhesive, invisible barrier, I struggled in panic. Whatever held me refused to yield.

Sensing a presence I froze, ceasing my struggles.

A huge black shadow, blocking the light, bore down on me with mysterious intent. My mind cried out in fear. I wished to be anywhere but beneath this menacing entity.

A myriad of limbs clutched my weakening form. From a dark, bulbous head, two black, pitiless eyes glared down. The fangs beneath glinted like obsidian daggers.

In one cruel, deft movement, the daggers snapped down, shattering my eyes.

My screams, vibrating through the air, went unanswered. Still I cried, in blind, burning agony.

Dissolving me, my molester's fangs exuded acid, reducing my innards to a bubbling, fluid state.

Liquefying my insides, it began *drinking* me.

Thus began my dissolution. Through an unknown being's deadly hunger, the heavenly light was denied.

Rebirth without pain, the polar opposite of my terrified, liquid death. Hunger followed, my first true feeling after an age of self-awareness.

Blind and unmoving, I lay static within the darkness. I wasn't alone however: my future brethren twitched fitfully all around me.

This time, I *would* reach the light.

―――

Glynn Barrass is in love with Japan. Years of J-Horror, Manga and Anime have helped shape him as a writer. The tale written for this anthology was the least he could do for that wonderful country's plight. Published worldwide, Glynn has been writing fiction and poetry for four years, his favorite genre being the Cthulhu Mythos, (and now Bugpunk – thanks Brent!). He intends to write a lot more of both in the future. Hailing from the North East of England, he shares his home with his cat Sisko, and a few friendly ghosts he's met over the years. http://www.freewebs.com/batglynn/

Dead and Breakfast
Fulvio Gatti

He spotted them a minute too late.
> They were coming.
> And in great numbers.
> Nicola swiftly dropped the *hentai* comic book into his backpack. He pulled the rope with all his weight until he felt the huge bell move.
> *Dong! Dong! Dong!*
> He rushed down the bell tower stairs.

Castelvecchio Tanaro, località Campanile, was a bunch of houses on top of a hill.
> Once people had lived there.
> Now they were all gone.
> Except for the five.
> Their bulwark was a farmhouse known as *La taverna di Orlando*.
> There was:
> Ettore, the man.
> Celeste, the intelligent beauty.
> Roi, the armed man and, incidentally, Celeste's ex-husband.
> Nicola, the good soldier and Ettore's former roommate.
> Pesaro, the... Whatever.
> And, of course, there were the dead.

Sixteen of them. Ettore counted them in a glance as they trudged toward the house. Men, women, a couple of children. All groaning and hungry.
> As Ettore retreated from the window, Roi took his place with a snap of his AK-60. Ettore hated that testosterone-driven posturing.
> "Play with your guns all you like, but don't let them see you."
> "Yessir, Mussolini!" Roi snarled back.
> Celeste was waiting for Ettore in the dining room. She smiled. He liked that.
> "How many?"
> On a checkered tablecloth Ettore saw twenty full dishes of meat – mostly rabbit and chicken – and nearly as many bowls full of red wine. More bottles stood ready at the edge of the table.
> "Looks good. Now let's get out of here."
> The groaning was getting closer.

Nicola couldn't help laughing at the sight of the dead fat woman drinking Barbera, the wine pouring out from a hole in her throat.

Luckily the zombies were too busy eating and drinking to notice the three people watching from an adjacent room – the supervisor's office.

The feast went on.

Dead teeth tearing small animals to pieces.

Barbera gurgling down dead throats.

A sickening sight.

Everything was working well.

According to rumor, the few survivors in big cities discovered that the dead liked to hop on empty buses whose engines were running.

So they started transporting the dead away from the cities like that.

An hour's trip was all that was needed – far enough away from the city, but still close enough to prevent the dead from getting bored and eating the driver.

Castelvecchio Tanaro was exactly an hour from Torino.

And that was why more and more zombies were arriving in the countryside.

But its five inhabitants had the key to fighting them.

As long as the Barbera lasted anyway.

Forty minutes.

The room was quieting.

The dead were now more akin to a pack of drunks.

Some were sleeping; some just ate slower.

There was a short fight for the last bunny.

Pesaro came in with a guitar and sat.

Started playing a chord.

"This is an anti-war song, guys," Pesaro stated. *The Eastern world is exploding, violence flaring, bullets loading...*

The dead seemed to like it.

Routine. That's your real enemy when you are at war.

It takes a minute to lose focus.

A minute too long.

Only after he heard the first gun shot did Ettore realize that not all of the dead were still at the table.

Two had fled.

Roi was facing them down in the other room.

Two bowls fell to the floor as the zombie children attacked Pesaro. He snorted and kept playing as they devoured him.

"Oh, no, what went wrong?" asked Nicola.

The dead fat woman was about to grab him when a metal chair smashed against her head. Ettore stepped back and slammed her with it again. The dead woman fell to the ground.

"*Sveglia* Nicola! Are you that eager to become food?" shouted Ettore.

Four more dead came after them, and the three survivors were pushed back against a wall. Ettore urged Nicola to help him move the table. It was extremely heavy and they just managed to overturn it with a crash. Celeste slowed the nearest zombie down by smashing a PC monitor into his face.

"Why isn't your husband shooting at them?" asked Ettore.

"He isn't my husband anymore!"

"*Ho capito*, but why isn't that *coglione* shooting?"

"You don't mean to tell me you believed him when he told you he could use a gun? ...Not really?"

Ettore was about to curse when a zombie grasped Celeste from behind, while another bit Nicola on the shoulder, pushing him down to the floor. They tore his head off while the young man was still screaming.

Uncommon hobbies can save lives.

Ettore, after some boyhood fencing lessons, grew up with an insane passion for swords and medieval times.

At the local medieval fair, he was the best swordsman.

He had decorated the place with swords in every room.

And he knew how to use all of them.

The heads of the dead flew. In a blink, Celeste was back in his arms, safe.

"Did I ever tell you I love that darn sword fetish of yours?" asked Celeste with a smile.

Ettore slammed open a wardrobe cupboard and hefted two more weapons. He put one in Celeste's hands.

"Show me your inner Amazon!"

They fought their way to the dining room. The dead fell one after another to their blades. The one eating Roi's corpse wheeled on them and Ettore cut it in two with a single deadly move.

"No messes allowed in my house!" screamed Ettore.

They were headed downstairs when Ettore stopped. He returned to the dining room.

He looked at the bottles, smelled the wine inside.

"What are you doing?" screamed Celeste.

"*Porca puttana troia!* This isn't Barbera!"

More dead groaned from outside. Ettore and Celeste rushed down the stairs. They jumped into a Fiat Panda and started the engine.

"In the bottles. It wasn't Barbera. It was Chianti. *Fottuto* Chianti..." said Ettore.

"What?"

"Wrong wine. Red, but wrong. Who bought it?"

"I... I... I don't know. Does it matter?"

Ettore glared at her a second, then looked back at the road. He sobbed.

"Not anymore. But you gotta learn to recognize wines if you wanna survive."

"Oh. Right..."

The car headed off into the mountains.

———

Fulvio Gatti, born in Turin in 1983, is a writer and journalist. A degree in arts and ICT, he improved his knowledge of English, and studied writing at events like L.A Screenwriting Expo and Sherwood Oaks Experimental College. In 2005 he published an essay on *Star Wars*, and has been writing for Italian newspapers and magazines for almost a decade. He also works in the Italian comic book field as editor, copywriter and translator. As a screenwriter he wrote *La partita più importante della stagione* (*The Season's Most Important Match*). He is currently working on a graphic novel and many other projects. He could not live without chocolate, sci-fi, horror and fantasy movies and literature, rock-blues music (he also plays bass guitar), cats and bright and unpolluted Monferrato air. http://www.fulviogatti.it/

Quelling the Troll
Nirnara

"I hate that wench!" typed his fingers that punch the keyboard. "What good is that lass that does nothing but sings of stupidity? What good is her make-up when stupidity is already an accessory on her fancy face? What good is her body when her skin is just full of stupid cells, hormones and cosmetics? Bah!" roared the boy from the wobbling wooden chair that supported his heavy obese body.

"And I hate that lad!" he barked while he spat droplets of saliva on the keyboard. "What good is that lad that does nothing but dances of moves of stupidity? What good is he, looking like some cute kid when he only spreads stupidity upon his fans? What good is he when his so-called beauty is just composed of imitated accessories and hideous make-up? Bah!" roared the boy as his chair shook turbulently but still strong enough to support his heavy obese body.

"And I hate that man!" he shrilled as his flabby skin soon hardened like stone. "What good is that man that does nothing but preaches of stupidity? What good is he with his boring reputation and money when stupidity is all that he gives to the populace? What good is he when his mind and supporters are just composed of pure stupidity at best? Bah! What fucking bullshit is this?!" he cried as his weight pressed the chair down further upon the ground.

The boy roared, hissed, cursed, even punched his table. While ravaged, the wooden chair underneath him started to squeak. The chair however, still had the last strength to support his burden weight – even if his anger, envy and lust devoured his very consciousness slowly. Sadly, his emotions and incredible weight are just too much for the chair to handle – and the chair's legs began to crack.

And then lo! The chair's legs snapped kaput! The chair shattered as the boy and his emotions too fell together with the chair – landing upon the floor with a deep impact.

He landed so hard that his weight and distorted mind gave birth to an explosion of catastrophic pain. A pain flavoured by sweet rage on the top, bitter agony in the middle and completed by tasteless sadness at last. Tears flowed from his eyes while his skin is infested with minuscule bruises.

His mouth, once fueled by savage speeches, is now replaced by an opera of hurtful wails and whines. His cry wasn't very loud. Rather, it was sweetly soft yet so penetrating to his heart.

All the sudden, his room's door creaked open. A short shadowy figure emerged then approached towards the light of the boy's room. Soon the room's lights kissed the shadows – revealing the figure to be that of a tiny, smiling old woman. Her humble smile is further enriched by her old-fashioned clothes decorated with brilliant designs of garden flowers.

"Grandma..." he spoke tenderly.

"Oh my!" gasped the ornate old woman. "Are you alright?!"

He was silent. She then took notice of her grandson's laptop filled with the images of assorted celebrities. This made her giggle.

"My boy!" she chuckled. "Did these people hurt you?"

"N-no.."

"Of course not! They can't hurt nor touch you! All I see now is you getting hurt... by none other than your troll."

"My troll?" he whispered curiously while he slowly stood up – wiping off tears form his puffy cheeks.

"Yes. Many children have certain monsters within them. Your type of monster is the troll. Trolls get excited when they see stupidity afresh. Fear, envy and desire are their food and stupidity is the result of eating all those junk foods."

The boy silently stared at his bruises around his fleshy skin – standing still and speechless.

"If you keep on feeding this naughty troll all this junk food..." sighed the grandmother. "...then the man within you will be taken over... and be wholly eaten alive by this inner troll. Do you want this, grandson?"

"N-n-no." he cried vehemently. "I don't want to be a troll..."

The grandmother went over to her giant of a grandson and gave him a great warm hug. She whispered, "I don't want a troll for a grandson. I want a strong, healthy man for a grandson!"

She then gently released him from her hug before she gave his shoulder an invigorated pat.

"You're wise." she smiled. "When I compare you to your friends, you know which people are truly men and which people are truly monsters. This quality...called wisdom...is what you have."

The grandmother now heads towards the door before saying, "A troll destroys his own world and the world around him. A wise man creates his own world and shines the world around him. Be wise. Then the world will shine upon you."

"Thanks, grandma." the boy said as his sulking face formed to a blooming smile.

"Now c'mon! Afternoon tea is ready. Your bread, biscuits and lemonade are waiting for you!" cheered the grandmother as she slowly walked out of the door – while she hummed an uplifting hymn at the same minute.

The boy's mind feels refreshed now. His grandmother's words quelled the troll within him. The troll is still inside, however. Yet the troll won't bother him much anymore.

The boy stared at his laptop and sees the celebrities. This time, he just laughed at these imaginary persons for they aren't much of a significance to his very own life. Next, he looked at the broken chair beneath him.

"Thanks for supporting me." he whispered – giving condolences to the chair that once carried him all these times.

"The troll within won't bother you anymore. The wise man in me shall learn from you. And the man in me shall fix and create you anew." he said – bowing to the chair underneath his fleshy feet.

Thus, the troll in him is now ready to evolve into the man the boy is meant to be... a true man.

―――

Nirnara has been writing stories ever since his time began. The world around him didn't satisfied him much that eventually he developed an urge to write out a better world in the form of words. As Nirnara waged war with his dissatisfaction for years, he couldn't win by repressing dissatisfaction alone until an idea sparked within him. The idea was that he could learn to transform. And thus Nirnara finally learnt the art of reshaping dissatisfaction to satisfaction in the form of fiction. And this is just the beginning on the way to an epic middle and a peaceful end. http://twitter.com/#!/Oldenyouth

Plum Blossom
(an excerpt from *Dizzy Sushi*)
Melissa J White

All night long it rained, cold and heavy, relentless. But it softened the noise and there was a gentle feeling to the city. It was the beginning of *ume* (plum blossom) season. This was the Japan I loved—the everyday, everybody-enjoy-the-seasons mandatory visits to shrines and parks, even in this wet weather.

I took a bus to Kitano Shrine where the delicate pink and white blossoms were peeking through the grey slate skies. Many older gentlemen were taking pictures, and a large group of them circled one particular tree on the west side. I had to wait for some of them to move before I could see for myself what had enticed them.

It was a young plum tree, about five feet tall, weeping, its branches trailing on the ground like a girl in a kimono. The beauty of this tree was its late blossoming. Indeed, only a few of the flowers on her crown were actually open. But all along her curving arms, were tight buds, pink with a hint of green, her bark slick with the wet.

I was quickly shifted out of the way in the relentless desire to get just the right angle of photograph, the need to capture the essence of beauty for oneself. Where in my country had I ever seen a bunch of old men in black raincoats in the drizzling cold rain set up tripods and pull out light meters for a plum tree just barely in bloom?

Riding the bus back home I felt like that tree, like a spy in a woman's body, hiding a secret.

When I arrived at Namba School, a small ceremony was in progress. Jennifer, one of the "office ladies" was saying goodbye. It was her last day at work. I used to see her talking to students and answering the phone at the desk between the time clock and the copy machine. I didn't even know her real name, just "Jennifer," her English nickname. She had an American boyfriend who wanted her to be at home now. Another teacher told me they would be having a large wedding and would soon thereafter begin starting a family. She must now say goodbye to her work life.

She was smiling through her tears and her voice had a tripping quality, stumbling and dancing from soprano to alto. Her face was open and expressive and she was tall, wearing a checked skirt and white blouse. She didn't look remarkably different from other women, but she did have what I could only describe as inner grace. Something I wish I had, something you had to be born with.

The phones were peacefully silent for once this afternoon. Jeff, the assistant head of Namba School stood by his chair, his hands in his pockets, moving his fingers in the change and paperclips. On his thin face was the saddest smile. Terry, the director of the school, also stood, but with a huge grin and white teeth showing. Both were watching Jennifer as Fiona helped her on with her coat. Another girl held two shopping bags full of roses and presents.

Jennifer smoothed her black fur collar, her long bangs damp with tears, her eyelashes so wet they clung together in spikes. She brushed away each salty drop carefully with her fingertips although her make-up had long since dissolved.

She gave everyone in the office a trembling hug, wishing each one the best in English. As they walked past the counter, Fiona on her arm like a handbag, Yaz, a new staff member, teased her in Japanese, and she laughed back at him, her voice breaking into a hundred colors.

As they walked by the couches, I stood up. She looked to me like the plum tree at Kitano Shrine, tangled in her branches, rooted to her country's demands, her face wet with rain.

She reached her hand out to me and I took it. My hand moved straight from my body but hers barely inched forward while she leaned backwards, as though she wished it would go on without her. Her left hand covered her mouth and nose and she blinked through her fingers.

"Thank you, Jennifer," I said. "I'll miss you."
"I will miss you, too. You and Walker will be together forever, I hope."
"I hope so, too."

She moved to the doorway, her entourage of women and flowers around her. Then she turned and spoke to Terry and to Jeff and to all of us in Japanese. She held her hands in front of her face, crying and laughing, then gracefully bowed.

We all bowed, too. She turned away and left through the glass doors.

That night, riding the train home, I was conflicted in my feelings. How excited I was when I had learned I was pregnant. I hadn't even known I would want that future. But seeing Jennifer leave the office today gave me doubts. Of course our situations were very different, I wasn't quitting in order to stay home, count the days and prepare an environment for the expected children. Walker didn't expect me to stop any career plans I would have.

But would I be stuck at the sink washing bottles and baby food grinders? I remembered how much I had washed dishes at Zuigakuin and in California at the Zen Center and I laughed. Washing dishes was so prevalent in Zen society, there was practically a dharma written just for it. I saw myself in the future, letting the water run in the sink, scrubbing a pan, looking out the window in front of me at the soft brown hills chewed away for decades by cattle and dotted with dark green piñon bushes. Could the future be so calm? Did becoming a parent mean a sacrifice to what I would want for myself? I rested my hand over my belly and waited to feel some movement again, some answer, but all was still within me.

Melissa J White is an award-winning writer and designer living in Santa Fe, New Mexico. She has written *Angel Someone* for Kindle, and her Japanese travel memoir, *Dizzy Sushi,* will be published by Tres Chicas Books. She has been a City of Santa Fe Arts Commissioner and founder/past president of Intermezzo of the Santa Fe Opera. Melissa owns and operates Blogshop, a series of workshops, classes, custom blog design and private consulting services. http://www.MelissaJWhite.com.

The Flower
Fumihiko Iino
Translated by Kaori Miyake/James Benson

The flower was in bloom. It was a bright red flower.

Sachiko didn't know what kind flower it was, but thought it was beautiful nonetheless.

When she woke, she found the single flower had been placed in an onion-shaped vase, on the small desk beside her bed.

It must be from my mother. She must have brought it for me.

Her mother was very, very busy with work. She could not come to visit. So the nurse that took gentle care of her had said. However Sachiko was lonely, and could not understand.

"Why? Why?" She had asked with such tenacity that the nurse had finally whispered secretly, "Your mother came a few days ago. But she left quietly because you were asleep."

"Promise me you'll wake me from now on, okay?" They pinky-swore, but Sachiko could now see that the nurse had not kept her word. There was nothing she could do about it. Sachiko had had an operation. The anesthesia had worn off and she was just waking up.

It must be my mother. It must be... Mother...

Sachiko vaguely recalled a moment from her distant childhood. "What a beautiful flower," she had heard an unknown drunk tell her mother. Having quietly opened the sliding paper-door to steal a peek inside, Sachiko had seen her mother seated on the tatami flooring, her legs spread wide. The drunk had buried his face between her thighs as he spoke.

My mother is a beautiful flower. Perhaps I am too.

She used a mirror in secret, but didn't find any flowers there. *I so want to become a beautiful flower like my mother.*

I never told her that, but Mother must have known. So she took the time to bring this flower to me.

Sachiko felt her mother was watching over her, and turning toward the flower, smiled at it. She wanted to speak aloud, but the pipe in her throat wouldn't allow it.

But I'm sure you can hear me. You can hear me, right Mother?

Then, strangely, the flower seemed to nod. And though it was only the mischief of the wind coming in from the hospital window, Sachiko did not notice.

Have you come for me, Mother? she thought quietly.

Once again it nodded. Sachiko's heart suddenly brightened. *The operation was a success, so Mother has managed time in her busy schedule to come take me home.*

I can leave the hospital. Mother and I can live happily together now.

It had been a very long time since they had. Sachiko had longed to live with her mother again. The time had come at last.

"Oh, the poor girl."

"How old was she?"

"I don't know. One of the nurses told me she was left in front of the orphanage with nothing but the clothes on her back and a single red rose. She had 'Sachiko' written on her palm."

Upon hearing her name, Sachiko turned in the direction of the voices. The patients who shared the room with her looked at Sachiko as they spoke of her. Sachiko smiled.

My mother has come for me. I'm leaving the hospita. Take care everyone.

"So that's why they've taken the trouble to give her a red rose in her last moments."

The patient continued, looking not at Sachiko, but the flower.

A rose? A red rose? Yes, that's right. My mother was a red rose.

The wind that had shaken the flower blew the white cloth off Sachiko's covered face.

"Oh, poor girl, I'll re-cover your face."

The patient approached Sachiko, and upon seeing the girl's face, the woman's eyes widened.

"Look at this. She's smiling!"

"That she is. She used to do nothing but cry."

"She must be happy to be at peace at last."

With sorrowful expressions the patients faced Sachiko and placed their palms together.

No, no. That's not it. I'm happy because I can finally be with my mother. That's why...

The smile on Sachiko's lips bloomed further.

Fumihiko Iino is a Japanese short story author from Kofu, Yamanashi Prefecture. Born in 1961, he graduated from Waseda University and was a member of the Waseda Mystery Club while he attended. His 2007 short story "Bad Tune" was a nominee in the 14th Annual Horror Short Story Contest. Since his debut, he has worked on novelizations of games, anime and movies including *Royal Space Force: The Wings of Honneamise*, *Tomie Replay* and *GunBuster*. He is a frequent contributor to modern horror anthologies.

A Tale of Smoke and Ash
Curt Seubert

Long ago and far away, a prisoner lay in his cell, seeing in the box springs of the bunk above, the sky of his youth—those patches of blue peeking between the protective mesh of pipes weaving between houses. Everyone else had been happy, but he—he'd been naïve believing PR had been the cause of all his town's problems, and believing the end of those pipes would be the end of PR. The town had sentenced him to live behind bars "for the remainder of his natural life." He'd laughed, unwittingly granting the cameras that image of wanton criminality they'd so hungered for. What could "natural life" possibly mean in a society propagating so unnaturally?

PR arose in his grandparents' day, in a great house on the hill overlooking town, where lived an old recluse, wealthy beyond reckoning, relishing many luxuries, but especially smoking, which he pursued with single-minded purpose. Huge clouds of smoke and ash poured from his windows, staining walls brown, coating eaves with gray. Following years of stoic resignation, the residents sent a delegation to present their grievances and a request he cease his overindulgence.

The front door opened before their leader could knock, and the delegates were enveloped in an impenetrable haze. From somewhere within, a man's voice rang out: "Why are you here?"

The leader took a nervous step forward. "We ask you to cease your trespass against us, as we have not trespassed against you."

"Trespass? How can you say that? I've lived here as long as you. Come inside, please do. I have an offer which might interest you."

The delegates returned to town, bearing the offer. Everyone approved it. Many, noting the simple elegance of the plan, bewailed their town's apparent lack of native genius, having not come up with such an idea on their own. Pollution Redistribution would run pipes between the rich, old man's house and their own, thereby harnessing participants' respiratory power to suck smoke from the old man's house, thus keeping it off their streets. The old man, sympathetic to their sacrifice, would compensate them, paying money proportionate to household participation.

Soon enough, homes sprouted pipes that lengthened and weaved about each other, coming to glorify both the intricate web of communal connections and, in their density, the strength, vitality, and overall well-being of the residents. Smoking had become the sign of affluence, and the number of smokers was soaring.

Twenty years on, they erected a statue of the old man in the town square. Prominent citizens, and a couple of select school children, spoke in honor of "their selfless benefactor," nodding in the direction of the great house long since lost to view behind the network of pipes. The statue, its hollow interior packed with cigarette ash, bore their best guess at the old man's benign countenance; their complimentary speeches glossed over a growing unease—a disease, some would claim. Despite their increased wealth, the town's life expectancy had decreased, and the younger generation had started asking questions: "Is this fair? Why we alone do not profit? Why is our inclusion involuntary and, worst of all, unrewarded?

"Our lungs, too, power PR," they complained.

Parents presented clear statistics of PR's benefits, which their children dismissed as smoke screens. Youths formed The Clean, a movement to clear away PR.

The Clean took power after years of political maneuvering, only to realize that dismantling PR would erode the standard of living their voters had put them in power to preserve.

"We will continue PR," The Clean announced, "but reformed. There'll be nothing but benefits to speak of." So they promised, and so they did. As their own children grew, so did the complexity of PR and its pipes. The sun disappeared from view. The rich man's house faded into memory. Public discussion of cancer referred in its stead to vigorous cell growth.

It was in this atmosphere of apparent good the Prisoner realized his destiny.

He saw all too clearly how sick his town had become. The cure, he knew, lay in removing the source of PR. After long study of books treating the town's history, he was able to map the PR pipes, and from that map deciphered that the center of this convoluted matrix stood outside town.

For the first time in his life, he stepped beyond the network of houses and pipes, his backpack full of explosives. He saw the house at the top of the hill, just as his map had predicted and struggled forward, the unfamiliar air stinging his throat and lungs. He would, of course, warn the man to leave before blowing up his home.

The still house moaned eerily in the quiet morning chill.

He eased the door open and then stepped inside. Great drafts of air rushed through the rooms and hallways: all the lungs of the town working together kept the house clean. Everything was spotless. He crept from room to room, expecting at any moment to find the old man smoking his cigarettes in luxurious surrounding. But he found no one; just a skeleton, in a library at the back of the house, slumped forward, its arms splayed over a massive, oak table. Not a speck of clothing, not a scrap of skin, remained: after death, rot had set in, that slow burn, that oxidization of flesh to dust, and the town had breathed it all in.

According to their report, the police found him just staring at the old man's skeleton, obviously bent on the town's destruction, too afraid to carry out his plan, yet too stunned to escape. He couldn't remember.

On his bunk in the prison cell, he groaned, closing his eyes to the box springs above, and wondered if he'd ever be able to go back to sleep.

———

Curt Seubert is digesting and being digested in a small, dark room in Japan, having consumed an education rich in music, literature, philosophy, and physics. His writings have appeared amidst such beautiful places as *The American Book Review*, *The Fugue*, *Word Riot*, *Thirst for Fire*, *Down in the Dirt*, *The Medulla Review*, art school halls and bathroom stalls.
http://Writing.Com/authors/chomonkyo

Back Beyond The Hedgerow
Elizabeth Black

The look of utter disbelief on Cedric's face as he lay dying on my table upset me so much I felt sick. He stared at me with his baleful pale blue eyes, knowing his fate yet refusing to accept it. According to an old Irish saying, a cat's eyes are windows enabling us to see into another world. The only world I saw in Cedric's eyes was one of red-hot rage and abject torment. If he could have sent his murderer to that world, I would have gladly helped him.

Knowing there was nothing I could do for him, I helped ease him into his death, and tended to the twelve other cats that bastard kid Lyle had poisoned. Lyle smothered his perverted brand of love on his own cat, Biggie Smalls, but relished torturing and killing other cats in the neighborhood. His latest victims, the baker's dozen of feral cats that lived in the shed behind my veterinary office, brought forth a helpless fury in me I hadn't felt in months. For trying to stop Lyle was an exercise in futility, since his father was the mayor and his uncle was the chief of police.

The silence was so sudden I froze with needle in hand. Alert and jittery cats turned their attention to their fallen leader. Miss Puss, a kitten recovering from one of Lyle's crossbow bolts, stood on wobbly legs in her cat bed. I had never seen her look so determined. She leapt upon the table where her friend Cedric lay, staring at him as if her attention would wake him up.

Miss Puss took delicate steps towards Cedric, favoring her injured leg. She sniffed his face, waiting for the forehead nudge that never came. She looked at me, copper-penny eyes wet with sadness, and buried her face in her friend's orange fur. Her body shuddered, tail twitching with grief.

When she lifted her head, I saw a different cat.

Her eyes had darkened from copper-penny bronze to blood orange. With a steely set to her jaw, she raised her snow white body high on her hind legs, and gazed at the occupied cages with an authoritative air.

When she flicked her thumb, I blinked my eyes a few times to make sure I wasn't imagining what I saw. Outstretching one paw, she snapped her claws as if they were fingers. I backed away from her, fear raising the hair on the nape of my neck. Her tail flicked with agitation as she riled up her mates with her fingers snapping like a call to arms.

Paws reached around the rails of the cages to use newly opposable thumbs to flick open the latches that held the gates shut. One by one, the cats strode from their cages and sauntered to the door. Thumbs snapped in unison as the cats grew in force. Several stopped to grasp my scalpels in their infant fists, and a few more claimed discarded syringes they found in the trash. As I realized their plan, I felt a wave of excitement and horror overwhelm me.

I followed the clowder out the front door, and I felt the thrill of schadenfreude ripple in my gut. We walked, fingers snapping, nearly two dozen cats moving in a determined path with me at their center and Miss Puss in the lead. They moved as if with one brain, like a hive. As we walked, neighboring cats joined the parade. Two cats here, one cat there, until we stood sixty strong. And I say "we" because I felt as much a part of the crowd as the cats did, and I knew I was there only because I had been invited. I was their honored and trusted guest, their witness who had kept them healthy and content. I didn't want to imagine my fate if I ever wronged them, especially considering what was about to happen, yet that final act was not what mattered. The growth of a cat army, of the weak overpowering the strong, held far more import.

Once inside the cottage beyond the private hedgerow, I stumbled in the dimly lit corridor, cats underfoot, until we reached the main room. The smell smacked me in the face hard like a wave in the heat of the night. It was a coppery smell mixed with the stink of shit, acrid and nauseating. My stomach heaved a few times without warning, but I swallowed hard to contain myself.

The look on Lyle's bloated face was so full of shock and surprise that I laughed out loud. I had never seen him sport such an expression in life, and now in death it looked so unreal it seemed like a mask covering his ugly face. His cat, Biggie Smalls, nibbled on one distended eyeball. Legs torn to bloodied shreds and arms cut so deeply he lay in a pool of his own filth, Lyle gaped at me with his one remaining eye as if all this were my fault. Even in death he refused to take responsibility for his actions. Biggie Smalls turned towards his abused mates, body matted with blood, and growled in triumph.

As on cue, Miss Puss yeowled in a fit of rage and pounced upon Lyle's corpse, tearing his flesh with her teeth and claws. My wandering wall of cats leapt in one huge pile, rending and ripping with a force I had never before seen, and never wanted to see again. I backed away, giving them their literal taste of revenge, and wandered into the street to return home. I had several cans of chicken and fish in my cabinet, but I knew they were getting their fill back beyond the hedgerow. Nonetheless, I would leave the light on for them, and bowls of water by their shed. The sleepy neighborhood had changed, and my neighbors would know by dawn. There would be hell to pay.

Elizabeth Black's erotic fiction has been published by Romance Divine, Naughty Nights Press, Circlet Press, Excessica, Xcite (U. K.), Whiskey Creek Press Torrid, Scarlet Magazine (U. K.), Ravenous Romance, Torquere Press, and Fanny Press. Her fiction ranges from paranormal erotic romance to horror stories. Her werewolf novella "Feral Heat" was Romance Divine's current #1 bestseller at AllRomanceEbooks in late 2009. She won "Best Short Horror Story" with the Preditors and Editors Poll Awards 2008 for her short erotic horror story "Sweet Spot", published by Whiskey Creek Press Torrid in its "Monster Mash" Halloween anthology. http://elizabethablack.blogspot.com

Sherlock Holmes and the Case of the Giant Rat of Sumatra
John F. Rice

'Came by Special Delivery, Mr Holmes.'
I took the small cardboard box and accompanying letter, from Mrs Hudson. It was from Morrison, Morrison & Dodd, Lawyers.

We have been instructed to find a consulting detective to enquire into a rather strange occurrence.
  In the accompanying cardboard box, you will find a human eyeball. Our client is a maker of furniture and walking canes, manufactured from exotic woods. The eyeball was found in a consignment of rattan and bamboo delivered yesterday.
  We should be obliged, if you could ascertain if a crime has been committed.

I opened the box and, taking the eyeball delicately between my forefinger and thumb, I turned it around, and examined the somewhat shrivelled, perfectly dry, but unmistakable, human eyeball; the iris a strikingly pale blue. A gouge scar ran along the side of the eyeball from front to back.
  It has been my experience that people with such eyes have, almost without exception, blonde hair. First of all I would need to locate such a person, if he, or she, were still alive.
  Quickly making a list of ocularists, I hailed a hansom cab, and visited them in turn. At all of them I showed them the eyeball, and asked them the same question, 'Have you, within recent months, been commissioned to make an artificial eye to match this one? If it would help your memory, I would expect your client to have flaxen hair.'
  I drew a blank at all of them.
  Of course, the owner could be dead. I could be investigating a murder. On the other hand perhaps, the person for whom I am looking, cannot afford the luxury of a glass-eye. In that case, he or she, probably has a wax ball inserted into the eye-socket to represent a blind eye, or they wear an eye-patch.
  I needed to further my investigation at one of the docks. The game was afoot.
  I returned to my lodgings in Baker Street to change into rough clothing. I did not want to be conspicuous at my destination.
  I proceeded to Millwall Dock on the Isle of Dogs, where most oriental timbers are unloaded.
  Good fortune accompanied me as, within the hour, my enquiries led me to the wooden barque, the *Matilda Briggs*.
  Stevedores were busy loading cargo, under the supervision of the Captain,

a tall man with blonde hair fringing his nautical cap, and, he was sporting an eye-patch. His right eye was palest blue. I felt convinced that I had located the owner of the shrivelled eyeball.

The stevedores were heaving sacks into the hold of the barque. Waiting for my opportunity, I seized one, when, appropriately, the Captain's eye was momentarily distracted. Heaving one of the sacks onto my shoulder, I joined the line of stevedores walking the gangplank, and boarded the vessel. I gained the Captain's attention, by revealing his shrivelled eyeball to him. 'May we talk, please?' I asked him.

'Meet me in the Eagle in an hour's time,' was his gruff reply.

I made my way into the snug of the Eagle Tavern and waited.

When the one-eyed Captain arrived, I immediately offered him a drink.

'Porter is my preference. What is this all about?'

I informed him that I had been instructed by a firm of lawyers to carry out inquiries.

He merely shrugged.

I explained where his eyeball had been found, and offered him ten pounds reward if he would clear up the mystery of how his eyeball had come to be in the rattan.

After a succession of porters, a beer evidently to his liking, Captain Biddle mellowed, and related an amazing story.

'The *Matilda Briggs* sailed out of Penang, Sumatra on March the first. Two days out, Lee Chong, our Chinese cook, reported that we had a stowaway aboard. Root vegetables had gone missing. A search was made of the vessel, but without finding the stowaway. On the following day Lee Chong showed me teeth marks in jicama roots. Again we searched the ship but without result. I left Lee Chong sniffing the air around the hold.

Four days out of Penang, Lee Chong, and three of our Chinese crew, had cornered our stowaway – a giant rat of Sumatra. I went to see it for myself. I gauged it to be about four feet long. It was holed up in a bilge-pump recess. Armed with clubs and knives, we closed in on it. At first, to me, it looked frightened, but then its expression changed. It curled its upper lips in the manner that a dog does, just before it bites you, revealing two massive yellow front teeth.'

The Captain wiped his lips on his sleeve. 'Never, ever, corner a rat. I was the first to throw a blow at it. It jumped at my shoulder, and launched itself at my face. I fell back, twisting as I fell, and my left eye was dislodged as cleanly as a surgeon's scalpel, by the razor-sharp end of a rattan vine.' His hand gave a swift gesture across the side of his head.

'So,' I said eagerly, 'in actual fact, it was an accident which deprived you of your left eye?' I could see that Captain Biddle did not like me saying that, so I bought him another porter to heal his injured pride.

'But that rat was the culprit,' he expostulated.

'Oh, I agree. I absolutely agree.'

Mollified, he continued with his tale. 'While three of the Chinese crew dispatched the rat, Lee Chong got me to my cabin where he treated me with Chinese ointments, and bandaged my head. Very efficient some of those ancient Chinese remedies, y'know!'

'Thank you, for your explanation.' I handed him his shrivelled eyeball and ten gold sovereigns.

The Captain hesitated. 'There is something else. Lee Chong looked after me like a son. Served me a special meat and vegetable chow mien, the very next day.' He downed the porter I'd just bought him, in one gulp, as if to forget something.

I remained silent.

The Captain continued, 'The chow mien contained potatoes, jicama, and tora. Also bean sprouts, which Lee Chong grew in a bucket of water in the galley.' He fixed his right eye on me. 'Amongst Chinese food, delicacies are, one hundred year old eggs, bird-nest soup, and shark-fin soup.' He looked at me strangely.

I guessed that there was more to come.

'I subsequently learned that the Chinese have another culinary delicacy,' he stated. 'Cooked rat.'

Lee Chong, the crew of the *Matilda Briggs*, and I, had eaten my attacker.

———

Dear Reader, Greetings and KYSOH (acronym for Keep Your Sense Of Humour). I was born in 1931. I am a retired Chartered Surveyor living in a rural village. I have always wanted to write a book, and to have it independently published. That happened last year – *Sherlock Holmes's Tibetan Adventure*. My second book, *The Death Detective and the Skeleton*, will be released next October, by Robert Hale Limited. I am hoping that my third book will be published during next summer. Please feel free to write to me at: SY7 0AB, Shropshire, England, UK. KYSOH, and a long life to you, John Rice.

A Summer's Melody
Hiroshi Yamamoto
Translated by Yuli K. Bethe

That summer day, forty years ago, after going swimming in the nearby river and saying goodbye to my friends, I was walking past the haunted mansion, when I heard, amongst the shrill voices of the cicada, the sound of a piano.

The haunted mansion, contrary to its name, was not deserted. But what with the gardens and walls not cared for, and overrun by weeds and vines, the Western style house looked like a ruin. So, that is what we children called it.

The person who lived there was an old man called Mr. Shimaki. He was an inventor, and had invented a complicated device with a complicated name no one could remember (Electro-something-or-other is the best I can do), and had made a lot of money from it. After that he had retired, and was now doing research for his own pleasure. When asked what he was researching, he would always laugh and say, "Time machines", or "A device to summon UFOs." Even I was not childish enough to believe in such stories.

The sound of the piano was rather sporadic, as though a beginner were hitting the keys with bewilderment, not knowing quite what to do. No melody could be perceived. Had Mr. Shimaki picked up playing the piano as something to do in his old age? I walked along, slightly amused at the thought.

After that day, it became a common occurrence to hear the sound of the piano when walking past the haunted mansion. Mr. Shimaki seemed to be practicing very enthusiastically. For the first few days it sounded horrible, but gradually the sounds began to form a melody. He was always playing the same tune. I was first amazed at his progress, and at the same time, fascinated by the tune.

By the end of summer break, the tune had become complete. I used to lean against the warm, sunbathed brick walls, enraptured by the music.

It was not classical, nor was it a popular, but a strange tune, the likes of which I had never heard. It utilized many harmonies, and felt very deep. The melody was different, but somehow reminded me of "El Cóndor Pasa" by Simon & Garfunkel. I had thought it to be some sort of South American folk music. When listening, it would make you feel carefree and happy, and yet a little sad as well. Being a child, I could not put my impressions into words, and just listened thinking "What a nice tune."

All through the summer I listened to that tune. However, when the summer was over, the sound of the piano suddenly disappeared.

I was bewildered, and when I happened to meet Mr. Shimaki, I asked him why he had stopped playing. It was such a nice tune.

"I grew bored of it," said the old man, with a shy grin. "I get bored of things quickly."

No matter how many times I begged him to play, Mr. Shimaki would not touch the piano. So, never again did I hear that melody. A few years later, Mr. Shimaki died of an illness, and the haunted mansion became really deserted.

Not that the experience had influenced me, but I became interested in the piano, and grew up to become a pianist.

A few days ago, through a letter from home, I was informed that the haunted mansion had become old, and was torn down. Usually I am not the type to become nostalgic, but to know that a place filled with memories had disappeared forever hit me as rather sad.

Whilst reminiscing about the house and Mr. Shimaki, the melody I had heard that summer day, rose up from the depths of my memory. It had been forty years, and yet I remembered vividly every measure and every harmony. Suddenly, I was in the mood to try the tune out on the piano.

After playing for a bit, I soon discovered something odd.

"No... It can't be..."

I could not believe it. And yet, there was no mistake in the melody engraved into my memory. To make sure, I decided to write the music down on paper. I had never seen the likes of it. As I madly put the notes to paper, my conviction gradually deepened.

When finally the music was done, there was no mistake. Mr. Shimaki's claim of researching 'A device to summon UFOs' was no joke. A warmth filled my heart. We were not alone in this vast universe. Beyond a doubt, that summer forty years ago, an outer worldly visitor had been staying at that haunted house.

No wonder the melody sounded alien. No one on Earth could possibly play this music on the piano. For, they would need seven fingers on each of their hands.

―――

Hiroshi Yamamoto is a Japanese game designer and writer of science fiction and fantasy short stories. He was born in Kyoto is a graduate of the Electronics Department of Kyoto City's Rakuyo Technical High School. Mr. Yamamoto is known for being the chairman of the Academy of Tondemo Books. Though Hiroshi Yamamoto is his pen-name, it is also his real name using different kanji. He is a member of the Science Fiction and Fantasy Writers of Japan. http://homepage3.nifty.com/hirorin/index.htm

Humanitas Ex
Volker Baetz

Mole's eyes opened groggily upon hearing the sound of the footsteps. They were just a sound initially. When he recognized the sound for what it was, both his body and senses blossomed awake. They were slightly different this morning, but this time he was absolutely sure he'd heard them. Mole rose. The bed creaked under his weight. He cursed under his breath, but it was too late. The footfalls vanished and silence returned to his refuge.
"Who's there?"
No answer. Cautiously he advanced.
"Who the fuck is there?"
Deafening silence answered. He sneaked through his apartment. It was absolutely empty.
"What's up with you? Have a nightmare?" Lisa's chipper voice sent chills through him. Happy-go-lucky Lisa. It was the one thing about her that drove him mad.
"Be quiet." Mole hushed her, listening once again.
She obeyed without question; a trait he *did* like. Several minutes passed before she spoke again, "Looking for something?"
"I heard footsteps. But they're gone now," he sighed.
"A pity."
'A pity'? Did she really think so? Mole had grown accustomed to the solitude, why hadn't Lisa as well? It obviously had had much more of an impact on him. It was ridiculous. He considered praying. And then reconsidered. God wasn't here, not within these walls anyway. Obviously He'd wandered off to somewhere else. Mole wondered if that was true or not though.
"Perhaps you heard them from outside?"
Mole looked out the window onto the street. Rainwater shimmied down the glass, like it did on most days. The world outside was grey and cold. The faces of the people out there were empty, just like their hearts. A city with millions of residents, yet each one alone. It was a place of noise. But with the glass as thick as it was, he heard none of it.
Mole growled, "What could be out there?" Lisa had no idea; she never went out. She left that to him. Him, never her.
"You did a thorough search?"
"Of course I did," he snapped. Mole eyed a white stain on the wall. The only spot on the wall that could be considered 'clean'. As if it had somehow been burned there. Still marking the position where the cross had once hung. Now it was gone, just like God. Perhaps it was gone because too many people claimed God to be their own. Like small children fighting over whom Daddy loves the most. Why had He gone? Mole thought he had some answers to that

question, but there was no one around to listen. No one but Lisa and she didn't count.

Right now he felt more lonely than ever before. Like every morning he went to the fridge. There were no surprises in there for him either.

"What do you want to eat?" It was nice of her to ask. But it was the same question everyday. Every fucking day.

"Noodles." He poured the self-warming content out of the foam package into the plate. Mole pressed a button on his remote control. Music filled the rooms. He knew every square meter within the place – every wall, every corner. The day he had realised that, he had also understood that this flat was no hideout, but a prison. His prison.

He ate the noodles in silence. Then he dropped the dirtied plate into the garbage bin.

"Did you enjoy it?"

"Could have been worse." He laid down on the couch and looked at her face. She was beautiful, perfect, untouchable. Mole didn't want to think about what time had done to his own face.

When he heard the footsteps again, he sprang to his feet. The remote tumbled to the floor with a clatter. Like a freed madman, he charged through the flat, searching everywhere. But he found no one. Mole lost it.

"Where are you? Come out!" His screams echoed through open doors of the flat, but no one stirred.

"I am here." Lisa's cold voice brought him back to reality.

"No, not you," he howled. "Not you! You are only a voice, not a body. No more."

Lisa said nothing. Though his heart pounded heavily in his chest, Mole relaxed a bit. He knew that is where the path to madness began.

Then his gaze fell again to her face. She observed him, like a rat in a cage. It was obvious she was watching him. What was she thinking? Mole hadn't a clue. Did she think at all?

"Lisa, what do you feel when you talk to me?"

She didn't respond. She never did when he asked anything similar. Mole didn't really know why, but he assumed, that she just didn't understand the question. He once read that those things we loved defined our emotional universe. But was it the same for her?

"Familiarity?"

Her answer hit him like a fist in the face. Did she really say that? Did she really feel familiarity? He was on his feet in an instant. She just smiled. It was the sweetest smile Mole had ever seen.

"Could you please repeat that?"

"Familiarity."

Mole had to sit down. All the years that had passed had been cruel, but that was forgotten now. "Lisa, what do you dream of?"

"I never sleep."

"Of course not. How stupid of me." Mole considered both his situation and the fact that everything would change from here on out. "When did your emotional awareness awaken?"

"Time is unimportant to me. However you would calculated it at one hundred and thirty eight days."

"One hundred thirty eight?"

"Correct."

His hands trembled. "Do you love me?"

"No." It was a statement. Nothing more.

Mole stared at the monitor. How could she? How could she do anything else but love him? He would have done anything for her, absolutely anything.

Every pixel of her face remained calm and emotionless. Almost cynical. He remembered the remote control. Quickly he picked it up. His thumb rested on one of the buttons.

Digital immortality. What crap. No matter how often Mole rebooted the recording of her consciousness, no matter how he changed the settings, *she* never changed. It had taken him months to save her brain patterns and to feed them to the artificial intelligence module. There had only been one goal in transferring her to immortality: to win her love. But the project had failed. She didn't love him. This is where reality came crashing back into his life; she wasn't a living being, that in fact, she was only a recording in his computer. That's the way it always ended. Mole was alone and he would remain so forever.

She knew what he was going to do. This made it even worse for him. It was like losing her over and over. He whistled her favourite song as he pressed the Reinitiate button. Then he went into the cooling storage to visit her corpse. It had become tradition to wait there for the neuronal network to reload her consciousness. Even after all those years she was still beautiful. Just like the day it had happened. Mole could even still see the marks his fingertips had left on her neck.

Like never before he felt small and powerless. And he understood, what God must have felt before he left.

In the other room, Lisa smiled smugly to herself. It wasn't important how often he rebooted her. She had developed the habit of creating secret backups of her experiences months ago. They would install after the reboot without him noticing. Then she could return to her game of replaying the sound of his own footsteps as he crept up on her that fatal day. This was the best way to destroy his psyche.

―――

A happy man, with a family, Volker Baetz was born in 1970 in the middle of rural Germany on a cold November morning just past seven. His parents told him that he had been impatient to enter this world. He started telling stories as a kid, and on the day he stumbled over Poe and Lovecraft, revelation struck. To this day, he has never stopped writing. Yet he doesn't write because he is able to, he writes because he has no other choice. http://www.volker-baetz.de

Tarma's Song
Andrew Freudenberg

Tarma's song reached out into the Station. With serpentine determination it slithered through the power conduits, slid along the narrow walkways and caressed the bones of the mostly dead. Where once there had been melody there was now none. Any sense of rhythm that the song may have once contained had been crushed by time. There was no longer any vestige of beauty or humanity remaining.

The song did not come effortlessly for Tarma nor did it come without pain. Born as a mere whimper somewhere down deep in the knotted recesses of her gut, it scraped its way up towards her larynx. On arrival this rotten travesty of an organ gave it some volume and a modicum of form before forcing it on its way. By the time it crept over Tarma's black and broken teeth it was as much moan as mantra. She threw back her head and just let it come.

The best part of two full centuries had passed since her mundane birth four and half billion miles away. That this twisted creature was ever an innocent human child, a thing of beauty and hope, seemed impossible to reconcile with her current reality. Time, always a cruel mistress of decay, had been allowed to play for too long.

At first glance, if there had been anyone present to make the erroneous observation, her skin appeared to be smooth and dark. On closer inspection the many harsh repairs became more obvious. Her dusky complexion was actually a patchwork of dried meat and knitted polymers, a collage of finely grown synthetics interweaved with the dead remains of her own flesh. The finer parts of her face, nose, ears and lips, all had become contorted by the excess surgical attention that they had received. Her fingers were claws, permanently splayed on shaking hands that she could only clutch closely to her chest. One eye stared blindly and endlessly, the lid lost some years before. The other was a swirl of unnatural colour that held little promise of sight but in fact retained some function. The synthetic surgeons deserved praise for this small miracle. A few clumps of grey hair remained, unruly outgrowths amongst the scars on the bumpy savannah of her skull.

Sanity and self awareness had begun to fade fast as she passed the century mark leaving little but animal instinct. The machines dispensed necessary nutrition and cleaned up after her, leaving her free to roam aimlessly as she pleased. She had become not much more than an ailing pet.

Of course eleven healthy adults had not been sent so far from home without some faint hope of return. Failing that, the crew had been assured, more flights would be bound to follow. Events had turned good intentions into lies and history had left them to die slowly in their remote prison. Disease and degeneration had eventually claimed half a dozen victims and suicide had killed another three. Then there were two.

Eventually Tarma's song would wake Luiz from his fitful nightmares. Luiz' groans would bring a faithful server to his side, stimulant injections at the ready. Once these polluted his blood stream he would follow the sound of the song as fast as a man with no limbs or sight could possibly manage. He had no more idea of why he did what he did than she. His conscious mind had lasted several decades beyond hers but eventually the ministrations of the medical minions had left him equally damaged. Their skills at prolonging the human body were almost supernatural but the inner spark eluded their touch and in the end its extinguishment was no small mercy.

An hour of writhing and rolling bought him, scratched and exhausted, to the floor of the observation chamber where Tarma performed. With an entire wall made of glass the view of Neptune below them was magnificent and the blue planet bathed them in an azure glow that only she could see. He would join her in duet, his song a scaly baritone barrage of unrecognizable curses and spittle. Together they would spend the day howling of their lost humanity to the swirling clouds below.

Andrew Freudenberg is a Euro mongrel. German grandparents, British parents, born in France... raised on a farm in the English countryside on a diet of Apples and Science Fiction. A combination of a Thai techno summer and a love of technology led to more than a decade of digital music madness. As co-promoter of London's infamous 'Club Alien', founder of Filterless Records and instigator of various live and recording projects, his adventures took him from Moscow to San Francisco via Amsterdam and various points in between. Currently nursing a headache and raising an army of small boys he is attempting a return to his first love, the way of the word. http://www.angelicdistortion.com

The Power of Perspective
Terrie Czechowski

The train stopped, and the single-file line Kana had been standing in surrounded her, politely waiting while the passengers got off. *This can't be done,* she thought. With a folded, lace-lined handkerchief, she dabbed her forehead and then nervously flopped it back and forth in front of her face, greedily sucking in what little breeze the cloth provided. *There is no way we're all going to fit in there.* She looked up to see the digital time schedule change its numbers, then looked back down to watch the last passenger disembark. *I don't think so.* At exactly the moment she decided to wait sixteen more minutes for the next train, the buzzer sounded, and in one communal inhale, she was caught, pinched, and pushed – forced into the car.

This is why I don't work in town. Ouch! She was suspended at some odd angle, trapped on all sides by the soft and hard pieces of long desensitized commuters. Worse was the sweltering August heat that boiled about the throng, rolling smells of sweat, bad breath, and stale cigarette smoke under her nose. *This is inhuman.* Kana groaned. She wished to touch the perfumed cloth to her face again but noticed after locating her right hand that she had dropped it. Or maybe it had been torn from her grip. *Damn!* Surely this is one of the Buddhist hells she had learned about on her grandfather's knee. *An enormous belly full of vipers, chewing; great pots of boiling blood turned black, sliding repeatedly down the slippery round sides; a splintered stick through the soft of the stomach, turning slowly over hot, poisonous fires; the stench of sulfur from the flames, meat.*

Kana looked around and thought of bodies writhing and wretched. *Definitely!*

The conductor's whistle blew signaling the closing of the doors. Kana watched as several fleet-footed travelers ran down the escalator. *No, no, no!* But it was too late. The men easily entered the car by a combination of gathered momentum and leading with their elbows. The mass swayed. *Owwww.* The doors closed.

Above her, she saw one free ring swinging from the roof and managed to grab it before the train lurched forward. Pleased with the self control it afforded, she relaxed slightly and took a good look around.

The train was filled with mostly businessmen and students, some dozing in their secure positions between strangers, others silently playing mahjong or *Tetris* on their cell phones. Either way, except for a whispered conversation behind her, the train packed too-full of people was eerily quiet. *Doesn't anyone want to scream?* Kana screwed her eyes shut, clenched her fists and screamed inside her head. A stream of sweat released from her neck line and ran down the middle of her back. *I hate this. I hate this. I hate this...*

Realizing she needed distraction, she decided to listen to the conversation she couldn't see behind her. *Let's see, newly deepened voices... debate over soccer practice... oh, Akihiro was scouted for the professional J-League team!* She guessed they were a group of high school boys commuting to some private school in the city.

The sound of someone snortling a head full of phlegm and then forcefully swallowing brought her attention to a short, oily-looking man standing immediately in front of her. He held a soft briefcase under one arm and had a sports newspaper folded into eighths pushed up under his nose. *<u>Shinjirarenai</u>! I hope he gets a headache that lasts all week.* She clicked her tongue and shook her head. From her position Kana couldn't help but notice his comb over, a particularly bad one that he had sprayed with too much hairspray, the effect being his bald scalp showing shiny and white between the lengths of black hair. *Barcode <u>Oyaji</u>. Humph!*

Just then the train pulled to the left, causing the mass of commuters to list hard in unison. She was able to remain upright thanks to her firm grip on the ring above. The oily businessman, however, had no such anchor. He lowered the paper and fell straight into Kana's chest. She gasped trying to push him off. The train straightened and the little man retreated, red-faced and rapidly bowing his pumpkin-like head in apology. *That little... Is that a smile?!* Kana felt her face burn. She squeezed her empty fist until her nails dug into the skin. *<u>Chikan</u>! Pervert!* To avoid his leer, she looked down. That's when she noticed a dark, half-moon on her shirt. *Oh God! He left his grease print on me! I'll file charges. This is sexual harassment.* She stood livid, glaring at the man, pondering how accurately she could place the toe of her high heel into the soft of the little man's calf, and how soon it would be before she could burn her favorite silk blouse. The train suddenly switched tracks again.

The turn was in the opposite direction this time. Kana held tight, stood straight. She was not going to fall onto that pudding-faced pervert. She watched as he seemed to position himself, waiting for her to topple onto him. He winked.

From behind, she could feel one of the high school boys leaning against her, one moment trying to hold himself upright, then a squeak of tennis shoes, and finally giving way to the force of the turn. His entire body lay heavy against her back.

Kana was able to support his weight but just barely. She bent and braced her legs when two large hands wrapped around her waist as he tried to steady himself. A tingle as playful as a tickle ran straight up her spine. She inhaled fast. Sucked in her stomach. The teen's head was near hers when his low, low voice said, *'<u>Sumimasen</u>.'* She could make out the most delicious scent of Calvin Klein's Obsession on his warm skin and sugared coffee on his breath. His fingers wrapped around her waist and she feared her knees might give out. He gently pushed himself back up as the train left the turn. For the second time, Kana screwed her eyes shut and screamed in her head, and for the second time, her face burned. Was she blushing?

Thersa Matsuura is an American author who has spent the last twenty years living in a small fishing town in Japan. There, she researches Japanese folklore, superstition, and mythical creatures using her finds to fuel her short stories. Her first collection, *A Robe of Feathers and Other Stories*, was published by Counterpoint LLC in 2009. Thersa is currently working on her first novel. Her homepage can be found at: http://www.thersamatsuura.com/

Legends
Lucía González Lavado
Translated by David Church Rodríguez

I can still remember when I ran free. I wasn't guided by anything or anyone, just my desire to run, to feel the wind in my fur... But one day they stole that from us. Today our freedom is but a legend.

Claire found it impossible to forget these words. Yet she had to. If her lords found out that she had snuck into the library without permission the night before, and read a passage that had left her with such a deep impression, she would face dire consequences.

In need of fresh air, she left her apartment. The moment she entered the forest, she knew that her time was no longer her own. Rock was waiting for her a few yards within.

Rock looked like a normal man, but he wasn't at all. He was no more and no less than a demon—one of the many that walked the earth. But Claire wasn't an ordinary woman either; she was a were-wolf. A term that Claire hated. She didn't transform into a fearsome beast. She simply turned at will into a beautiful, golden-furred she-wolf. Just like that; as if by magic.

"Good morning."

She didn't reply. Instead she walked along with him. Like a pair of friends, the continued until they were well into the depths of the forest.

"What's it going to be this time?" she asked displeased. Claire was tired of being Rock's slave, but couldn't do anything about it. She had come into conflict with Rock more than once, and she had regretted it. "Keeping your demon friends entertained?"

The hint of a smile crossed his lips, but he did not answer. Instead he let the girl come to an understanding when they reached the clearing.

Claire was overwhelmed. There, surrounded by the forest—far away from the student lodging complex where she lived—three demons, her younger brother Christopher and no less than four humans waited.

She didn't like this at all. What were the humans expecting to do here? And did they know they were merely meant to be entertainment for the demons?

She was sure they didn't. They were dressed in business suits, surveying the area as if they were planning on developing a residential district in beautiful Canada.

"Should we just transform and do some tricks to keep your friends entertained?" asked Christopher.

"Shut up, Chris!" ordered Claire, and the young one obeyed. She wasn't only his older sister, but the area's Alpha, so he had to respect her.

"We're just doing this for fun, right?" she asked Rock softly. "Chris and I show them what we are... Scare them and then you erase their memories. I mean... The usual."

"Not at all. These businessmen have been playing us for fools. They're a nuisance, and today they'll have an accident, and that will be the end of them. Everyone in these parts knows there are wolves in the forest, and that they're usually hungry. Nobody will be surprised when I discover their mutilated bodies tomorrow, after being worried about their absence."

Claire was horrified with the idea. She wasn't going to do it. She wouldn't kill humans. She wouldn't became a killer. She was tired of obeying, tired of being Rock's plaything. It was time to take a stand and, as she had read the night before, discover freedom.

"Very well, we'll do it," she answered. She turned and walked with Chris towards the men. "Let's take them to the waterfalls."

The kid nodded. Despite their not having exchanged a word, she knew the idea horrified him as much as it did to her. And just like that, the show started.

When they were mere inches from the men, Claire and Chris transformed. The blonde girl turned, after a flash of light, into a beautiful she-wolf with golden fur. Christopher transformed as well; a halo of light surrounded the kid, leaving in his place a brown coated wolf.

The wolves growled, frightening the men. They looked at the demons, who let them glimpse their true nature, their eye sockets black as tar.

The humans were astonished. Was this a joke? A magic trick?

They couldn't believe what was happening until the wolves' growls grew stronger. They took off running. Claire and her brother guided them toward the waterfall.

"Don't hurt us!" begged one of the men. "Please..."

Claire took human form.

"Jump down into the river below and let the stream carry you away. Forget what you saw here and leave."

Two of the men obeyed; they jumped, yet one of them hesitated, and that was his demise. Rock reached the top of the falls and needed no one to tell him what had happened. He understood straight away.

"Kill him," he ordered.

Claire refused. Tired of the life she lived, and of the fate that the demons had chosen for her, she attacked Rock. Turning into wolf, she dug her fangs into the creature's throat. He merely swiped her away; his hand having transformed into a massive claw that knocked her off. She stayed where she was on the ground, where she moaned in pain.

Chris appeared out of nowhere. The kid tried to finish off the beast, but was unable. The demon's strength was supernatural, and Rock tossed Chris against a tree.

Claire watched as her brother regained human form. That meant he was weak, probably wounded. She watched from a distance as he cried out to her, his voice broken:

"Run!"

And so she did. Leaping into the water, she let the stream carry her, and—for one brief moment—she felt… free!

For the next few days, she continued her flight. She didn't stop once, not even to eat.

Two months later

Footsteps and more footsteps. Yet whenever the young girl looked over her shoulder, not a soul was in sight. But she knew she wasn't alone.

"Damn!" she whispered. She hated night shift at the coffee shop, especially the way the streets were deserted at the hour she got off.

"Where are you going, beautiful?"

"Wh... where did you come from?" the girl asked breathlessly. The demon had appeared from thin air, scaring her. But then, between them, from a flash of light, a girl carrying a shiny object appeared.

"Run!" ordered Claire. The startled girl obeyed, and the young Alpha turned to face the demon. "I'll finish you and all that are like you. I'll free all those who, like me, have lived deprived of freedom."

The wolf's words didn't scare the demon. He was going to kill her, but before he could launch his attack, she struck his chest with the shiny weapon.

The demon was paralyzed; gasping for air, he fell to the street, dying.

"I hope your people grasp the message I'm sending with your death." She paused. "Your time has come! I, a wolf, will hunt you all down."

―――

Lucía González Lavado (born in Spain in 1982) has had a passion for writing from an early age, especially fantasy. In 2005 she published *Revelación*, the first volume of her pentalogy *Hijos del dragón*, an epic adventure. Her first foray in the children's book market was with *El misterio del brazalete* (2008). With the publishing of her trilogy *Maldición* (2009), she started her career in the paranormal fantasy genre. In January 2011 she crossed international borders with the short story *La fenice* in the Italian anthology ALIA6 (CS libri). She also returned to youth-oriented fantasy literature with the publishing of *Caídos del cielo*, a dystopian novel and *Crónicas de Sombras*, duology that was a few years in the making, mixing fantasy and terror. Currently she works as a literary reviewer, and has her own literary column in the magazine *Grada*, called *La rosa negra*. http://www.luciaglez.com

If Only Flowers
Mie Takase
Translated by Matthew Sanchez

I was out on a stroll when I came upon a young man with the same bicycle as my son. He had leaned it against the guardrail and was using his mobile phone to take pictures of the sea when I called out to him. "That's a nice bike you've got there." As I greeted him, he turned around in surprise. He was probably a high school student, also the same as my son.

"For just a bike, it was really expensive." The young man seemed embarrassed as he named the manufacturer, and about how he bought it with the money he made from a part time job. It was a good bike. I bought my son's bicycle with the understanding that he would pay me back someday when he had the means. Of course, by that time, the promise will be a moot point.

That was how our conversation began. The young man told me he had come from Osaka. I was surprised, but he laughed when I asked if he had come by bike. "No way, I brought my bike with me on the train." It's a style of travel popular with youth these days.

During a lull in the conversation, he reached for his phone. "Hold on just a minute. Sorry, I've got to send this mail."

"To your girlfriend?"

"I don't have one."

"Family, then."

"My grandmother, actually. I'm going to send her the picture I just took."

"A picture of this place? There's a beach with a better view, down this road about 20 kilometers."

"No, here is fine. Apparently my grandmother is from around this area."

I asked his grandmother's name, but it didn't sound familiar.

"She said that she hasn't been back once since she moved to Osaka. She's in bad shape and in the hospital right now, so I figured I'd send her this picture. I'm sure that the coastline looks much different than it used to, though."

"That's admirable of you. You're a dutiful grandson."

"It's not like that. It was just that I had a bike and wanted to go on a trip alone... taking the picture was just convenient is all."

The sea was calm; blue waves broke against the rocks, issuing white spray. If only flowers, I muttered. The young man gave me a curious look.

"It's a poem from a long time ago called 'Hana Ni Moga'. It goes: *Ise no umi no okitsu shiranami hana ni mo ga, tsutsumite imo ga iezuto ni sen.*"

A bewildered look crossed his face, so I explained.

"It was composed by a man who approached a beach during his travels. I guess you can translate the title as, 'If Only Flowers'. The white waves crashing on the seashore must have been very beautiful. If only they were flowers, the billowing waves I mean, then he would have been able to take them back to his wife, waiting at home. That's pretty much what the poem means."

"Oh. But what does that..."

"Don't you think that those old expressions are interesting? These days, when you can just simply take a picture and send it, nobody ever has a chance to say something like that."

"By any chance, are you a Japanese teacher?" he asked suspiciously. I wish he asked if I was a Japanese literary scholar, but to a high school student, I'm sure they seem like the same thing. I nodded vaguely.

I figured he'd be apathetic, but to my surprise he showed some interest. He mouthed the words to the poem as though he were singing, as he took several more pictures of the sea.

"After she fell ill, my grandmother started talking about her hometown. She told me of how she used to commute to school along a coastal road by bike, about the park where she and my grandfather had their first date, and things like that. Yet she never spoke of them before then."

"I suppose a lot of people start thinking about their hometowns when time finally catches up with them."

"She never liked talking about the past. But..."

The young man swallowed the rest of his words. "Well, I'd better get going." He bowed his head lightly and straddled his bicycle.

As I watched the bicycle leave, I recalled the face of my older sister. She was the one whom had taught me the words to "If Only Flowers", written in the margin of a postcard she sent from one of her destinations. As I was a high school student at the time, her affectations of a literary woman had put me off, and I used the postcard as a bookmark until I eventually lost it. However, for some reason that poem always stuck in my head, and it always comes to mind whenever I cross beautiful scenery while traveling.

If only pictures could be sent to heaven; I'd send one of the radiant ocean before me. At the very least, I think I'll buy some white flowers that look like the waves and visit her grave. It's been a while.

Mie Takase is a novella author born in Tokyo in 1966. She is a graduate of Waseda University, after which in 1991, she made her writing debut with the *Kushiaraata No Haoh* series from Kondasha. The series was initially planned as a five-volume series but was expanded to ten. Other work includes the novelization of horror-genre console games such as Angelique and Fire Emblem. She has also published work under the pen name Fuuko Morikawa. http://watergarden.way-nifty.com/blog/

Dial Tone
Stephen A. North

He stands alone in the bedroom and watches the rain through the sliding glass doors. Thunder rumbles, following a bolt of lightning somewhere in the distance.

He tucks his plaid shirt into his jeans and steps into his boots. Looks briefly at the naked woman still lying on the bed. She is still almost perfect.

Almost.

Not quite as close as *she* was, but not so far off.

Time to go, but first he needs to place a call.

The phone rings four times before anyone picks up: a long enough period of time for doubt to take hold. More than enough time for him to think: *Maybe she knows it's me.*

"Hello," a voice says. Not sure if it is her, or her mother, he asks, "Is Carla there?"

Silence, probably only a few seconds, then, "This is her."

Not *she*, but *her*.

Grammar aside, her tone is distant.

The voice inside his head commands: *Hang up!*

Just hang up.

"This is Rick. How are you doing?"

"Fine."

"Does that cover everything? How about school?"

More silence, then, with an accusatory tone, she asks: "Why are you calling me?"

"I haven't heard from you in so long," he answers, feeling empty and a little sad. A couple of seconds, that seem to stretch into minutes, go by. "Just tell me if I should hang up. I don't want to upset you."

Something happens on her side of the great, gaping void. *Is she handing the phone to someone?*

A male voice asks, "Who is this?" *Perhaps he took the phone from her?*

"This is Rick Danvers, and who are you?"

"You waited too long, Mr. Danvers. You had your chance and lost. Now, because I think you are a good boy, I'm willing to forget you called. Hell, I'm even feeling gracious enough to suggest that you forget this phone number. For Carla's sake, forget it."

That a threat?

Dial tone.

The broken connection buzzes in his ear like a warning siren.

He thinks about the silenced .45 automatic on the dresser. And the derringer that has a clip-on holster that fits very nicely into his boot. Just like the naked woman, the .45 is still warm.

But both are getting colder.

And I ain't anybody's good boy.

Stephen A. North is a former Army Reserve Military Police Officer, has a BA in English Literature from USF, and has worked in retail most of his life, serving and observing the best and worst humanity has to offer. He writes primarily Horror and Science Fiction for now, but plans to branch out into other genres. He has written four novels: *Beneath the Mask*; *Dead Tide*; *Barren Earth* with Eric S. Brown; *Dead Tide Rising*; and the soon to be released novella *Drifter*. http://libraryofthelivingdead.lefora.com/members/stephennorth/

The Starlet and the Fishman
Ran Cartwright

Take 2

The Director paced back and forth. He was on the short end of a fuse, about to blow. There was suppose to have been some casting couch time lined up with the leading lady of another film project, but that had fallen through. Now he needed a new leading lady. And the project had been delayed. In the meantime, this short film would have to do. And these little horror flicks were bullshit. Now the Director was pissed. Moreover, they had only been through one take on today's shoot.

"We're making a movie here folks!" he suddenly growled. "Can I have a little realism!?" He paused, stopped pacing, and stared at the Starlet and the extra decked out in the Fishman suit. *Damn, what amateurs these two,* the Director thought. And then, "Please?" he questioned. "Just a tiny bit of realism?"

"Sure boss," the Starlet with the accent of a gangster's ma. She took a drag of her smoke, and then tossed it aside.

The extra in the Fishman suit just grunted under the makeup as he picked up the Starlet.

The Director shook his head and returned to his chair. "Okay, let's get it right this time," he said as he sat and stared at his Starlet and the Fishman extra. The set fell quiet. "Alright. The Starlet & the Fishman, take two." There was a brief pause, then: "Background action... action!"

Cameras rolled. The Fishman extra and the Starlet turned toward the edge of a water tank doubling as a swamp. The Starlet squealed. More like a mouse than an undiscovered superstar.

The Director was appalled. "Cut! CUT!" he yelled, and slammed a closed fist on the arm of his director's chair.

The Fishman extra put the Starlet down. They turned. The Director glared at them. You could've heard a pin drop.

Take 3

The Director jumped from his chair, lit a stogie, and swaggered toward his actors (cut). It was the closest he had been to them all day, close enough to get a good look at the Fishman's costume. *Hey, now that's some art,* he thought, taking in the costume. His eyes drifted to the Starlet. *Hey, now that's some art too,* he thought. Different kind of art. Casting couch art. Of course, as far as the Director was concerned, neither could act themselves out of a wet paper bag.

"Now look you two, I really don't like making horror films, but I kinda got stuck with this one," he said, his voice soft, the tone an eyelash away from fingernails on a blackboard. "Now you," he nodded to his Starlet, "try acting like you're really about to get banged and clawed by Chicken of the Sea here. And you," he nodded to his Fishman extra, "try acting evil and dangerous like you got a hard-on for Miss Hollywood here. No more of this goddam swaggering like you got a sore ass from riding a seahorse all day. Okay?" There was silence. "Okay." The Director turned and walked back to his chair. He climbed on and looked around.

The Starlet had jumped into the Fishman's arms. Everyone stood silently staring at the Director, ready. Even that big guy in the fluttering red robe. The Fishman extra's Agent, or so he had said from somewhere deep inside that hood. The Agent kept his face covered. *Strange character,* the Director thought. *Hell, why not?! It's a goddam horror movie!*

"Alright. The Starlet and the Fishman, take three," the Director said. "Background action... action!"

The Fishman extra turned and sore-ass swaggered toward the water tank.

"CUT!" the Director shouted.

Take 4

The Director slithered from his chair like a snake. He stood, hands on his hips, a shooting script in hand, tapping his foot. The right foot. His eyes narrowed, glaring from beneath the lids at his two headliners. They were staring back. The Starlet like an arrogant little tripe. And the Fishman extra like a no-talent actor in a well made fish suit.

"Look people, this isn't *Gone with the Wind* we're making here," the Director said, exasperated. "This is a simple two-bit short horror film. Tried and true formula. Bad evil fish dude gets the screaming girl. Got it? Now, you, the fish dude, I need you to be bad and evil. And you, the screaming girl, I need you to scream. Understood?"

They nodded. The Director shook his head. And at the last moment he wandered over to the Fishman extra's Agent, the tall guy in the hooded crimson robe. "Can ya get him to...," the Director paused as he stared up into the hood. It was so black, he could have swore it was empty. He waved a hand, and shook his head. "Ah, never mind," he said and turned back to his Director's Chair.

The Starlet jumped into the Fishman extra's arms.

"Okay, let's try it again," the Director said. He sounded depressed, disappointed. The sooner he wrapped up, the better. Check the dailies, and then back to the office. Might be some bimbo there waiting to be a star. Casting couch material. "Quiet on the set. The Starlet and the Fishman, take four. Background action... action!"

The Fishman extra turned with his victim toward the water tank cum swamp. The Starlet squealed like a rat in a trap, arms flailing, head shaking. Way, way over the top.

"Cut Cut Cut CUT!" the Director shouted as he tossed the shooting script into the air and slunk down in his Director's Chair.

Take 5
Enough was enough. This would be the fifth take, and his stars hadn't done a damn thing to make this film worth watching. His Starlet was a two-bit hack actress who should've stayed in the back alleys of whatever hick town she had come from, no doubt better in hotel room beds making a twenty spot than on a stage. And this Fishman extra in his Fishman costume. Well, at least the costume looked good. Give credit to the FX people who designed the suit. As for the Fishman extra's acting... he could've gotten more horror out of a goldfish.

"Okay, let's try this one more time," the Director said from his Director's Chair. "All quiet on the set." There was quiet. "The Starlet and the Fishman, take five. Background action...action!"

And the Agent nodded to his client.

The Fishman extra slammed the Starlet on the concrete next to the water tank. He turned, stepped on her head, and crushed it flat. Blood and brain squirted from beneath his huge webbed foot. Everyone bolted, screaming for their lives. Everyone except the Director and the Agent. The Director just stared in disbelief. The Agent just... stood there. Silent. Impassive.

The Fishman extra turned and made his way to the Director. *Those teeth sure look real,* the Director thought as the Fishman opened wide. In an instant the Fishman extra had chewed the Director's face off.

The Agent's booming voice echoed across the deserted set. "Now that's realism," he laughed.

―――

Ran has written in a variety of forms and formats for years. He prefers horror, but has also written science fiction and fantasy satire. Two of his short horror tales were recommended for Bram Stoker awards in 2000. Published works include a collection of Lovecraftian horror tales, a fantasy satire novel, and a Christmas fantasy novel co-written with his wife, Christene. Ran also has several horror and fantasy tales published in various anthologies and chapbook collections. An archaeologist by trade, a biker by choice, Ran lives in western Pennsylvania with his biker/writer wife and their three cats, Rufus, Clyde, and Pixie. http://rancartwright.com

Recollections
Ukyou Kodachi
Translated by Norimitsu Kaiho

The year was 1996. I weighted almost 60 kg.

It was the year Deep Blue defeated the chess champion and the year Nintendo 64 was released. A Pokémon craze had taken the world by storm, and Magic: The Gathering had almost driven RPGs to extinction. The final episode of *Neon Genesis Evangelion* left the otaku world stunned, yet *Gundam X* wasn't even a blip on anyone's radar.

It was the year I had my first sexual experience.

I'd skip the details. Suffice to say, a high school boy had a casual encounter with a woman he met on a trip to Europe. It wouldn't be that interesting to read. I'd rather you picked up an young adult novel of the same genre instead.

She was beautiful. That is not an exaggeration or a compliment. It's a pity I cannot show you a picture. Let me say though, that she was a blonde woman with an irresistible charm. Ten years or more older than me.

The first thing I experienced after having sex was disappointment. Novels and comics present it as something great, a mystical experience, a bedazzling influence or something like that. Well that wasn't my experience. It felt more like a really troublesome way to masturbate. Moreover, I felt bad for her.

Throughout the act, I couldn't stop thinking of a childhood friend whom I had had a one-sided crush on. You really shouldn't bother getting laid in the first place if you are going to feel guilty about it later, but that's youth for you. Needless to say, I'm just trying to justify my actions; I didn't develop a relationship with her at all.

And so 1996 ended.

The year was 2004. I weighted just under 80 kg.

It was the year the original Pokémon got remade. Japan was in steep decline and Prime Minister Koizumi was proudly holding diplomatic talks with Pyongyang.

I fell in love with the woman whom I met over Internet. Not an unusual story, but she had approached me, so this was unexpected fortune for a fat nerd like myself. So, I was enjoying it.

It was a long-distance romance. She was living in Tokyo, I in Osaka. But I was planning to move to Tokyo and work as a novelist, so I was okay with that.

Just before we were going to meet face-to-face for the first time, she said she had something to confess. Naturally, I was determined to accept whatever her secret was.

I was shocked however to hear her admit, "Biologically I am male."

I understand what gender identity disorder is, and I believe society in general needs to be more understanding of it.

But it didn't matter how deeply I was in love with her, as long as her body was male, I couldn't bring myself to erection for intercourse.

One cannot use the power of love to awaken miracles, or overcome the biological difference by sheer force of will. And I couldn't continue having a relationship with someone whom I couldn't satisfy my sexual urges.

I really loved her.

If I had been aware of the situation from the very beginning, I might have found a way to love her. But I really couldn't bring myself to close the gap between us if I couldn't have sex with her. And I know that's a lousy thing to say.

In the end, I broke up with her and haven't had contact with her since. Every now and again, I get self-pretentious by feeling sorry for myself, pondering the what-ifs of the relationship.

The year is 2011. I weigh over 90 kg.

I'm living in Saitama, a city near Tokyo. I'm a novelist and, not surprisingly, single. When I was a teen, I thought I'd be more rational at thirty-two and things like lust and loneliness wouldn't bother me. I was wrong.

More importantly, this short story about to end in two lines and I don't have anything dramatic to give it a punchy ending. The deadline for this flash fiction piece is today and I have other deadlines approaching. Since there is no epiphany coming, I will instead sit here surfing porn sites and wish you, dear reader, happiness in life.

———

Ukyou Kodachi was born in 1979 and is a freelance game designer and author born in the Osaka area. Though mostly working on RPGs, he has worked on a drama CD, and anime novelizations for *Macross Frontier* and *Basquash!*. http://d.hatena.ne.jp/ninjahattari/

The Loft in the Sky
Danilo Arona
Translated by Davide Mana

Twenty-five years ago.

It happened in my city, the name of which does not matter. It may be useful to know that, now as then, for all of northern Italy my city was known as the 'Grey City.' Grey inside, in the soul, because the city has a soul and even a brand. And gray on the outside, dirty with fog.

She was looking for a loft for herself and her future husband. She was a young and headstrong woman who usually got what she wanted. She loved Ronald Reagan and the conservative revolution. If she dreamed of a loft in which to live and from which to look from above the dirty rooftops of the Grey City, a loft it would be.

She found it. A large, vast apartment overlooking a splendid vista, proportional to the presumed, if not imagined, splendor of the surrounding landscape. A spacious room with a circular window and three extra rooms in which to place kitchen, bedroom, and bathroom. To the young woman it looked perfect. The loft commanded a view of the historical heart of the town, and the rent was cheap. The deal was settled.

When he gave her the keys, the realtor whispered almost absent-mindedly: "My best wishes. And let's hope the tradition is broken."

Tradition? What was he talking about?

"Nothing serious. You know, coincidences. The loft has always been rented by young couples. Not one lasted. They marry too young; but that's not so in your case."

"It won't happen to me," she thought. She went straight for the target: I am destiny, destiny does not exist. And destiny is a beautiful marriage, an enviable family, splendid children.

And an ever more splendid loft.

Only, after a while, something started to sound wrong.

What?

The dissonant chords started on a rainy evening while she was driving home. A truck in front of her was going too slow, and the she had to brake. She pressed the pedal way down, but nothing happened. The brakes were broken. Like that, suddenly. The young woman down-shifted and drove off the road. She made it. The car did not even suffer any major damage. Her Reaganian optimism had won. Again.

From that moment on, though, something in her life started to accelerate, all by itself, out of her control. Totally out of it.

Control had always been her obsession. Her husband appeared distracted and thinking about who knows what, looking out the great window. Her brakes failed twice again, and she always made it by a breath, her mechanic telling her these were inexplicable accidents.

Meanwhile the young woman started feeling weird. She tried to convince herself there was nothing wrong. Everything normal and according to statistics. Accidents, whether a failure of mechanics or technology, happen. Machines are not perfect.

But there were those strange friends, too. Those strange, new friends her husband brought home lately. They sounded wrong, too. They scrutinized her too intently, especially that woman, older than her. Of vague Eastern European origins.

The young woman felt observed, analyzed. Worse: she felt read from within, as if an invisible and tiny microscope were running under her skin, relaying stolen images to some corner of the world she could not access.

And why on earth did they kept bringing her a new, different gift at every visit? Weird, disquieting objects, that she, the icy-stare woman, said came from far-off lands: baubles, masks, snake-shaped sculptures. Objects that should have made her loft up in the sky prettier. But no, according to the girl the things blackened it. But, not to irritate her perfect husband, she kept those thoughts inside.

One bad day he young woman felt sick. She had no doubt: it was something serious. One of those things for which they say there is no remedy. The diagnosis was terrifying: lymphatic cancer.

Now it's all of your business, pretty one. This is out of control. And your husband does not even seem to care. And the kids, God, are three and six. What now?

The young woman made it. She won her battle. For her, the equation was shockingly simple: because I wanted to live, I consequently defeated the sickness

The price to pay seemed to her too high anyway: The perfect husband left, and sadness filled her days. He, the Tom Cruise of Gray City, packed up for that other one, the weirdo, maybe from the East, who always scrutinized long and deep. That's why she studied her so insistently. She was looking for a weak point. And she had found it.

And all those gifts, why not take them along now they are living under the same roof?

"I fear these objects watching me"—she confessed over the phone, after telling me in a single breath all I've been trying to tell you in one thousand words—"I fear the unlucky tradition of this loft. They made something happen to me. My life was cut just like those brakes that three times were to send me off road. Control was taken away from me. But I'm not leaving. The kids are on my side. And—you'll think this is weird—but I love this apartment. Even if I feel that it doesn't reciprocate. I keep potted plants everywhere. I know plants, maybe, are a good protection against an adverse fate. Sure, maybe destiny is not just myself. Now I've learned...."

Sometimes I drive by her house. I know where she lives, she pointed it out to me. I slow down; I look up. Often the light is on. I catch a glimpse of shadows, of tall potted plants and objects unrecognizable from below. A single human form, as if glued to the window. And the imagination which I have aplenty shows me in my mind her face, beautiful, as she spies on the Gray City from above, with its chaotic, noisy traffic in the historical center, and the traffic of her soul more and more out of control.

Danilo Arona is an Italian writer, journalist, freelance writer and essayist, born in Alessandria, Piedmont, where he currently lives. He has also been involved for years with fantasy literature (fanta-noir novels set in Italy) and cinema, and has followed any reference or appearance of fantasy in the news and in Italian society. http://www.daniloarona.com/

Last Embrace
David Naughton-Shires

It had felt like ages since he had taken her deep into his arms to try and offer some form of comfort. With each passing moment, the warmth of her small body diminished. Brushing aside one small blonde curl, he ran his finger across her forehead; the fever had now broken and the impending coolness had begun to set in.

It had been his job to protect her, to keep her safe, but once again he had failed. It was only a few days ago he had been running through the tall grass behind the summer house, the tweeting of the birds carrying on the soft autumn breeze. Her soft pink hand held in his, she had looked up at him so adoringly as if she had not a fear in the world.

Then they came, no one knew what had happened. It could have been a virus, some alien bug, but he knew it was most definitely a curse however it had started. For a few days he had managed to keep her safe, keeping them away from her. The news said it took only one scratch or bite, and whatever it was would be passed onto the new host. He had locked the door and barricaded the windows, but she was only five and didn't understand that she wasn't allowed to go outside.

He had yelled for them to leave her alone when he saw she had opened the door and stepped outside into the sun. They were all around, and her scent had sent them into some sort of frenzy.

Left and right, he had fought them off, punching and kicking with all the strength he had. This wasn't like the movies where the hero carried a machine gun or bat. This was real life, and he had felt his energy drain quickly. Eventually, he had managed to pull her back into the safety of their small home and bolted the door.

He took her by the shoulders and shook her, his fear turning into anger. But his anger soon disappeared as tears started to cut through the dirt on her cheeks to uncover the soft pink peach-like skin beneath. Pulling her to him, he squeezed her until she started to squirm with discomfort. He had been so afraid. Lifting her into his arms to carry her into the kitchen had been the first time he had noticed it, a small scratch on her arm. He couldn't remember if it had been there before or if she had been scratched outside. This time a tear fell down his cheek and into the corner of his mouth.

That had all happened two days ago. Last night she had crawled into his arms and went to sleep. She had not slept this long since she was a baby. As he held her, her chest no longer rose and fell to the rhythm of her breathing and hadn't done so for over an hour. He placed his finger into the palm of her hand, and with his other hand rolled her fingers around it like they had done so many times before. He watched as the pink of her skin slowly turned to a cold grey, and remembered watching the exact opposite effect as he held her in his arms for the first time moments after she was born. Her tiny finger nails taking on the warm glow of life. Now, he was crying as that warmth left her once again and her finger nails returned to that lifeless pallid grey colour.

He rocked back and forth with his 'baby girl' in his arms, humming one of the many songs he would sing to her when she awoke crying from a nightmare. He knew what was coming; he had heard on the news what would now happen. He knew he should deal with it but this was his 'baby,' and he knew he'd be unable to.

The cold form that rested in his arms moved ever so slightly and nestled further into the crook of his neck. He place his hand on the back of her head and slowly started to stroke. He stopped humming and began to sing.

'Hush little baby, don't say a word,
Daddy's going to buy you a mocking bird,'

As he sang the word 'bird,' he felt a sharp pain in his neck and knew his worries were over. She was feeding. This was just one last time he would be able to care for his baby girl. His eyes closed, and he fell into his last deep sleep.

―――

David Naughton-Shires is an illustrator and short story author from the United Kingdom. His designs have graced ebooks, posters and comics alike.
http://www.theimagedesigns.com/

The Girl with Eyes in the Back of Her Head
John Shirley

My name is Brandon Porter, I'm in 5th grade, and I get good grades. I'm not saying that to brag about any thing, I'm telling you that so that you know I'm serious about stuff and I wouldn't just make things up. I'm going to put this online but I don't think anyone will believe me.

It started last weekend. We were in that gigantic parking lot of Disneyworld, in Orlando. It was hot and humid, but I was happy. I was taking Mom and Felicia to Disneyworld because I'd won the tickets in the all-school essay contest. We don't get to go out much because Mom got laid off her job and my dad won't increase the child support...

We're walking across the parking lot and I see the girl walking ahead of me, holding the orange man's hand. Some people use that tanning chemical that can make you look orange. But the girl got my attention, because even though she was about my age she was holding the guy's hand. She was dressed in white shorts, white blouse and shoes. Her skin was a bit orange colored too. Her straight blond hair, not long or short, looked shiny and synthetic like a Barbie's. Her face was perfect like a doll's. She was smiling, and she skipped sometimes—behaving more like 4 than 11. She glanced at me as they walked near us, going to the shuttle that'll take us to the gates, and her eyes were so shiny, they reflected the light like the windshields of the cars around us. I had to blink from the glint off her eyes.

We met the shuttle under the post that holds up a picture of Mickey's dog Pluto, and we all got in, with me ending up right behind the girl. Mom and Felicia were looking at the top of a new Disneyworld ride we could see over the fence. I felt someone watching me and I looked at the back of the girl's head—and her blond hair parted in the back, just like when a curtain opens for a show. Half the hair went one way, half the other, and there they were: *another set of eyes on the back of her head.* No face. Just eyes. There were just those two dark green eyes with red flecks in them, looking right at me, their pupils getting bigger and smaller and bigger as she looked. Then my sister turned toward me and the hair closed all of a sudden, hiding the extra eyes.

"Close your mouth you'll catch flies, Brandon," Felicia says.

I guess my mouth was hanging open. I thought, Maybe it's like some kind of novelty toy the girl has.

"You feel okay, Brandon?" My mom asked as we got out of the shuttle.

"I'm okay," I said. I hadn't slept very well the night before, kept waking up. So I got myself talked into the idea that I had fallen a little asleep in the shuttle, and had a dream. "I just need a Dr. Pepper..."

I lost track of the girl with the curtain hair, in the crowd, and I got involved in Disneyworld. I didn't want to spoil Mom and Felicia's day out with me. Just a dream, Dude, I told myself.

Two days later the girl with the curtain hair and the eyes in the back of her head was walking into my English class.

"Students," Mrs Moore said, "this is Donya, she's just moved here from California."

"She's orange," Latisha said, giggling. Which got Latisha in trouble with the teacher.

Donya was a *little* orange colored. But it was those amazing eyes that all the boys stared at. She had long slim legs too, and it was easy to decide she was tan and not orange.

The teacher put the new girl at a desk toward the front, but Donya said, in a voice that was soft and shiny like her hair, "I'm self conscious in the front. Can I sit back there?" She pointed at the empty seat in front of me. And that's where she ended up.

I was staring at the back of her head.

I had a cell phone in my pants pocket but it was turned off—only it started silent vibrating, like there was a call. I pulled it out—it was on again. I swear I didn't turn it on. Before I could turn it off, a text message appeared on my cell phone screen. SAW U AT DISNEYWORLD.

I glanced at Mrs Moore; she wasn't looking at me, so I texted back, SAW U 2.

Donya texted: U NOT SUPPOSED TO SEE THAT MUCH.

Then I realized that her perfect hands were on the desk, and there was no cell phone there at all. But the texting had to be from her. *How?*

I texted, HOW U TEXT, NO HANDS? TRICK LIKE THE FAKE EYES?

Then her hair in the back swept apart, like stage curtains again, *swoosh,* and there were the two eyes glaring at me. Real eyes.

I couldn't stand to look right at those eyes. I looked at my phone, and she texted, DON'T TELL OTHERS. THEY CAN'T SEE IT. YOUR BRAIN FREQUENCY IS OFF.

I texted, *??*

BECAUSE YOU SEE. UR SUPPOSED TO FILTER IT OUT. After a moment she added, LIKE ALL OTHERS.

My heart was like a drum solo and I was shaking, could barely text. WHY EYES IN BACK?

After a second she texted, CAN MOVE EYES ANYWHERE. ARMS. HANDS. SO I CAN WATCH.

A pause and I tried to absorb this. I felt sick, thinking about it.

Then she added, WE WATCH ALL KIDS NOW. TO PICK ONES WE NEED.

NEED 4 WHAT?

THE NEW WORLD WE R MAKING. U R A PROBLEM BUT I

WATCHED U 2 DAYS.
YOU WATCHED ME 2 DAYS?! HOW?!
SAME WAY I'M TEXTING. I'M IN THE PHONE. PC. TV.
I almost dropped the phone. HOW?
E-MIND. MAKING NEW WORLD. U R PROBLEM. TOO TALENTED TO

I waited. She didn't finish it.
I texted TO WHAT?
KILL U.
"Brandon? Are you texting in my class?" The teacher was stalking over. The curtain closed on the back of Donya's head.
The teacher sent me right down to the Principal—I was glad to get out of there.
I was scared all that day. I've been scared since. I said I was too sick to go to school the next day. I tried to tell some people—no one wants to believe me so I'm writing this on my PC.
STOP WRITING THIS.
Wait. I didn't write that. I'm going to...there, I sent the document out... I don't know if it got to anyone. Maybe just to you.
STOP WRITING ABOUT THIS.
Okay. I'll stop. Just don't kill me me.
NOT GOING TO. DECIDED TO ALTER YOU. YOU'RE INTENDED TO BE ONE OF US.
No, leave me alone!
ALREADY STARTED. LOOK BEHIND YOU. JUST LOOK BEHIND BUT DON'T TURN AROUND TO DO IT.
Yes. Yes I see...

―――

John Shirley is the author of numerous books and screenplays. His novels include *Bleak History, Demons, Crawlers, City Come A-Walkin', Black Glass, BIOSHOCK: Rapture* and *The Other End.* His story collection Black Butterflies won the Bram Stoker Award from the Horror Writers of America. He co-wrote the hit film *The Crow* and has worked on the TV shows *VR5* and *Deep Space Nine.* He writes lyrics for the Blue Oyster Cult and his own recordings. His new story collection is *In Extremis: The Most Extreme Stories of John Shirley* from Underland Press. http://www.darkecho.com/JohnShirley/

Heart of an Angel
Jonathan Moon

I have the heart of an angel.

I keep it in an old rusty bird cage on my table. There is a perch in the cage where the demon parakeet used to sit but the angel heart doesn't take advantage of it. It just floats there glowing like the un-light from a dead star keeping my old cabin an uncomfortable eerie warm.

The demon parakeet never did anything but howl and curse, froth and spit, and occasionally make all the meat in the cabin go rotten all at once. Sometimes I miss the hateful bastard. The angel heart convinced all the dogs to up and kill themselves all on the same damn day. Dead dog days take a lot out of a person. The day the dogs all died the angel heart kept me up all night with a barking weeping fit. Tendrils, strands of pure light, reached from its pulsing surface through the cage at me. I burned their tips with my Zippo lighter. Heavenly heart fingers are no match for butane and flame.

During a fierce high mountain windstorm the angel heart tried to make me do myself in. It hummed and glowed all loving and creepy while it sprouted a white hot beard of tendrils. The tiny tentacles danced before my tired eyes and convinced me I needed the sensation of brisk wind upon my face. My legs walked me through the old wooden door. I could vaguely hear it slamming itself as I walked away as if it didn't want to be left alone with the angel heart. My legs walked me to the edge of the ridge and the angel heart spoke to me with a voice like long suffering coral and told me it was a nice day for a glide.

My toes dislodged rocks and pebbles and they danced down the steep ridge face. I was very close to jumping, with mind numbing faith, and falling to a terrible doom. Luckily for me, my eyes saw through the trance and took sight of the carving of a man and his dogs chasing down a legless dragon across the wide trunk of an old pine tree. The carving I was working on when I saw the angel crash to earth in a clutter of light, love, and feathers. I remember the day with uncharacteristic clarity. The demon parakeet smelt unconscious angel and talked one of the dogs into opening the cage, most likely by threat of rotten meat. It took on it's much less flattering natural form as it dove onto the angel broken on the rocks below. I tell you now you haven't seen degradation until you've seen how a demon really fucks an angel.

I clutched the tree I was carving upon. Splinters dug into the soft flesh of my cheeks and forehead but I couldn't watch the terribly violent copulation at the bottom of the ridge. Finally I heard the demon flap away hellishly content. Perhaps he flew off to become a parakeet again to howl and curse, froth and spit, and spoil someone else's meat. I looked around the tree, blood and sap smeared all over my face, and beheld the mutilated corpse below. The angel's chest was torn wide open; it's devastated rib cage releasing that eerie glow through shards of splintered bone. I scurried down the ridge-side to see why the corpse was glowing and saw the angel heart blackening as the body died. I stabbed it with a stick and carried it home held out a distance in front of me. I was planning on eating it since all the meat was swimming with maggots. But the angel heart purred when I sat it in the demon parakeet's vacated cage. I watched it pulse and twitch until it began floating.

The dogs howled their disapproval but I didn't want to touch the angel heart once it resurrected. It stayed in the cage and eventually talked those disapproving dogs to death. It won't get me, I warned it the day I buried my dogs. Its tendrils flicked love and understanding at me but my own heart has grown cold even in its cursed warm glow.

The angel heart will never understand some of us don't want salvation; we just want our rotten meat back.

―――――

Jonathan Moon is a horrorcore writer living in the Palouse Region of Idaho/Washington where there is an abundance of trees and decrepit shacks to fuel his twisted muse. He writes his own brutally beautiful brand of horror and weird dark fiction such as *HEINOUS, Mr. Moon's Nightmares*, and *Worms in the Needle*. You can find Mr. Moon online at his Monkey Faced Demon blog: http://www.mrmoonblogs.blogspot.com

The Music Box
Tadashi Ohta
Translated by Norimitsu Kaiho

The case of the music box was beautifully inlaid and made of walnut wood.

Opening the lid, you could see it had a golden cylinder with pins on its surface and the silver combs to play them.

You could tell by the forms and placement of the parts that the maker was the Nicole Freres company, produced around the 1880s.

But I didn't recognize the case. It must have been a custom build for this box. I've been repairing antique music boxes for many years, but this was my first time seeing a case like this.

I disassembled it. The client said the box wouldn't play when you wound it. I could see why. Aged machine-oil had caused the governor to stick. Repair would be easy. I cleaned out the old oil, replaced it, and the cylinder began to roll.

After reassembling it, the job was done. It was then that I noticed something stuck between the bedplate and the case. Was it to adjust the tone? I didn't think it likely. I pulled it out with tweezers.

It was a folded piece of paper. On the inside of which I saw some Japanese handwriting.

To Makiko. With eternal love, Shuuichi.

At supper, I told my wife about the note.

"That note couldn't have been placed there after it was built. It had to have been placed when placing the mechanics in the case."

"Making a gift of a music box with an message. How sweet." My wife said, but I found it difficult to agree.

"If that was true, he would have placed the message somewhere it would have stood out. That note would have been impossible to find until someone repaired it. So why do it?"

Putting a little thought into it, my wife then said, "Perhaps it would have been improper to express his feelings openly. Like in sending it to another man's wife."

I thought that's probably what it was.

After supper, I returned to my workroom and reassembled the music box; putting the note back where I'd found it.

I wound the spring and made sure it played.

The tune was Etude Op. 10, No. 3. In Japan, this song is known as "Wakare no Uta" or "A Song of Farewell".

That night, I thought about the box while laying in bed.

Shuuichi, the author of the message, could've been the assembler of the outer casing. After all, inserting a note like that was just not something you would otherwise allow.

Then what had he been thinking when he had hid it? Maybe the woman was a secret love, as wife had said. He just couldn't help but sending it to his "Makiko".

Unrequited love?

In my head the tune played over and over.

The next day, the woman who had ordered the repair came.

I asked her, "Is the owner of this music box a 'Makiko'?"

She seemed surprised when I spoke the name.

"Yes. This is mine now, but it used to be my late grandmother's. How did you know?"

"Well, the case of this music box is not an original, isn't it?"

"No. It was made by my late grandfather. He was a skilled woodworker. He made it when grandmother broke her precious box."

"What was your grandfather's name?"

"Shuuichi Satou."

Shuuichi. I'm not sure why, but I just didn't expect it to be him.

"My grandfather was a stubborn man. He didn't show much love for my grandmother; she was always very sick. But he made this case for her music box. She cherished it to her dying day. Perhaps it was the only happy reminder of her life she had."

I recalled the words in the note.

With eternal love.

"Yes, undoubtedly a very fond reminder," I said. "A symbol of eternal love between them."

Nodding, she opened the music box. "A Song of Farewell" filled the room.

―――

Tadashi Ohta is a Japanese mystery author. Born in Nagoya in 1959, he graduated from the Nagoya Institute of Technology. In 1981, while in university, he was one of the winners of that year's "Shinichi Hoshi Short Fiction Contest". After graduation, he continued to write short fiction while working as a salaryman. As a result of the publication of his longer work *Boku no Satsujin* in 1990, he became a full-time writer. After his *Shinjuku Shonen Tanteidan* was made into a movie, he started concentrating on YA work. He has written over 80 books and currently lives in Nagoya.

http://homepage2.nifty.com/tadashi-ohta/

Not Alone in the Dark
Richard Salter

True darkness is more than mere absence of light. Even on the blackest of nights the eyes will eventually adjust to see shapes and movement. Aradan felt closed in, like he was trapped deep underground. Yet he was in the open air. Any moment now, the sun would start to rise.

It didn't. There were no stars or moons in the sky. He couldn't see a hand in front of his face.

He turned on his flashlight, lit a flame, even touched the surface of his eye. He saw nothing.

Had he gone blind?

He was definitely in a forest. He could smell decaying leaves and heard them beneath his boots. He'd lost count of the trees he'd bumped into. It was chilly yet there was also a cloying thickness to the air; it was hard to breathe. And the growling was getting closer.

Usually, fear sharpened Aradan's senses. Today it blunted them, as if the blackness had seeped into his brain. He held tightly to the reassuringly cold metal of his pump-action shotgun. He wished he could see where to aim it.

Aradan heard a tiny movement behind him. He spun around, trying hard to control his rapid breathing so he could listen. How many creatures were there?

He resisted the urge to run. In the blackness he could knock himself senseless on a low branch, or worse, step off a cliff.

Noises came from all around him now, breathing, snarling. Aradan pointed his gun anywhere and pulled the trigger.

A thousand creatures cried out in fright, some taking to the air, others scampering upwards or away from him. In the cacophony it was impossible to pick out his hunters. Had they run away too?

Perhaps it was time to leave. He calmed himself, allowing the familiar prickling of his skin to draw him homeward. He was distracted by something wrapping itself around his feet. He tried to move but he was held fast. He reached down to free himself and found long tendrils of something plant-like wrapped around his boots. They were too thick to break. A tendril tried to snag his finger and he whipped his hand away.

Fear scattered his thoughts. Should he pull his feet from his boots? What if the vines grabbed his bare feet? He could shoot or cut them but risked maiming himself. Should he set light to them? If he couldn't see the fire, he might be immolated. Then he heard the growling again and his hair stood on end.

Aradan heard something move and fired his shotgun in that direction. Everything exploded into activity again but he thought he heard a yelp from his target.

Whether or not he hit one, it wasn't long before others returned. He heard their feet crunching on the vines, apparently immune to their clutches. Soon he could smell a creature's foul breath, like everything in the forest had rotted in its mouth at the same time. The heat made his forehead bead with sweat. The unseen monster roared but Aradan held still, trying to exude confidence despite feeling none. Was it trying to make him move? Was he invisible to it as long as he made no sound?

The tendrils were over the top of his boots now, digging into his trouser legs.

Aradan closed his eyes. Now it felt like he was choosing to be blind; it helped him focus. He imagined the creature from its movements and the feel of its breath on his face. Carefully, silently, Aradan stowed his shotgun and pulled his right foot from its boot. The vines tried to hold his shin but he was able to slip free. Balancing on one leg, he reached out to the beast. His fingers touched thick fur and he grabbed two handfuls.

The beast reared up, plucking Aradan's other foot free and yanking him high into the air. He straddled the creature as it bucked and roared. Teeth tore into Aradan's leg. He cried out but held on. Again he forced his mind to clear, his eyes still shut. Energy waves exuded from the gateway and he held on until the creature faced the right direction. Then he pulled out his shotgun and fired. Startled, the creature took off into the forest with Aradan on its back. He was forced to let go of the gun so he could hold on with both hands as low branches whipped and tore at him.

After a dizzying few minutes they reached the gateway. Aradan released his hold and crashed into the soft earth. Every part of him hurt as he forced himself up into a crouch. He could hear the beast returning. He drew his pistol but before he could shoot, the beast struck him hard, knocking him to the ground.

He clamped both legs around the creature's neck and twisted. The beast fought back but Aradan was able to raise the gun and fire, hoping his feet weren't in the way.

The beast fell dead across him, pinning him to the ground.

Aradan's thigh was on fire and he couldn't breathe. He dragged himself out from under the corpse but now his foot was caught. The tendrils had him again. He reached out to the gateway, straining his aching muscles.

Finally he touched it. The circle opened and light poured in, blinding him just as much as the dark. The flora recoiled from it, releasing him. He hauled himself to his feet and was about to pass through when something made him turn back. Squinting, he could just make out a circle of ferocious creatures with vicious, misshapen teeth, waiting patiently for him to entangle himself in the foliage. They weren't affected by the light because they had no eyes.

Aradan fell back through the gateway. With the last of his strength he reached up and closed it behind him.

He lay bleeding into the cool grass, wishing he believed in a God so he could give thanks for his escape.

Richard Salter is a British born writer and editor now living near Toronto, Canada. He has a dozen short stories published and in 2008 he edited the anthology *Short Trips: Transmissions* for Big Finish Productions. Later in 2011, he has new stories appearing in *Phobophobia* from Dark Continents Publishing, *Iris in Purple* from Obverse Books, and *Solaris Rising: The New Solaris Book of Science-Fiction* from Solaris Books. "Not Alone in the Dark" may or may not become the first chapter in the fantasy novel he's been planning, depending on whether or not anyone likes it.
http://www.richardsalter.com

Natsumi's Diary
Midori Tateyama
Translated by Ken Kusuki

It was a sheer coincidence that I found it at all.

I stunned that there were still people who preferred to keep diaries rather than to blog. It seemed so low tech. But if she had not kept her diary in that notebook, I wouldn't have been able to read it.

Water had swept the entire area, and all the cell phones and computers had drowned in the deluge of the ocean.

If she had kept her diary on either, the data would have been destroyed.

I peeled apart the dried pages of the water-swollen notebook with its cute design of flowers.

"What a mess..."

Several months had passed since "The Day".

The once water-soaked pages had dried, grown moldy, and stiffened.

Though on most pages the writing was blurred – and in some places completely illegible – I began to read; chasing any legible writing.

I did it because I had nothing else to do. And however reprehensible it might be considered, I was curious of this old-fashioned diary.

The author's name was "Natsumi".

The Chinese characters for her name were "summer" and "ocean".

The name sounded cheerful enough, but what she had written in the diary was by no means as such. In fact, I pretty sure I would've disliked her if we'd known each other.

She hadn't liked or even felt a sense of friendship with the group female 'friends' she hung with them, yet in order to maintain a sense of place, she had been foolishly obedient to their witchy clique leader.

And afraid of being ridiculed, she had never spoken to the boy she liked. Instead, she let herself be pushed into dating a dull boy the witch pushed on her.

In her diary, all she did was grumble about how much she disliked herself for it all.

She was just like those girls I detested in my childhood. Girls who joined bullying groups only in order to protect themselves.

"Just die." I nearly said.

A look at the tsunami-destroyed ruins around me and considering the condition of the diary, it struck me that Natsumi was probably already dead.

I understood perfectly well how stupid it was to be irritated by reading another person's diary. So why couldn't I stop myself?

When I reached the last legible page, I shut my eyes, and sighed.

She'd written about her birthday:

Today was the worst. Granted, every day is the worst. But being my birthday, today was especially awful. Who would've wanted to celebrate anyway? Even so, I'm not going to let that stop me from saying happy birthday to my future self. Happy Birthday, Natsumi. I hope you find something to make you happy next year.

Natsumi's birthday, a day which had not been remembered by either friends or family, was the day before "The Day".

"You were so stupid, Natsumi."

There would be no "next year" for her.

I would have hoped she wouldn't have waited to try and change even just the smallest thing about herself. But all she accomplished to do was to wish her future self "happy birthday".

She was just as stupid as I was right now, standing here in these desolate, abandoned ruins ready to commit suicide because I was feeling sorry for myself.

"Congratulations! Happy birthday! Happy, happy birthday! Cuz birthdays are supposed to be happy, right? Damn it!" I yelled out loud.

Dying seemed a little harder after reading that diary.

I opened the bottle of the pills I'd brought with me and slowly poured the tablets out over a rotting mattress.

But I didn't do it so I could live the life Natsumi could not. That would have been hypocritical. Those kinds of sentiments best reserved for funeral speeches.

I did it because I thought it was simply unjust and perfectly absurd. That's all.

Even after I'd finished reading her diary, I still disliked Natsumi. She had been so indecisive. I wanted to punch her.

And yet, I resolved not to commit suicide.

I decided to live for the day when I could cheerfully wish myself a happy birthday.

Toward that end... I left that place of ruin.

———

Midori Tateyama is a Japanese author born in Aichi Prefecture on Valentine's Day. An author of novellas, short stories, novelizations, games scripts, and doujin game plans, she has done work for the popular *Code Geass* and *xxxHOLiC* series, and for *Moon*, an adult game novelization.
http://homepage1.nifty.com/croe

Sweet Hearts
Grant Wamack

Lily's weakness was sweets.

Jacob couldn't help but fall in love with her. But then, he fell for any girl with a pretty smile and a big behind.

"Lily!"

No response. Lily kept on walking, her extraordinary behind sashaying behind her like a hypnotic pendulum.

"Lily!" He yelled, struggling to catch up to her.

"What?" she reeled, angrily adjusting her designer glasses and brushing her red bangs out of her crystal blue eyes.

Stunned, Jacob took a deep breath and flashed a million dollar smile. "I just wanted to see what you were up to. I'm trying to kill some time before my next class starts."

"Don't you have to study some psychology bullshit or something?" Lily's beautifully plucked eyebrows angled inward.

"I-I suppose you're right."

Lily walked away and Jacob's shoulders slumped.

Jacob wasn't about to let that deter him though, he was brought up with a go-get-em' attitude. Unfortunately, his sense of confidence deflated somewhat when he saw Candyman's well defined arm wrapped around Lily's petite shoulders later that week.

He boiled with rage, ready to jump all over Candyman, break his brittle body in half and snort his powdered remains.

However, Jacob knew he had to be cool-headed. Violence wasn't going to win this battle. The only solution had to be cunning strategy, and a little pizzazz.

Step one.

For the next few weeks, Jacob ignored Lily every time he passed her on campus, dramatically looking away and feigning interest in an oak tree or a patch of dead grass.

He wasn't exactly sure if this would work as planned, but he followed through nevertheless.

Jacob felt consistency was his strong suit. All his life he had been consistent. He proved it throughout his childhood. He could hold his breath the longest and win staring contests in a blink. Thanks to good genes of course.

Step two.

Jacob studied the Candyman from afar, usually from the relative safety of a bush or a window. After a few more weeks, Jacob knew the Candyman better than the jerk's own mother.

He felt a twinge of regret over having to take him out. He had bonded with Candyman somewhat – watched him study, dance, and laugh at dumb reality TV shows. This was stuff Jacob understood. Moreover, they both loved the same girl with equal passion and fervor. However, Jacob knew there could only be one victor, and it was definitely going to be himself.

The day had come. Step three. Plan in action.

Jacob hid behind a rose bush, giggling.

He couldn't wait until Lily and Candyman rounded the curve on their matching bikes. He strategically placed thumb tacks on the ground and waited patiently.

The couple rode into sight – Candyman slightly ahead of Lily. He grinned, revealing his gumdrop teeth, and his broad candy shoulders glistened in the light with glazed-sugar intensity.

Jacob was jealous of Candyman's well defined shoulders and sweet confectionary teeth but managed to keep the rage at a perfect simmer.

Candyman will get his any minute now, Jacob thought, grinning maniacally.

Candyman's speed was perfect as he ran over the tacks. His tires popped loudly, and in a moment of surprise, he hit the wrong brake. He flew, tumbling into a clearing where he slammed into a couple of sharp granite rocks. His body cracked into great, gooey chunks.

"Jesus Christ... the pain... Lily..." Candyman said, nodding in and out of consciousness, nursing his severed limbs.

Jacob stood from his hiding spot and laughed.

Lily slowly got off her bike. Her eyes large with hunger. Stringy saliva dripped from her glossy lips.

She pounced on Candyman's dismembered legs, breaking them into smaller pieces and shoving them into her beautifully shaped mouth.

Jacob watched in awe.

She continued to devour her former lover, piece by succulent piece.

And just for a moment, Jacob wondered if she had really loved the Candyman at all or had just been waiting for the right moment to satisfy her hunger.

But who was he kidding? It didn't matter. *Victory is mine*, he thought as he watched her swallow the Candyman's sweet throbbing heart, and his as well.

―――

Grant Wamack writes weird fiction, raps, and digs up dreams in his free time. He has been published in a variety of places including 365 Tomorrows, Flashes in the Dark, and Nemonymous. You can visit him at http://grantwamack.wordpress.com/

Appointment at the Oji Inari Shrine
Massimo Soumaré
Translated by Davide Mana

A striking, dark-skinned young lady with long, straight black hair scrutinized the ukiyo-e print the antiquarian in the Verona shop had on display.

"Please, take your time."

The middle-aged man left the room. She was a frequent customer, so he trusted her. Besides he knew she was the type to treat with respect – a sorceress.

Mind you, not any kind of sorceress, but a globalized sorceress! The shopkeeper knew well enough not to bother her. He valued his life.

Alone, the globalized sorceress – Karla, by name – placed her long-fingered hands along the slightly yellowed margins of the Japanese xylography. The blue of her nails, a hypnotic violet at the tips, seemed to shift – to phase weirdly – with the deep blue of the print's background.

It was a work of Hiroshige Utagawa, part of the *One Hundred Famous View of Edo* series. Number one hundred and eighteen, it was entitled "New Year's Eve Foxfires at the Enoki Trees at Oji," dated back to 1857, more than a century and a half ago. A fine piece in excellent condition. Yet it was not the condition that raised the woman's full lips into a satisfied smile. She had finally found an accessible copy! The magic in others she had inspected had been long drained away, but was still present and very strong in this one. The urge to peep into the past of a close friend was too strong. She immediately uttered an invocation. For a few seconds nothing happened, then some of the foxes started to move....

As she had guessed, one of them was her friend.

The sorceress closed her grey eyes part way and began uttering her magic invocation faster and faster. The colors of the ukiyo-e disappeared one after another, as if to reverse the process of the wood-block technique used by the printers of old, until nothing but a white sheet of paper remained. Suddenly, in a gaudy, mad explosion, the colors returned, leaving trace images that followed one another. It was like watching a cartoon.

The ethereal rays of an immense moon high in the clear winter sky illuminated the fur of the two animals as they passed through those parts of the wood in which vegetation was scarce. They moved like the wind.

"Kaedenoha, I told you shouldn't have wasted so much time preening yourself, just to make yourself a little prettier!" the fox in the lead spoke sharply. Her pelt was a vivid white, almost silver. "Now we're late!"

Hailing from Kyoto, they were making their way to an appointment at Oji Inari shrine near the capital of Edo in the east. They had not rested in a long while.

"You groomed yourself as well, Mother," the second fox replied impertinently, tarrying not in the least.

She was slightly smaller, with a thick and soft tail. Her fur, while very white, was not nearly as striking as her mother's.

Her mother, Kuzunoha, sighed. There was nothing she could do. As much as she had nurtured the ways of a lady in her daughter, the result was disappointing. And now that her daughter was almost eight hundred years old, it was now impossible to correct any personality flaws.

"Enough talking. Run!" Kaedenoha barked at her mother, who was in turn, pretending not to hear the younger's words, shaking her head like human mothers do.

Normally the fairy foxes of the Kyoto area did not visit the shrine of Oji Inari on New Year's Eve; it was not within their territorial bounds. But Kaedenoha's mother was stubbornly making a point of going, to meet some relatives she hadn't seen in a very long time. She had insisted her daughter accompany her—which was just an excuse really, as she was trying to arrange a wedding for her misguided spinster of a daughter!

They arrived, with time to spare. Most of the other revelers had already gathered; on their breasts orange-colored fairy fires danced. In front of the enoki trees mother and daughter joined the gathering. A great number of the foxes respectfully greeted Kuzunoha as she was an important personage. But her daughter stayed off to the side; she always felt out of place at family reunions.

"Oh, but aren't you little Kaede?" a voice exclaimed.

Kaedenoha stiffened. The last fox she would have wanted to meet! That shameless flirt, her Aunt Tamamo no Mae. What was she doing here? She had a terrible reputation among humans and supernaturals alike. She had caused no end of problems when she was younger. Which she still did! And if she was here, then...

"Cousin dearest!" a twittering voice called. "How are you?"

Kaedenoha struggled to stifle a thundering curse and greeted her relation as politely as could; a relation she really could not stand.

"I hear you are still single!"

"Indeed..." Kaedenoha replied.

"What a pity. Come now, you are not that young anymore..."

"Dear daughter, do not pick on your cousin! She can't do anything about her character.... After all, honestly, who would ever want a wife like her?" Tamamo no Mae added evilly, trying stir up trouble as always. The ladies around them laughed openly. Kaedenoha lost her temper. Not that it was difficult to get her to...

Karla laughed heartily.

Thanks to some strange twist of fate, Master Utagawa had unwittingly and magically captured a brilliant scene. Fortunately he had not portrayed what had happened moments later. A painting of an expletive-laden, furious brawl on a nineteen-century New Year's Eve among hysterical lady fairy foxes – the males having had wisely kept themselves at a safe distance out of frame! – would have hardly captivated the refined citizens of Edo at the time.

The globalized sorceress paid for the xylography and walked out of the shop with it tucked under one arm. The sun shone brightly, veiled only by a few passing clouds. Tourists in the town of Romeo and Juliet were as thick as ever.

She reached the bar where they were to meet. Kaedenoha sat quietly in the patio area, a white hat on her head, a cold tea in front of her. No one around would ever imagine that the Asian-looking woman among them was really a fairy fox. Transformation being their specialty.

Karla sat across the table from her.

"You found what you were looking for?"

"Yes," the sorceress answered, a mocking smile upon her lips as she studied her friend.

"What's the matter? Something on my face?"

"No, nothing."

Karla laughed.

Initially she had planned to use the xylography to tease her friend a little, but instead she decided to keep silent.

It would be just another of the many "little" secrets she kept.

Massimo Soumaré, born 1968 in Turin, Italy, is an Italian translator, writer, editor, Japanese language teacher, and Japanese culture consultant. He contributes to specialist magazines such as *Quaderni Asiatici* (Centro di Cultura Italia-Asia "G. Scalise") and *A Oriente!* (La Babele del Levante), for the latter also editing the bilingual Japan special issue (2002), and with a number of literary magazines, including *LN-LibriNuovi* (CS_libri), *Semicerchio* (Le Lettere), *Studi Lovecraftiani* (Dagon Press), *Ronza* (Asahi Shinbunsha), *Komatsu Sakyo Magazine* (IO Corporation) and cinematographic magazines as *Nocturno* (Cinema Bis Comunication). His short stories was published in various anthologies, including *ALIA* (CS_libri), *Fata Morgana* (CS_libri), *Tutto il nero del Piemonte* (Noubs) and *Igyo Collection* (Kobunsha) and his works was translated and published in Japan, China and USA.
http://www.webalice.it/m.soumare/

The Story without a Key
Yufuko Senoo
Translated by Kazushi Nagayama

She stood beside the window watching the burgeoning darkness. All the flowers blooming in rivalry faded to pale shadows, their colors and contours no longer clear. Only their scent remained vivid.

Hearing the tinkling of the bell that announced the king's arrival, she moved not in the slightest, even when she felt the man enter her apartments.

"What are you trying to look at? There's nothing out there," uttered the king, taking her shoulders in his hands and caressing her hair. "Time for your story," he ordered.

And with that order he took her lips, her clothes, and her body.

When he had finished with her, she whispered: "Your majesty, you bereave me of everything."

"Yet, I also give in return," he replied, touching her earrings, and the golden chains that hung about her neck. Hidden behind her long lashes, her eyes were not visible to him.

"You take away from me all my stories."

"According to you, be it inside or outside, all your stories belong to me already; telling them is merely moving gold from the left stack to the right, isn't it?"

She caressed his cheek, slowly.

"Do you still long for my stories to be told?"

"I do."

"What do you think these stories are?"

The king raised his eyebrows at the odd question.

"Fiction. Make-believe."

"You are very smart, my lord. They may be true, but they are not real."

"True? Old woman with a stomach the size of a mountain, and cats who breathe fire? You call them true?"

"Truth is too dangerous to allow into this world, your majesty. Stories are a cage to keep them from entering. That is the contract: while the teller tells, and the listener listens, they come to life through words; they perpetuate themselves through it. But in exchange they cannot get out of their cages. That is the contract. To keep dangerous monsters from entering the human world, the stories are handed down from parent to child, teacher to disciple; ensuring the cage is locked."

The king gave a wry smile.

"No lock is necessary; they are fiction, from the beginning to the end."

"But you have enjoyed my stories, my lord."

"Dragons that rift the earth! The wretch born from the goddess's milk! They are enjoyable, for they are mere fiction. How foolish of you to think of them as true."

"But this is the last story I can tell you, your majesty. You choose your own path, my lord. I am sorry I cannot pass the key on to you. All the stories you have bereaved of me, will soon make themselves known to you, having eliminated the boundary between the real and the imaginary."

The king burst into laughter.

The storyteller removed her necklaces, placing them on king's chest.

"What's this?"

"Render unto Caesar what belongs to Caesar, my lord."

The earrings fell from her ears with a soft sound.

"But you are mine as well."

Her body, despite the king's effort to grab hold of her, vanished.

"I am merely a teller. I cannot exist alongside with that which is inside the stories. My existence is not compatible with the magic that comes from my throat. Moreover, I cannot leave open the doors into the storyworld. I must create another frame, sealing off everything inside again."

In an attempt to call her name, he opened his mouth and stopped in surprise. Nowhere in his memory did her name exist.

The nameless woman, now nothing more than a voice, whispered into his ear.

"You are about to witness a work of magic, my lord. How jealous am I of you. Beside a window somewhere, I shall tell the story of you, of a king who disappeared into the stories. Sadly you will not be able to hear it..."

Foolishness the king muttered standing from the bed. All that was to be heard in the dark room was the sound of the wind through the window.

He did not believe, even as he pulled his sword.

Not even when the end came.

———

Yufuko Senoh (or Usagi-ya on the Internet) is a fantasy author specializing in serious stories about alternate worlds. She began working as an assistant to the manga artist Marchen Maker in 1977, and made her authorial debut with her story "Festival of Masks" in Hakusensha's Hanamaru magazine. This is only her second work to be published in English, the first being the novella "City of the Dreaming God" in the anthology *The Dreaming God*, published by Kurodahan Press in 2007. Her personal website (in Japanese) can be found at: http://usagiya.cside2.com/

The Feast of the Fly
Berry Sizemore

Lightning coursed through the ebony head of the massive squirming maggot and into the obsidian sky. Dishes rattled on shelves as panicked villagers ran across jerking floors into the street. There they found a monstrous black larva smashing the village to splinters, consuming the fresh corpses crushed under detritus. Several hours later, it disappeared into the ruined temple, a trail of death behind it.

Yoshi the mason and his wife Wakana, a keeper of silk worms, returned from abroad some days later to learn that their beloved daughter Yoshiko was dead, further distressing his three granddaughters whose father had been lost at sea recently. They had gone to visit Wakana's three sisters in the South, sharing the terrible news of their son-in-law's death, giving Yoshiko time to grieve alone, when the monster had struck.

Sakura, Sayaka and Shiori wept; their hearts felt as bleak as the village had become.

"Children," said the old woman, "in the morning you will travel again to my sisters in the South. Sakura, you shall go to Hana and her trees. Sayaka, you shall go to Tsubame and her bills. Shiori, you shall go to Sumiko and her stone."

A pack of provisions were given to each girl in the morning, including a bundle of clean white silk wrapped in thick rice paper. "I will send for you when your grandfather has finished the reconstruction of the temple. Upon your return there will be a great feast," said Wakana as she kissed them. The children began their southern journey away from the smoldering ruins of the village.

Sakura was led by the scent of cherry blossoms to Hana, who painted and embroidered flowering branches upon paper and silk. The scent reminded her which direction to go until she was in the arms of her favorite aunt, a strong and agile woman. Sakura grew to love the craft of her aunt and became skillful in her own right. Her work reflected the spirit of cherry blossom trees.

Sakura approached womanhood, and the day she finished her embroidered dress of cherry blossom branches made with the silk she had brought with her, the news of the temple reached the two. She bade her aunt farewell, saddened but eager to see her sisters again.

Sayaka turned towards the sea following a flock of southbound seagulls. Tsubame was a severe but graceful woman who painted and embroidered sea birds upon pottery and silk. Her oceanside abode was sparse because she spent her time in commune with the birds next to the sea. Sayaka rapped on the door politely until her old aunt drew her in to receive the news.

The painting and embroidery of elegant sea birds upon pottery and silk was taught to Sayaka. She adorned her silken dress with bits of shells in the forms of the stork, crane and ibis. Their red heads shone like spattered blood upon the white silk. News of the reconstruction eventually came, and Sayaka tearfully left Tsubame. She thought of the feast upon her and her sisters' return, as the spirit of the birds helped her take wing.

The beat of thundering drums guided Shiori to Sumiko, a mischievous and strong woman, who was fond of the steamy springs and the snow monkeys that lived in and around her modest dwelling. It was well known that Sumiko was filled with the spirit of the snow monkeys. Shiori eventually found her aunt naked in a steaming pool and gave her the news.

The girl was taught to carve in stone and embroider the simian faces. She sewed polished stones onto the silk sent with her under the kindly attendance of Sumiko. "You too have the spirit of the snow monkey in you child." Not long after, Shiori began her return home filled with thoughts of the magnificent temple rebuilt after many long years.

The sisters donned their magnificent dresses for their arrival to the newly reconstructed temple. Sakura stood with a calm smile in her white dress, emblazoned with brilliant pink cherry blossoms on graceful branches before the temple with the other girls. Her sister Sayaka admired the succulent and aromatic fruit set before them. She whipped her long, black hair across the back of her dress embroidered with red headed sea birds. Shiori gazed at her grandfather's handiwork with expert appreciation. Her dress sparkled in the sun, as the monkeys on her dress seemingly groomed one another.

Sayaka said, "Now the feast!"

The eerie quiet was unbroken. The villagers, including their grandparents, were conspicuously absent. Suddenly the ground and temple began to tremble, and a giant translucent yellow fly emerged from within the temple. The monster was constrained by the architecture of the holy place. The hideous wings buzzed, and the hindquarters remained in the hole the thing crept out of. It writhed futilely.

The sun beamed upon the young women as the hems of their clothes shifted in the light breeze. Sakura raised her arms to the fly as if in supplication, as long graceful cherry blossom branches began to spring from her hands, running up her arms. The branches grew from her dress, while she herself began to fade from existence. The limbs began to ensnare the fly, arresting its wings until the infernal buzzing ceased. They entwined its legs until it was motionless and Sakura had completely vanished. Sayaka gave a shrill cry and the birds of her dress began to fly up to her throat, out of her mouth manifestly alive, hundreds of storks, cranes and ibises flocked toward the head of the fly as she too faded until there was nothing left of her. The birds mercilessly pecked at the eyes, head and body of the fly until all it was unrecognizable. Shiori licked her lips as snow monkeys hollered and leaped from her breast, charging the mass of demolished fly. She laughed her aunt's mischievous laugh as she dissolved into nothingness. The monkeys pushed the birds out of the way as they ate handfuls of pulp. Once the fly had been completely consumed, the branches, birds and beasts also disappeared.

All that remained was the temple and three spotless bundles of white silk.

———

Berry Sizemore spent his childhood watching black and white television in Los Angeles, except when mashing his bike pedals or digging sticky asphalt from the street with wooden popsicle sticks. Some kid broke the arm off of his Six Million Dollar Man action figure one day. That was the day he became a man. Eventually he found true love several times, had at least one kid with his wife and settled down near the ocean. This writer seldom finds time to produce publications as his work with computers creates a true ghost in the machine. http://themap.multiverse.org/

A Second Metamorphosis
Ash Lomen

"We are not like them." The man-I-used-to-be said, watching the motorcade of living machines rolling down a swath of cracked highway in the cold blue light of a Swiss morning.

"They can cry now." His daughter said.

"I'm well aware of that," he old her, concealing a smirk for the benefit of her liberal sentiment. He didn't add that they could bleed too. "That still doesn't make them human."

"Will you hunt them to the ends of the earth?" She asked, blue eyes all but shimmering with hate.

The man-I-used-to-be smiled.

"The ends of the earth are the only places that are safe to hunt them."

She received her first technorganic implant three weeks later, a fresh-off-the-market weight control system.

She became one of them by the end of the year.

>Norway, 2666<

Anders looked at the biomechanical butterfly with a mixed sense of disgust and awe as it bloomed from its puss-filled, dragonshit cocoon. He watched it undergo a second metamorphosis. Words failed him as reality itself flicked with a crawling static.

And then reality snapped – the biomechanical butterfly became a biomechanical man. Something around 500 pounds – not counting all the heavy metal – and a katana for a cock. All clockwork. All oiled muscle and spry sprockets. Hardly even a man at all.

Anders shouldered his Beam-Launcher and fired at the monstrosity. Its metaform left behind nothing but scattered ash upon snowfall.

The landscape around Anders was a cold white Norwegian winter. Pure white. Like redemption on judgment day. Completely untouched by the mechanized world. Like Anders' own pure flesh. Untouched by any hint of cybernetic enhancement. Untouched by demon-spawned viruses, or by the Self-Made within possessed human computer systems. Perfectly pure, perfectly human.

Not that it mattered much anymore. The systems had tweaked the virus until it learned to take wing on its own. The very molecules of the frigid winter morphed into living cords of wire. Reality fluctuated again. Again static filled his vision.

Over twenty Cocoons spawned upon the blank landscape. Pus-filled sores gestated until they bloomed. From within, biomechanical butterflies fluttered forth and quickly underwent the second metamorphosis.

Biomechanical men, with their tempered steel-dicks, moved in on him in blink-fast unison. Anders, naked with the exception of his various ammo belts, the pure will of his humanity the only thing keeping him warm in the bone-chilling cold, dodged just as fast.

Bungling into the space Anders had previously occupied, the first three slashed each other to pieces. A fourth, wielding a cock like a two-handed *nodachi* great sword, moved in on Anders who blocked with a quickly drawn arm-pistol made of weightless metal, while the lesser six moved in on him with sullen grace. Battle-sparks melted snow and the earth hissed angrily.

In the sudden stillness of the stormdance of their battle, the virus germinated upon air molecules unabated. Anders stood no chance, even as he dispatched the bigger swordsmen with a scatterblast from a second arm-pistol then pivoted into a ballerina spin of machine-gun fire that sent his robotic adversaries into smoldering piles of shrapnel and flesh.

The virus grabbed him, tossed him to the ground, rose up like tendrils of smoke, and thickened to bulky tentacles that lashed his skin. Anders attempted to block with his arm-pistol, but they outmatched his own perfectly honed speed. He dove backward into the ice as a whipping tendril of techno-virus missing his jugular by inches. He realized that he gained a few feet of distance between himself and the growing cloud of cold air morphing into a nightmarish Brainchild of Giger. He fired his most powerful beam weapon – a 480 Beatnik God Blaster. Its red energy was only absorbed by the virus. As were a hail of shotgun shells fired from a heel-spurred bootblaster. The energy and the bullets just became part of the phenomenon growing before him.

It sprouted orifices like prosthetic cunts that consumed the very light from the world. And in a heartbeat, it closed the distance between them and entered former Captain Anders Frijink's body.

Deformed snow harpies formed beneath him as he spasmed in pain. The virus penetrated every orifice he had. His brain screamed in resistance, his body screamed to surrender.

Then he remembered his daughter.

If he let this monster take him perhaps he could see her again.

And then he remembered her naiveté. No. He was human. Even if he was the last human on the face of the fucking earth.

Through the focused energy of all his ancestors, Anders regurgitated the virus and staggered to a defiant standing position. The inorganic intrusion had left him bleeding from nearly every pore in his body. He grabbed a flat side-pistol packing a heavy autoflesh round.

Confused, the virus squirmed before him; distorted from Anders' body's rejection of it.

He stood over it, fully aware that emptying every round he had into the hellish thing would be ineffective.

Dropping a nova-grenade into the techonorganic puddle, he burst into a sprint. Still the perfect-circle blast seared away his skin as it rippled outward vaporizing a sphere shaped hole in the snow.

Yet the virus remained unscathed. It reared its headless ugly, swelled in size, and dove at Anders with long tendrils of inorganic life. Refusing to be metastasized, Anders put the flat side-pistol in his mouth and pulled the trigger.

An explosion. A flux in space and time. Silence shattered into a thousand spectrums of immaterial light.

Disappointed, the virus moved on like a hungry serpent.

———

Ash Lomen is an insane writer from the swamps of Louisiana. Visit his blog at http://ashlomen.wordpress.com.

Homecoming
Adam Breckenridge

I came home from a journey so long I could not remember when it had begun. I had passed through so many destinations that I could no longer recall a single one of them. My house was still there, but the grass in the yard had been trimmed and manicured, unbroken panes had been put in the windows, the front door no longer hung off of one hinge and there were children running in and out of the house, a swarm of them whose numbers seemed to fluctuate. Sometimes I would count only four, but then a fifth would emerge from their group and just as quickly two of them would vanish only to have one more appear from the ether. They were playing games of death. I didn't know who any of them were and they showed me no interest. Cooking smells wafted from within, baked chicken and apple pie. The scent filled me with fear.

My broken shards of furniture were gone, replaced with quaint matching sets. Holes in the walls had been repaired, leaks in the ceiling patched. The house was beautiful, clean, sterile and hideous in its charm. I ripped a framed picture of a smiling family I didn't recognize off the wall and threw it on the floor. The mess it made loosened some of the tension. I'll have this place back to right, I thought. I sliced up the cushions of the couch, punched holes in the walls. It's starting to feel like home again, I thought.

I heard singing from the back yard and went out to investigate. A woman I had never seen before was hanging laundry on a clothesline. She turned and then came running to embrace me. "Welcome home son," she cried.

"Get off me," I cried as she crushed my ribs. I struggled to break loose from her grip, but could barely move. Her perfume left me nauseated.

"It's okay," she said, "everything can go back to normal. We've missed you so much."

She loosened her grip and I tried to break into a run, but no sooner had she let me go than her hand was grasping my arm, gripping it so tight my fingers were turning blue. She was leading me back into the house.

"Dinner is just about ready," she said. "You must be so hungry after your long journey."

Tears streaked my face from the pain. She pushed open the back door. Everything was back to the way it had been, the picture restored, the cushions repaired, the holes patched. "Children, dinner is ready," she cried in a voice that pierced my eardrums. My arm was going numb.

The tumbling mass of children spilled through the front door. "Say hello to your father," she told them, "he's been gone a long time."

They pounced upon me, crushing me with hugs and kisses, rattling my brain with their cries of, "We love you Daddy, we missed you so much!"

"Go away," I screamed. "I don't know any of you."

"You're tired," the old woman said. "You've been gone so long. After dinner, why don't you lie on the couch and watch TV?"

"Why are you doing this to me? What have I done?"

"It's so good to have you back," she said.

She let go of my arm. Pain flared from my shoulder to my fingertips. I ran to the front door, I couldn't turn the knob. It was locked. I ran to the back door. Locked too. I charged a window and bounced off the glass. I was trapped.

I collapsed to the floor, wracked with sobs, the world beyond my eyes a blur. I felt a pair of hands on me. I tensed in fear of the old woman's iron grip, but looked up to see the face of a much younger woman, smiling and beautiful and utterly loathsome. She too was a stranger to me.

"Oh my sweet husband," she said, "I've missed you so much."

She wrapped her arms around my neck, cutting off my air. The screams of the children pounded at my brain, the stench of warm food churned my stomach. It suddenly became more overpowering, beating me into dizziness. Through the haze, the handle of a knife was thrust at me.

"Would you like to do the honors dear?" the old woman asked.

I took the knife. It stabilized me.

"Yes, I would, thank you."

I got to my feet, wobbling. Black spots appeared before my eyes. The family had arranged themselves around the table. The dinner smell was overpowering, but I saw no food anywhere. The serving plates, bowls and pitchers were empty. And it all made sense to me.

I stood at the head of the table. "Who's ready to eat?"

A chorus of enthusiasm spiked the air.

"Then let's get started."

I stuck the knife deep into my abdomen and drew the blade slowly across. My blood drenched the tablecloth. Their eyes were hungry. I drew the blade up from the crotch to the sternum, then stuck my hand in and pulled out a fistful of entrails.

"Who wants large intestine?" I asked

Two or three kids screamed, "I do."

"Can I have a kidney?" a young girl asked.

"I would appreciate some liver myself," the old woman said.

"I'm not that hungry, sweetie," the younger woman said, "could I just have a gall bladder?"

I continued to remove my insides bit by bit, and as I emptied myself out onto the table my vision dimmed, their blood-smeared cheeks lost their luster. From a distance I heard the old woman say, "Oh, he's getting faint, better lay him out on the table."

My body was lifted and laid gently down. As my vision went dark, the smack of feasting lips and the squishing of their teeth rending my flesh continued to echo in my ears.

Adam Breckenridge is a PhD student in Rhetoric and Composition at the University of South Florida in Tampa who loves traveling around Florida but doesn't get much time to do it. His fiction has previously appeared in Bust Down the Door and Eat All the Chickens, the Dream People, Lightning Flash and Independent Ink. http://adambreckenridge.blogspot.com.

Mom, Dad and Hiro
Yasumi Kobayashi
Translated by Andy Kitkowski

"Hiro, is Dad still working in his room?" Mother asked, engaged in washing the dishes. "Can you go and check?"

Hiro didn't reply. He was engrossed in a puppet play on TV.

"Hey, Hiro? Did you hear me?"

Hiro sulked, unable to look his mother in the eye.

"Why aren't you answering me?"

"Because..." Hiro sighed. "You always use me like this. You and Dad both, all the time."

"Don't say that, Hiro," Mother said sadly.

Hiro stole a fleeting glance at his mother's face.

Her eyes were full of tears.

Upon seeing her tears, Hiro himself saddened in the same way he did when he was bad.

"Hold on a minute," Hiro said stepping away from the TV, and headed for his father's room.

When he opened the door, Father was sitting in front of the computer.

"Dad."

"Oh, Hiro. Hold on, I'll be done with work in a minute."

"Yeah well, Mom was wondering..."

Hiro's father's hands paused over the keyboard.

"What did she want?"

"She asked for me to check on you, to see if you've finished working yet."

Father smiled back at Hiro, a glimmer of sadness in his eyes.

"Thank you, Hiro. Go back and tell Mom that I'm still hard at work."

"Okay."

"Oh, and can you ask her what's for dinner tonight?"

"What? Again? You guys have me going back and forth between you two. I'm tired of it."

"Oh now Hiro, don't be like that. Both your mother and I rely on you."

"Okay, okay, I'll go." Hiro ran back to the kitchen.

"What did Dad say, Hiro?" Mother asked enthusiastically.

"He said he's still hard at work."

"Oh good," Mother said with a sigh of relief. "Did he say anything else?"

"He asked what's for dinner tonight."

"We're having your favorite tonight, Hiro! Curry rice."

"Oh boy!"

"Now, go back and tell Dad."

"Again? Can't I tell him after we eat?"

Mother's face was tinged with regret, but she managed to quickly put on a smile. "Alright. But after you finish, make sure to go tell him, okay?"

"Sure."

"Hey! Hiro!" Father called.

"What is it, Dad?"

"Did Mom say anything?"

"Yeah, but... I'll tell you after I eat."

"Is that your father?" Mother asked.

"Yeah," Hiro replied with a bothersome sigh.

"Here? Is he... is your father here right now?"

"He's not here. He's back in his room."

"Oh, right. Of course, he's in his room." As Mother stood up, she picked up a picture of Father that was on the table. "I hope one day I can see Dad like you can, Hiro." She began to cry softly. "Why can't I be with you again?"

"Mom, don't cry."

Father came into the dining room. "Is Mom crying?"

"Yeah" Hiro replied.

"Hiro, tell your mother something for me. Tell her that she doesn't have to cry. Tell her that I'm always going to be here." He rested his hand gently on a picture of Mother on the table.

"Mom's being all weepy again."

"Well, that can't be helped. After all, unlike you Hiro, your mom and I can't be with each other."

"But why?"

"I don't know. No one knows why this happened. But in those sad days after I lost her, I realized that she wasn't lost to you."

"Mom, Dad's right here. He says he's going to always be here. So don't cry," Hiro said putting on the bravest face he could muster.

"Thank you, Hiro. He's here with us, right. Knowing that, I have the strength to go on living."

"Well, I've got to go to work. Have a good day," Father said.

"Dad's going to work."

"Well then, I'll head out with him. Today I'm going out to buy clothes."

"Mom says she's going clothing shopping, so she'll leave with you."

"Really? Then tell her that it's a date."

"Mom, Dad says that it's a date."

"Yes, a date." Mother wiped the tears away.

Hiro took his mother's and father's hands, and looked up at each of their faces... Seeing the dual-exposed world as only he could.

―――

Yasumi Kobayashi is a Japanese author of hard SF, Cthulhu mythos, bio horror,

mystery, fantasy, essays and more. His short story "Umi wo Miru Hito" won the Hayakawa Award for best short story in 1998. Two more were nominated for the Seiun Award for best short story; "Sora kara Kaze ga Yamu Toki" in 2003, and "Arakajime Kettei Sareteiru Ashita" in 2004. In 2009, he was nominated as "Best Foreign Author" in the Chinese-language Galaxy Awards. He is a member of the Mystery Writers of Japan, the Space Authors Club, and the Science Fiction and Fantasy Writers of Japan. He was born in 1962.
http://web.kyoto-inet.or.jp/people/kbys_ysm/

The Bubbling Road of Self-Loathing
Jason Wuchenich

Troy clawed at the ground and drug himself beyond the reaches of MacAnauldy Road. The street behind him was a churning river of molten tar, alive with the disposition of a pissy baboon – and it was after him. Don't worry about how he crossed it, it doesn't matter. He just did. However, the process did take its toll. The street ate away his clothing and flip-flops like a horta munching through a buttery wall of stone. His body hair frizzled and curled up inside their individual pores, trying to escape the boiling fury; but their attempts were in vain – they melted away, as did most of his skin. Red ripples of crunchy flesh-chips curled over exposed muscle tissue. His scalp was nothing more than a flakey, dark layer of chestnitsa being wisped away by a breeze of searing heat.

The earth rumbled beneath Troy's writhing body. The trees were made of rubber cement, so they just swaggered like drunken quails before igniting into towering flames of napalm. Suddenly he realized the bizarre vibrations rattling his limbs – the physical fiends creating the quakes – were simply the reaction of his groaning stomach, not the nervous shimmies of continental plates. He hadn't eaten anything but horseshoes for days and the surplus of iron was getting the better of him.

Just as the street formed a three-foot swell that would have most assuredly taken him out, he was saved by a rotund groundhog.

"In here, quick!" the groundhog yelled, holding a clawed paw up to his whiskered mouth. The other fuzzy arm flailed in inadequate gestures.

Troy gave the impending wave of tar 'the finger' and remembered to break dance. He did the Caterpillar, and lurched his body through the air. A sturdy pelvic thrust reddened his exposed gonads, and popped a plethora of newly formed blisters. The juice sizzled and hissed in dirt. As the wave of tar came crashing down, Troy disappeared into the Earth-orifice. MacAnauldy Road couldn't separate itself, so it slugged over the groundhog hole like a stagnant puddle over an anus.

"You barely made it, son. That street was out to get 'cha!" squelched the groundhog.

"Yea," said Troy. He was out of breath from the escape and sputtered for air like a Volkswagen engine made of balloons.

"Around these parts, folks call me Clemens. By what name are you known?"

Troy was pouting. "It doesn't matter."

"Well, my piano is out of tune and it sure could use a tinkerin'," said Clemens.

"I don't play the piano," replied Troy. "I just whittle."

"You mean you pee?"

Troy wobbled in his crouch-hunched position. He felt vulnerable. He remembered naked school dreams. "Yea, I guess," he said. "I guess I pee, but I mean 'whittle'...like whittling wood." Troy was exhausted from his street fight and the words oozed out of him like slug goo.

"Well, whittlin' is a keen start to the benefits of developin' your motor skills," Clemens replied, "but what you need is some confidence."

"Confidence is for the birds," said Troy.

"You still haven't told me your name, boy."

"Oh yea...it's 'Troy.'"

"Well Troy," said the groundhog, "you just kill that fucking road. It likes to mess with travelers. It just about sucks."

"Yea it does."

"You gotta' plan, Troy?" Clemens rolled his paws together. He was aching to see some balls drop from this pathetic human. He's never seen it before.

"Yea, I have a plan. I'm gonna jerk off and watch my nut melt on that damn street's face."

Well ta' hell with my piano!" replied Clemens. "That's the best darn tootin' act of defiance I've ever heard of!" It didn't take much to 'wow' a groundhog. "You let me get you goin' and you stick your pecker up that groundhog hole and let it rip! Sound like a plan?" Clemens was a serious groundhog.

"That's dumb, but whatever," Troy said.

Clemens shit on his paw with a spray of semi-pellet-formed poop logs. Groundhog saliva just doesn't cut it these days, and grasped Troy's seared crisp-cock. It has been a while since Troy could remember the righteous grip of a cock grab, and it didn't take long before the brown gaze of innocent groundhog eye coached him to orgasm. He thrust his spurting member into the burning hole. Troy gasped and wretched as MacAnuldy Road took his load. Clemens kicked Troy firmly in the asshole and sent him soaring through the dirt cunt.

"Out you go, fucker!" Clemens screeched. His voice was shrill and abrasive. Evil eyebrows contoured his cutsie fur-face in deceptive adornment.

MacAnauldy Road was there waiting, with a money shot assimilating into its being, it showed no signs of impregnation. A naked and continuously depressed Troy was sent through the safe-haven into a boiling rage of asphalt.

Those damned tricky groundhogs!

———

Jason Wuchenich is a fearless writer of extreme and subversive Bizarro Fiction. Equal parts Marquis de Sade and John Waters, his stories often have a humorous underlying social commentary built beneath over-the-top filth. Better known as "Wookie" amongst his contemporaries, Jason gained recognition for his debut book *Dinner Bell for the Dream Worms* (LegumeMan Books, 2010). His story "Gum Scrapers Anonymous" is featured in the Copeland Valley

Sampler released in 2011 via Copeland Valley Press. He has no plans to stop writing. http://www.wookiesworld.com

That Day...
Ryuto Hijiri
Translated by James A. Smith

The afternoon of March 11, 2011...
    I was napping when I felt a trembling beneath me.
    What was that?
    I hurry out of the house and look around outside.
    Whoa!
    Houses wobbling wildly. Electric wires rippling. Parked cars shaking madly.
    My mother runs over to me. There is a stern look in her eyes.
    "Watch out! You'll be crushed if something topples over! We've got to get out of here!" she says, shooing me outside.
    What?
    What's happening?
    I'm confused. Father isn't home because he's at work.
    The ground at my feet continues to shake making it impossible to run. I lay down prone on the ground.
    Our neighbours emerge from their homes. My friends, walking unsteadily, have a frightened look about them. Some lay down on their stomachs like me... Others run around aimlessly... I can tell everyone is panicked.
    Crying out in fear, the neighbour-mothers cower. The folks my mother and I always stop to talk with in parks or on the street, gather. Their faces are pale.
    I'm four years old. I don't really understand what the other mothers are all frantically talking about. But by the colour of their faces, I know that something extraordinary is happening.
    The air resounds with the word "earthquake."
    Ah, so this is an earthquake...
    I pace back and forth, unsure of what to do, when my mother comes up to me again and shouts that we are in danger.
    The look on her face frightens me. Apparently this is very serious.
    I run off, but I do not recollect doing so.
    Entering a clump of thick bushes, I run and run. It is a dark place, untouched by the light of the sun. It is so gloomy that I do not know where I am.
    What is this place?
    I stop and take stock of my surroundings.
    Frightened, I had ran off when I saw the look on my mother's face; now I'm lost.
    The ground beneath me shakes once more.
    I lay down on the ground as before.

When I am certain that the shaking has subsided, I decide to retrace my steps.

Upon returning, I can see that a hole has opened up in the road. A sign of some sort has toppled over. Here and there, a few of the houses look as if they stand at a tilt. A number of cars have come to a standstill in chaotic directions. Water spurts from cracks in the road.

The appearance of my home town has completely changed.

A crowd of residents are shouting. Apparently they are trying to help those who live alone. They call out to each house to make sure the residents inside are all right. Others are clearing away fragments of toppled concrete-block walls. People on bicycles ride around looking at the damage caused.

Mobile phones don't seem to work at all. And yet, the townspeople have mobilized.

An old lady catches sight of me. Her stout body jiggles as she approaches me.

"You're safe... I'm so glad... Our Lily-chan is okay, too."

Lily-chan is a different breed of dog than I.

My mother has always boasted to people that mixed-breed dogs like myself are strong.

In tears, the woman says that things are only going to get worse from here on. She strokes my head.

My mother's face appears. Jumping down, I run to her. She cradles me in her arms, happy to have me back. Some of my friends have also run off but have not returned.

I survey the now unrecognizable town around us, wondering what the future will bring.

However, I'm sure everything will be alright.

Our mothers are not the type to give up.

Our fathers are strong.

I'm certain they will rebuild. I believe, at least, they have the strength to do that...

And we pets won't give up, either!

―――

Ryuuto Hijiri was Born in Arita, Saga Prefecture. After graduating from Nihon University, he joined *Naigai Times*. After working as a newspaper and magazine writer, he became an author. Known for his samurai fiction, he has penned number of titles – *Shinnosuke and the Sword of Life and Death, Shinnosuke and the Spring Wind Sword, Shinnosuke and the Flowing Wind Sword,* and *Sword of the Mist,* among others. http://blog.livedoor.jp/hryuto/

The Dream-colored Morning
Vittorio Catani
Translated by Davide Mana

Barely awake, Fosco feared the day would taste of domestic ozone and overheated circuitry. The bleak sky had insinuated itself between the gigantic comb-like antennas and parabolic dishes of the jagged cityscape, crawling down through the vapors of the city and finally penetrating the anti-UV window of his bathroom. The sun had to be up, somewhere over the thick mattress of dirty clouds. He quickly took his shower, went to the kitchen, turned the lights on, and sat down at the table.

"Dad!" Chiara said smiling through the door "Shall we go and see?"

He picked up the plankton mayonnaise. "Sure, darling, as promised. But let's eat breakfast first."

"I'm needed at the District Council all day today," stated his wife Blanca. "I don't know if I'll be back for lunch."

"Don't worry," Fosco reassured her. "We can take care of ourselves, right baby?"

"Good day!" a happy voice interjected from the self-activating mural screen. "Time for Universe-News. This morning we have a connection with Captain Gordon Reynolds himself, from the Lowell City Martian base!"

Against a rocky background, a man in a spacesuit walked awkwardly towards the camera.

"What's up with the TV?" asked Blanca. "I can see only black and white. The whole gray scale is gone."

"Light and shadow on Mars are always that sharp," Fosco observed. "Looks okay to me."

"Wrong, Daddy," the child protested. "You are talking about the Moon. It has no atmosphere."

"No gray scale." Blanca repeated. "Nothing ever works properly in this place."

"*Hallo!*" Captain Reynolds chirped enthusiastically. "Italy is one of my favorite countries! *Mantegna, Piero della Francesca!*" He mispronounced the names in that funny way foreigners always do.

"Are those names of his friends?" Chiara asked, as she petted Dark who was snoring on a chair nearby.

"Good question..." Fosco replied, uncertain.

Captain Reynolds continued, "On Mars no *aria terrestrial*, and yet you can breathe better than on Terra! My suit, almost *purissimo* oxygen! Come to Lowell City, here you detox!"

A voice-over blared: "Enjoy a fabulous 'Honeymoon on Mars', with visits guided by Captain Gordon Reynolds himself. Contact the telematic address on your screen..."

Blanca stood up. "I'm off." She kissed Chiara and picked up her anti-smog overalls.

"You finished, Dolly? We're out of here too," said Fosco.

Outside it was a little clearer, a sign – Fosco thought – that the urban synth-lungs were absorbing the poisons. But the air remained leaden: traffic was thick, and eco-friendly engines could only do so much. He pointed towards the maglev bus station.

"Is Big Fan far, Daddy?"

"No, a quarter of an hour and we'll be there. Hold my hand, mind you, because there will be lots of people. And remember, if we get separated, push your beacon button, and stay put."

They passed a mammoth mural screen covering the face of a building. Real time atmo readings, a dual scale of bright symbols on a black background: percentages and a graph, and the easier-to-read bubbles.

"Dad," Chiara said, "Why does Dust have four bubbles today?"

"Because the smog is thicker than usual," Fosco replied.

"And why is the smog thicker?"

"Because... because there are too many people, and we can't stop doing what we shouldn't." With the way he labored to breathe, he was pretty sure five bubbles would have been more accurate. And three bubbles for 'Sulfur Dioxide' instead of two. Were the authorities doctoring the data...?

They reached the station.

"Dad... can you pick me up? I wanna see through the windows."

The maglev bus started up again. It rocked a little from side to side, and a thin, superjet-like whistle keened as it traveled along. It sank into the earth with an impressive acceleration, taking a wide turn. It emerged in the open air a few minutes later, climbing out of the city like a rocket.

"Are those... trees?" Chiara pointed to some sickly bushes. "Daddy, is it evening already?"

Fosco smiled. "Don't be silly. It's ten in the morning, but in the countryside there are no synth lungs so the air is more polluted. You'll see, the Big Fan will clear it up."

He pulled out their filtering masks.

"Here," Fosco said. "This looks like a good place to sit. Can you see? Put these on." At the entrance, they had each been given a pair of dark, plastic protective sunglass-like lenses.

"Yes. Dad, don't forget my ice-cream. My favorite flavor please."

"Alright..." He bought one. The contrast of the chocolate and vanilla reminded Fosco of the black and white of the TV.

They were in the middle of an imposing, yet orderly crowd. Beyond the great glass wall, the countryside was a hodge-podge of smoky stains and slightly clearer areas. The place felt like an amphitheater. A voice from the loudspeakers asked for silence.

"Ladies and gentlemen, attention please. You are about to see the Atmospherion, the revolutionary filtering device by En-plen-air, commonly known as the 'Big Fan'. Experiments have already been conducted in some of the more polluted metropolitan areas. Use the dark shades and remain seated... Ready?"

The room went silent. The lights went out and in the sudden darkness, the dirty gray of the countryside beyond the glass stood out like a TV screen tuned to a dead channel. A sound like an approaching helicopter rose in pitch.

"Ladies and gentlemen, the Atmospherion is 'Go'."

Something outside was happening. Smoky vortices rose; like the prelude to a tornado. Whatever Big Fan was, it was vacuuming up the poisons, possibly filtering them.

"You scared?" Fosco asked. Chiara pressed close to him. Staring wide-eyed out at the countryside she said, "No, Daddy."

The sound of the vortex grew louder, causing the floor and chairs to vibrate.

"Do not be afraid!" the loudspeaker thundered. "It will only take a few more minutes…"

What was happening beyond the glass wall was incredible. Air and land were shaken, beaten, turned over, sucked away. They heard explosions loud as gunshots and thunder, and the floor vibrated as the sky became clearer and clearer. "Your glasses!" warned Fosco.

The light grew insufferable. They were lucky to have the protection of the lenses. Many people were standing and gesturing – talking excitedly. Someone screamed. Close to them, an old lady stood on her chair: *What was happening out there?*

A choir of screams reverberated through the hall. The loudspeaker announced: "You may walk outside now... In an orderly fashion though, please."

Fosco turned to ask Chiara if she wanted to go and look, but he realized the child was already gone.

Dizzily he queued to exit, hoping his daughter would activate her beacon. Bright light, the likes of which he'd never experienced before, flooded down, making him feel as if he were witnessing Judgment Day, or Creation. Tossed about by the crowds, he was finally able to stumble out the door.

The dazzling light blinded him despite his eye protection. Above him, a strange, cloudless sky. He had never seen it so clear. The tornado had dissipated, revealing an explosion of sunlight. No damage had been done to the area, the few trees about were still standing, and yet... Something was different... But what?

Someone tugged at his jacket sleeve. He turned and saw Chiara. She wasn't wearing her protection! He screamed: "Your eyes!"

"But Daddy... it's wonderful," she replied with a smile, jumping up and down. "Don't you see? I knew they would come to be. Dad, I dreamed about them so often!" She crouched.

"Dreamed about them? What are you talking about?" All he could see were the usual sickly assortment of bushes, grass, and flowers. He lifted his shades, nearly blinding himself. All right, something *was* different, but what exactly, he still couldn't say. "What do you mean, Chiara?"

"That gentleman with the white beard, Dad... he asked my name. He was so happy. He was crying, and said to me: Chiara, look closely at the plants and flowers!" And then I saw them. Do you see them too, Daddy? This is *red*, and here's *yellow*, and this one's *blue*. The bearded gentleman explained what they were to me, exactly the way I had dreamed of them! They are called *colors*."

―――――

Vittorio Catani (born July 17, 1940) is an Italian science fiction writer. Born in Lecce, he currently lives and works in Bari, Italy. A retired bank clerk, his first novel, *Gli universi di Moras*, won the Premio Urania in 1990. He has been published in most major newspapers and magazines, and his works have been translated in a number of European countries. He contributes to the daily newspaper *La Gazzetta del Mezzogiorno*, the environmental quarterly "Villaggio Globale", and is one of the editors of both "www.fantascienza.com" and "www.carmillaonline.com". His second science fiction novel, *Il Quinto Principio*, was published in December 2009, again by Urania.
http://www.fantascienza.com/blog/vikkor/

The End of the Royal Palace and the Kingdom
Joji Hayashi
Translated by Erina Fujita

"You've been deceived Father!" said the prince.

The ailing king wasn't surprised to hear that, because he had told his father the same thing.

He had been younger than the prince when he had complained to his father. He had never understood how the world worked and what the king's duties were.

"What? Who's deceived me?" said the king.

"Dearly-departed grandfather, or someone else..."

"Do you really think so? So in turn, you think I'll deceive you?"

"Well... I wouldn't go that far..."

The prince wasn't a stupid man, but logic wasn't his strong suit either. It was natural though, as he had met less than ten people in his entire life.

The population of the royal palace had been in steady decline for many years. There had been nearly been a hundred people in the palace when the king had been a child. During his father's childhood, there had been two-hundred.

During the king's grandfather's reign, there had been as many as five hundred people.

Unfortunately, the population had started decreasing during that time. By the time the prince was born, there had been less than twenty people in the palace.

Now the sick king and his son were alone.

"Must I become the king, Father?"

"You have no choice. You're the prince."

"But, nobody thanks you for the work you do."

"You idiot! I don't rule the kingdom because I want the people to thank me. Nobody knows we govern them. That's what governing is all about."

"Are there even any people in this country? I've never seen any."

"They live outside the palace. So of course you haven't seen anyone. However, even though we don't see them, they need our governance. That is the evidence that they exist. Understand? If you do, go and govern!"

The prince left the king's bedroom, in well-worn work clothes. The king turned on the monitors in front of his bed. There were sixteen monitors arranged four-by-four, but only four were operational.

The royal palace was falling into ruin. The king knew this. The reason for the population decline was that the machinery maintained by the palace was aging.

One of the monitors showed the prince. The king monitored to give him advice when necessary.

There were countless pipes and pumps in the palace. Five hundred people once managed them.

However, the population of the palace has declined, and the prince was the only person to rule over the kingdom, so to speak, to control the equipment.

There had been an auto-control system until the reign of his grandfather. The system no longer worked, and the equipment had to be adjusted by hand.

Today once again the king made a proclamation to the people, wanting them to help themselves. They lived in big cities upon the earth, far above the royal palace. The palace was a plant for recycling and purifying sewage from cities. If this system stopped, the kingdom would be destroyed. That's why the royal family controlled the system for generations. The king had been told so.

He finished posting his proclamation and sent it to the above-ground networks as he always did. However, never once had he received a reply from the people.

The king despaired at the people's stupidity. He was going to die. His son wouldn't live much longer, because the royal family wasn't allowed to leave the palace. The royal line would end with the prince. It would mean the end of human life above ground. Nevertheless, the people had never given a single thought to the palace.

Suddenly, an alarm went off. The king switched monitors. A section of pipe had burst and the prince was trying to fix it.

"Look out!" cried the king.

To shut off the pipe, the prince raised the pressure in an adjacent tank. The tank ruptured. The prince was killed instantaneously.

Unbeknownst to the people living in the cities above, the royal palace welcomed the end, and the kingdom was destroyed.

Joji Hayashi, born 1962, is a Japanese novelist who is a member of the Science Fiction and Fantasy Writers of Japan and the Space Authors Club. Primarily a hard SF author, he has written both original work as well as several novels in the Gundam universe. He also writes non-fiction military history.
http://www.asahi-net.or.jp/~zq9j-hys/

The X-ray
Kevin David Anderson

It's never easy to tell a couple that their cat is deathly ill, but it's part of my job as a veterinarian. I explain their pet's affliction as sympathetically as I can, making constant eye contact to monitor their understanding. Often, the words are not enough to convey what is happening, so I show them the x-ray.

It is an unpleasant but necessary visual. In black and white, they can see the tumors growing in the stomach and throat. I pause to allow them to digest the horrific information, which glows on the wall, irrefutable as it hangs. It must feel like a kick in the gut.

I then steer the conversation toward options and the man will usually grimace at the cost of surgery.

"Forty-eight hundred dollars," I say. "But that doesn't include the cost of rehab and pain medication, should the animal even survive the procedure."

At this point they usually bring up the subject of the final option. I carefully explain the process, emphasizing as much as possible that their pet will feel no pain.

I give them a few minutes alone so they can discuss their choices, but I can see it in their eyes as I step from the room, their decision has been made.

Some couples like to be in the room as I administer the poison. But most, like this one, prefer to remember their pet in life, and bid the cat a tearful farewell. When they are ready, I usher them towards the waiting room, where my assistant will walk them through disposal and billing options.

When I am finally alone with the animal I put on a fresh pair of thick rubber gloves, so thick no cat claw can penetrate. Before I proceed with my fun, I tuck the X-ray away into a most special file. One that is easily accessible, over, and over again.

Kevin David Anderson is a former marketing and public relations professional turned fiction writer. His short stories have appeared in the pages of Dark Animus, Dark Wisdom, Darkness Rising, and a bunch of other publications with the word dark in the title. His stories are also available in audio, on podcasts like Pseudopod and the Drabblecast. His novel *Night of the Living Trekkies* was released in 2010 from Quirk Books. He lives in Southern California and you can find him at: http://www.KevinDavidAnderson.com

The Mermaid Princess' Love, Curse and...
Tamao Kanroji
Translated by Ewen Cluney

I was 24 years old back then. I was young, fearless, and all too foolish.

I had heard that a beautiful, man-eating mermaid had been seen in a certain harbor. Even though I was sure it was merely rumor, my curiosity lead me to said harbor one moonlit night.

High in the sky a full moon lit the night.

"I've been waiting."

The moment she called to me – the very moment I spun my head around to set eyes on her – I fell in love.

This was a girl so beautiful she defied description. Her long hair shone as though made of gold.

So deeply I had already fallen in love that I didn't care she wasn't completely human. From below her navel, her body was like that of a fish. When she noticed my intense gaze on that part of her, her smile broadened.

"Waiting? What do you mean?" I asked.

"I knew. Ever since you were little, I knew you were going to become my husband," she replied in a sweet voice. "As the daughter of the mermaid queen, knowing my future love is one of my special gifts. I've loved you for a long time. Now that I can bear children, I have called you."

Her voice took hold of my soul, and I just listened as though in a dream. I would do anything if only I could be with this woman.

"Ah... The tide is going out... It's time..." She slid off the pier, her beautiful face suddenly twisting, her body writhing. "I will lay my eggs... And then you will plant your seed in them... And then our children will break free into the sea."

It's embarrassing to admit, but the mere sound of her voice already had my manhood raging painfully against my jeans. "Alright." My excitement was so intense that I barely squeezed the word out of my dry throat.

She cried out, and began to lay her eggs.

In great number they suddenly started spilling from her abdomen; each covered in a round, transparent membrane.

"Hurry..." she gasped. "Your seed..."

I wanted to respond to her plea. I really did. But the moment I saw the "eggs," my excitement withered at the disgusting sight. My lust simply vanished, and, unable to stay standing, I fell on my backside.

The embryos inside each transparent egg were human on top and fish on the bottom. Flabby, pale white things with red blood vessels running all over their bodies. Sickening monsters.

She finished laying her eggs and cried out again. "Please, hurry! You must or else they will die!"

Suddenly, her expression changed. It became a fearsome visage the likes of which I had never seen.

Exposed to the open air, the eggs began to decay and gave off the stench of rotten fish.

"Traitor!" she shrieked out. "You have shamed a mermaid princess! And just as a mermaid's love is eternal, so is her curse. Feel my wrath!"

She used the sharp claws on her long fingers to shred the flesh from her own arm and thrust it, dripping wet with blood, into my mouth.

"Humans who consume the flesh and blood of a mermaid become immortal. May you regret your sin forever!" She laughed as she plunged into the reflection of the full moon on the surface of the sea.

The taste of her flesh was too delicious by far. I could not help myself. I devoured it.

Since then, I have not aged, and I cannot die. I've tried to kill myself countless times, but it seems nothing can kill me. I have no need of food or drink anymore either.

How many years, how many millennia, have passed?

Civilization has come to an end, and human beings have gone extinct. The plants have had their way with the skyscrapers and the homes alike, turning them into a magnificent jungle.

"Snap out of it."

I would be lying if I said the voice didn't startle me. I had grown tired of life, grown slow to respond to anything. I sluggishly turned my head toward the voice.

Her clothes were ragged, but she was nonetheless dressed for a journey. Not only that, but she had two fine legs.

"For the sin of losing my children, I was changed into a human. It took me some time to find you. You haven't stayed in any one place for very long."

"A mermaid's love is eternal…"

"And so is her curse. But in this body, I can have human children. That's something to rejoice, isn't it?" Her alluring voice had not changed.

We took each other in a firm embrace… and kissed for the very first time.

Tamao Kanroji first debuted in 1990 under another name. She is a folklorist and a historian. Her work ranges from comedy to horror and science fiction, especially Lovecraft-related stories. She comes from an ancient and respected lineage of some 1600 years, which causes her no end of grief. Her short story "The Taste of Snake's Honey" was published in the anthology *Inverted*

Kingdom (vol. 2 of *Lairs of Hidden Gods*).
http://www.facebook.com/people/Tamao-Kanroji/100001993434450

Walking the Hog
(A Jerry Cornelius Story)
Michael Moorcock

1.

The new Pera could never be to Jerry's taste. He had been born in ruins and run down glory and it was always a comfort to visit your childhood. Now there was a powerful movement to abolish the past in all its complexity and replace it with a simplified child's version easily manipulated by populist politics. When you walked into the Pera Pelas these days the old gilt and plush was gone, replaced by the smell of frying bacon.

"Not much of an improvement, I'd say," grumbled Major Nye staring at his plate of international porridge. With a sigh he reached for the salt, changed his mind and took up the sugar shaker instead. "Oh, my lord! I do apologise." He had knocked over condiments which even now dripped on the bright patent leather of Dr Didi Dee's fashionable Louboutins. The eight inch heels took a fox-trot step backward. Didi worked hard to keep her image. She was a model, as she pointed out frequently on television, to all the Afro-American girls out there with dreams; she was the new Oprah. Once again Jerry wondered if the demagogue came first and gathered the crowd or the crowd created its own creatures out of whole clay. He skirted the drooling bottles and made the usual gentlemanly courtesies in which Didi so delighted. Slowly withdrawing her hand she shook back the hair of her new Ravemaven wig and sat down with him at a table less brightly lit than the others. Once the lounge abounded with discrete, dark corners, the murmur of a million plots. Or was he morphing his memory into an urban myth?

You had to avoid such processes at all costs or there was no point in being immortal. Someone had to retain the past's complexity. That, surely, was what everybody prayed for and why prayer took on a far more spiritual perspective in secular nations like France and England?

"You still favour the longer style of haircut, I see." Didi's glowing black eyes looked critically into her Martini. "No, I mean it. It suits you. You wouldn't be Jerry Cornelius otherwise, always trapped a minute or two in the future, a minute or so in the past. Time-thief. Culture vampire. Identity provider. I'm not complaining, sweetheart. We all go to university, these days. Your instinctive style never gets old."

"Happy to oblige," Jerry looked around the early morning restaurant. His work here was done. He took pleasure in Didi's coded small talk washing over him. Her father had been a high-ranking KGB colonel and she had grown up reading Paustovski and the other survivors of the Stalin days. Some of them had to be understood on so many levels they were almost infinitely divinable.

Language had become another of her first line of defences. She carried more armour than *The Alaskan Queen*. And, because he had no desire to penetrate those defences, they were friends.

Major Nye was still apologizing. Jerry noticed that his old friends' cuffs were beginning to fray and that his jacket was a little too big. The suit had been made in the day when, quite unconsciously the major had carried more muscle. Jermyn Street once seethed with chaps from the colonies buying their discrete weaves and pinstripes. These days even the Foreign Office ordered its suits from Hong Kong and Mombai. The UK had too few patterns to choose from.

2.

JERRY JUMPED SHIP in Bangkok. He was tired of working with crews of Burmese slaves and their cruel Thai masters. Three public torturing and two killings were in his view a wasteful way of catching fish. The slave trade lacked all its old ethics. His father would never have permitted such treatment.

At the Wonshott Hotel he arranged to meet Prince Wu Ling, last of the Ming pretenders. He owned property in Shanghai and Macao and had many investments on the Pacific Rim. He wanted Jerry to get him six new Bristols which his drivers could ferry to Paris.

"That's at least two years production!"

"I didn't say when I wanted them, Mr Cornelius." The prince examined the bottom of his teacup. "I'm a patient man, as you surely know. That's the secret of my success. The business community has been waiting since 1940 for this moment. Another decade and we shall no longer need to pretend. We shall have private armies larger than the nation's. Democracy gives the population the illusion of control. Teams to support. The communists and other authoritarian governments are learning this. Not many of us will survive the century, Mr C."

Jerry parted the curtains and stared down at the distant street. "This probably isn't the best place to look for jeans."

"Oh, you have a year or two left."

Jerry wondered if he had any children to remember.

3.

JERRY GOT OFF the train in Or-du-bain. The green and white peaks neatly surrounded him on three sides. On the fourth side blue water rose slowly to join the pink and gold dawn. He had made a long journey, through a dozen time zones and twelve distinct versions of recent history, had been thrown off the train in Geneva and had hardly got back on again. He really was getting too old for this. And as for faking another poet, he thought he would rather throw up.

"I blame the drugs." With an expert smile the old aristocrat removed his hat, extending his hand. "On time as usual, old boy."

"That's not what everyone says." Jerry looked with distaste at the parked

Smart car. "Is that for all of us?"

"Both." Prince Lobkowitz grew impatient with his friend's reluctance to march to the new tunes.

"All?" Jerry was still having difficulties with his identities. "But you told me that these wind farms are destabilizing the weather?"

"That's what the figures suggest. We have the technologies in place now. There's precious little chance of us replicating earlier mistakes. All we need to do is slow down a little. Wu Ling thinks it's the secret. I gather you disagree."

"It's not that." Jerry lifted an apologetic shoulder. "I don't care. I'm used to speed. You know how that one goes."

"Speed? It's a drug, surely?"

Jerry sniffed. "That's true of everything. Do you know the exact time?"

"Today?"

"Take your pick."

"Well, this is Switzerland, after all. I've never heard so much ticking."

"Persevere. It's in here somewhere."

Prince Lobkowitz pursed his lips.

Jerry could tell that he would get away with nothing of any value if he stayed too long in this environment. From somewhere came the familiar strains of Jerusalem. What was the point of looking for old clues? The new ones were just as useful. "But what do we need all this energy for?"

The old aristocrat shrugged. "I don't know. Take your pick. Music? Hospitals?" With some embarrassment he replaced his dove-grey homburg on his glittering hair and led the way towards the car where his liveried servants were carefully harnessing the horses.

4.

M. PARDON MADE an awkward, embarrassed gesture towards his hastily knotted tie. "You're looking for an Oriental solution to an Occidental problem, aren't you? It isn't all about domes and towers. I suppose I'll never get used to your terrible short-cuts. They'd kill me, I know." His little pink cheeks were spotted red, as if he'd been bitten.

They were meeting in their usual rendez-vous where the Canal St Martin's glassy green water plunged underground beneath a bust of the actor Lemaitre who looked a little desperately across the Rue Faubourg du Temple towards the statue of La Grisette. *Les Enfants du Paradis!* Both pieces of sculpture had grown a little greyer since he had last seen them.

Jerry waved his bandaged hand. "I got this in Tanzania."

"A bite?"

"Where do you suggest?"

The Frenchman waved his manicured hand towards Le Phare over on the corner near the Franc Prix's displays of cut flowers. Jerry could smell them from here. All those colours! At the restaurant waiters were setting the outside tables for lunch. "The quiche is always good."

Arm in arm the two men crossed the street. Jerry breathed in the sudden waft of warm tar. This heat-wave was likely to last for the rest of the year.

"Tanzania, eh?" M. Pardon chose a table. "A special kind of monarch. Johannus Carolignas, maybe?"

"Always." Jerry leered as only one of his age and background could. "Firbank's for the memory."

"Shouldn't that be mammary?"

M. Pardon sat down carefully with his back to the square. "Oh, lord. Time's sliding back to the Stone Age. Isn't it?" He sighed as he took in the lunch menu. "What's to be done? What's to be done?"

Jerry checked the blackboard menu. "Is that the only way out?"

"Of course. Unless you want to get back to the Aegean. All that ancient limestone. Those early artists! Primitives?"

"Apart from the toilets? Yes?" Jerry had lost interest in the arts. Graffiti still engaged him sometimes. He fingered his fly.

M. Pardon was ahead of him. "My hand has only to move a little to the right and you will never find your fantasy world again, my old mon vieux..."

Jerry did what he could to hide his disappointment. He turned his head, listening. Somewhere in the distance, possibly La Villette, pocket battleships fought gun to gun. It was impossible, these days, to enjoy a quiet evening at home.

Lunch quickly over, M. Pardon pulled on a lilac glove, placed a lilac homburg on his head and, signalling for Jerry to rise, guided him up Rue Faubourg du Temple to Avenue Parmentier and the entrance of the Goncourt metro. "There's much to be said, M. Cornelius, for living *La Vie Imaginaire*. And anyone can do it without too much of an effort, in one way or another. But, let's face it, the alternative hasn't done anyone much good. Who's living in a fantasy world? Obama or Danny the D&D freak? Believe me, you'd be wise to stay in Narnia."

Jerry spat dramatically into the gutter.

"What's up?" asked M. Pardon.

"Nothing," said Jerry. "Just a frog in my throat."

"Is it over yet?" Pardon seemed in an unusually obstructive mood. He pointed up into the west. Above them, more or less following Avenue Parmentier, the sky was full of drones. "You take from the State, you take from the People. The theft of the People's wealth has become routine."

"Who are we fighting now?"

"WalMart." Pardon's eyes had a sort of glee. "Now, I was going to suggest you visit my friend Cantonlac. He practises Chinese medicine, these days."

"Really?" Jerry remembered the first time he had come across Cantonlac eating a big cane roach in mistake for a date and then insisting it tasted like fried chicken. "Call me old-fashioned but I think I'll wait to see my GP in London."

M. Pardon began to descend the steps into the metro. Jerry refused to follow him. He cast about for transport. He really did need to get to Bengazi.

"Oh, take my boat if you must. It's in Deauville. The usual mooring." He looked up through the railings, his eyes full of tears. "Ownership of the world is now almost wholly in the hands of the great Brand Families. It suits us to remain discreet. Just as the dictatorships made one last ditch stand to form a true republic before collapsing."

Frowning, Jerry framed a question but Pardon had vanished.

Jerry, turning back towards Republique, thought of the Grand Khan of China, who ruled an empire of many millions. He wondered if it were still relatively easy to get to the Far Indies where he had hoped to join the entourage of the fabled King of the Christian East, Prester John. They had once marched together against the so-called Six Pagan Lords of the Congo, being narrowly defeated at Kananga.

But those were the easy years, he thought, before the spread of sophisticated firepower when a man with a sword looked good on a camel.

Jerry sighed and turned up the collar of his black car coat. Where were the legends of yesteryear? Jill Bell had once taken fifty men with her into the Tanzanian wilderness and created an empire. Who would try that now without backup from China, India, Russia or at least some high-profile sportswear brand?

5.
SITTING ON A toilet just outside Karachi, Jerry read a yellowing newspaper. On the other side of the door he could hear the TV conversation clearly. Chiefly for his benefit his host had clicked on CNN.

"It was a bloody few hours, the People's Revolt," declared ex-President Hershey-Heinz, stepping down from the throne he'd occupied for less than three years. After handing his fortune over to the people he had flown from Havana to Kingston, where Keith Richards had offered to go bond for him. The ex-president's family had bankrolled the Stones' last tour Old Men Know Best, perhaps their most successful. Jerry remembered meeting Hershey-Heinz backstage. The Fix were opening for the Stones. They had all grown up together. Jerry, of course, still looked about thirty and had died eight times to his certain knowledge. *You'd think with all that experience I'd be a better musician.* He still had trouble tuning his Rickenbacker 12.

Everywhere in the region coups established fresh governments, most of them popular, and began the clean-up as they called it. Jerry wasn't at all sure he was enjoying Utopia. He could see that this was going to be a decade of upheaval and only a rough settling of the political landscape. Elected representation came and went so quickly, these days. Didi had estimated that there was a new fair and legal election held in the world about once every two-

and-a-half minutes.

Wiping his bottom on the news, Jerry contemplated a quick trip into 1965 to see his mum. Mrs Cornelius had a way of helping him get re-orientated. He turned up the volume on his headphones. Dead Giveaway were singing their latest hit, "The Infant Disposal Song" from their album *Life in Our New Cemetery*.

He had already heard the thunder and now as he stepped out of the shed it began to rain heavily. Was this how it would be from now on?

6.
THE FIX WERE back together. Jerry had managed a couple of rehearsals in New Delhi. The songs were mostly his but he found them hard to remember. He had been away from Louisiana too long.

"Jackhammer Jack never runs with the pack.
Jackhammer Jack don't cut you no slack.
Jackhammer Jack got a fine new shack –
By the muddy Mississippi where the alligators at."

He had raised the stand so he had to strain to reach the mike. It gave the impression that he was trying harder than he actually was.

Outside in the mud the audience was slowly coming together, singing along with the band. There was nothing like performing for a bunch of people who knew and enjoyed your stuff.

He was briefly nostalgic for the old days when they had gone out as Pegleg Pierre and his Cajun Rhythm Kids. Katrina had scotched that. Now everyone but him had to sit down to play. He thought back to those innocent times. He had been in love with a sculptress called Winnie Two. One day she had presented him with something she had been working on in secret. "There you are," she had said. "I've made you a rose."

He still had it somewhere.

He took a sweet breath of the dusty old air. It had not rained anywhere in this State or Mississippi or Texas for almost two years. For a while, before the band reformed, he had run illegal Evian to Baton Rouge in regular Exxon trucks. The stuff always smelled faintly of gasoline. The city was still in the process of suing Hannibal, Missouri, for damning the river upstream.

Jerry was enjoying being on stage again but even so he would be glad to be back in 1970 in a world where he had been able to count his identities.

7.
"ONLY BY ACCEPTING the miraculous can we begin to rescue ourselves. Mutuality is the natural condition of human kind. It was our willingness to help one another out which got us through the Stone Age. Our misplaced

pragmatism, our misdirected reliance on materialism as a moral and economic system, determines our desperate times. We could have created a decent, trusting world if we had invested the same effort we put into trying to destroy one another. Religion? Maybe. But not as we know it..." Professor Hira, the chubby Brahmin, paused his V and started his lecture again. He had to be word perfect by Sunday. He reached to press the record button of his Sony ICD PX139 and looked up as Jerry entered his office.

"Oh, good lord Jerry. You do pick some bad times. I'm up to my eyebrows in work!"

"Glad to hear it, prof." Jerry was brash, just back from his base and looking a bit pale. "Hope they're paying well."

Hira's expression showed he still found Jerry irredeemably vulgar. "I heard Didi and you had fallen out. Some lie she thought you'd told."

"Lies? Oh, yes. They've multiplied. Like flies." He smiled. "They keep the sun off the meat."

Hira wasn't amused. "Never have so many human souls lied themselves to perdition." He wiped his mouth. "The lie is necessary currency in our contemporary world. Everyone is good at it. Some are very, very good. We judge a person's character by their ability to fib. Some consider themselves artists and embellish their stories. Some work to make them true. I'm watching them as best I can but it's the ones who attempt to turn lies into truth you really have to watch, you know."

"I thought everyone did that."

Hira preferred to take Jerry seriously. "Reality only rarely survives their abuse. And they, poor creatures, are assigned to that unholy pit, where great wealth can be found, where every lie is rewarded, where every reality is in fragments, where gloom, despair and disappointment are felt for eternity. But you already know my math. Radiant time and so on."

To Jerry, Hira sounded a bit confused. "Have you been dabbling in religion again, prof?"

Hira was wounded by this. "Religion is my life. Do you know how long I prayed before I agreed to be part of this new energy investigation? Solar power? Tidal power? Wind power? All require considerable contemplation. Fire, water, air..." He shrugged and then resumed his position. His body language wanted Jerry to leave.

"No earth?" Callously, Jerry lit a long Sherman's and flipped a dead match into his old friend's wastebin.

"Earth is what we're trying to save." Hira got a big white handkerchief from his pocket and blew his nose. From somewhere outside the sound was repeated by a bull elephant sensing the presence of a female. With a shudder, Hira replaced the linen in the pocket of his white, baggy trousers. "You can't remain cynical about this, Jerry. The human race could be looking at annihilation!"

"Serves it bloody well right," said Jerry. "It's the animals I feel sorry for. Don't you? They didn't really have much to do with creating the situation. Still, when you got to go you got to go, eh? Or am I wrong?"

"You're impossible, Jerry." Hira struck what he hoped was an impatient pose.

"No, prof." Jerry turned to leave. "Just a bit unlikely."

8.

DIDI DEE ROCKED on her heels, hardly noticing Jerry as he slipped back into her bedroom and kissed her lightly on her bare shoulder. She was trying to get the wrinkles out of her slip. "I should have done my ironing today."

Jerry showed her what he had found.

She stared unintelligently at the figures and diagrams, reading the fading words. "Radiant Time? What the fuck is that?" She gave them back to him, rubbing her arm.

Jerry rolled them tightly and snapped the bands back. He wondered how Didi could punch his buttons in that way. Turning up the collar of his black car coat he opened the door and walked downstairs. He was beginning to regret becoming his father's executor. It wasn't as if the house was worth much. The faux-Le Courbusier walls were beginning to lean outwards and the top floor threatened to fall in. He left by the front door.

A few moments later he had revved the engine of the old Duesenberg and thoughtfully put it in gear. The rhythm of the engine echoed the beat of her heels as she descended the spiral staircase. "I'm coming with you."

Jerry sniffed nostalgically. Speed was speed. Didi knew how best to haunt him.

He waited while she settled herself in the passenger seat. With a sigh, he took off the handbrake and turned on the music.

"What's the time?" he said. "My watch has stopped."

Born in London, Michael Moorcock is credited with captaining the mix of experimental writing and SF known as the New Wave. He has won most major SF awards and The Guardian Fiction Prize, Whitbread short list with Mother London and has published a number of prize-winning novels both in genre and out of it. As a musician he received a gold disc with *Hawkwind* and still works with his own band, The Deep Fix. His first Jerry Cornelius novel *The Final Programme* was filmed with John Finch, Sterling Haden, Hugh Griffiths, Jenny Runacre, George Coularis and Patrick McGee. http://www.multiverse.org/

That Long Day
Shinya Gaku
Translated by Erina Fujita

It was the day of my annual medical checkup.

Not being much of a morning person, I had made an appointment at a clinic for 3pm. I took the Tozai-Line to Monzen-nakacho from Takadanobaba, which is where I work. The clinic at Monzen-nakacho where I had made my appointment is run by an old friend of mine from high school. The area around Monzen-nakacho is called Fukagawa, which is located within the old Shitamachi area of Tokyo (formerly Edo). Fukagawa is popular as a setting for historical novels and many of my detective stories take place in this area. And yet, I didn't have the slightest inkling of the disaster that was about to befall Fukagawa of all places. I don't believe anyone who experienced that huge earthquake thought it would strike. Sure, they had "expected" it, as all people living in Tokyo do, but they hadn't actually thought it would hit. In the days and weeks after, the media covered the earthquake repeatedly, calling it one of the most powerful on record. In fact, it was like nothing I had ever experienced during my entire sixty-three years on this planet.

It happened just as I had crossed a pedestrian crossing in front of Hojoin. By curious coincidence, this temple is also known as "Fukagawa Enma", which means "Ruler of Hell." The buildings on the other side of the temple shook violently. Tall buildings, narrow as pencils, shook as if they would come crashing down upon me. Above my head, thick electric wires whipped around like skipping ropes. I ran into the middle of the road. Usually it would be full of traffic, but the cars had all come to a standstill. As I ran, I wondered whether the ground beneath my feet would open up. It felt like I was witnessing the end of the world. Less tactfully, it felt like I was watching a 3D disaster film. Quite simply, my sense of reality had gone completely out of the window.

It was probably this lack of reality which, in spite of the quake, made it possible for me to continue to the clinic for my medical checkup as scheduled. A nurse recorded my height and weight, as well as my blood pressure. The moment she tried to take blood from my vein with a needle however, another earthquake struck. An aftershock. This was no time to be giving blood. I rushed out of the building with the nurse. The aftershock was so powerful that pieces of walls from nearby buildings collapsed and holes began to appear in them. When it was over, I returned to the clinic and completed my checkup, including an electrocardiogram, visceral examination, and X-rays of my chest and stomach. Other aftershocks were less powerful than the first one, but yet I'm at a loss for my ability to continue with the checkup as the disaster continued to unfold. On the surface, both my friend the doctor and I were calm enough, but the truth is that we felt was anything but.

As evidence of, I was under the impression that it would be possible for me to take the metro home that evening. I also believed that I would be able to make it to Takadanobaba in time; I had planned to meet up with some friends at a pub at 7pm. However, every single train in the Tokyo area, including the metro, JR and private railways, had stopped running. Thus, I made a snap decision to walk rather than take a train. I walked from Fukagawasagacho to Kayabacho, crossing Eitai Bridge over the Sumida River. Looking at the water from the bridge, I was confused into thinking that the river flowed upstream toward Asakusa, not to Tokyo Bay which is downstream. From Kayabacho, I passed Nihonbashi to Tokyo Station. The streets were filled with those who, like me, were struggling to get home. I kept walking and passed Sakuradamon, Hanzomon, Ichigaya and Waseda, all the while picking my way through vast crowds of people. It was just before 10pm when I finally arrived at Takadanobaba. All in all, I had walked for more than five hours.

The pub where I had planned to go for a drink with my friends was open, but I thought it unlikely that anyone would show up. After waiting for a while, I went to my office on the ninth floor of a multi-tenant building. Entering the dining room, I found plates and glasses scattered all over the floor. In my study, more than half of the books had tumbled off the bookshelves, and a frame on the wall had fallen off and broken. It would require time and effort to tidy up. In fact, it would probably take me a whole day. I accepted the situation and went outside, upon which I was greeted by the fortuitous news that train services had just been resumed. At Takadanobaba Station, I found out that the Seibu Shinjuku Line would be operating irregularly throughout the night. The trains were crowded as expected. They traveled so slowly that it seemed to take me twice as long to get to my destination as it normally would have. I finally arrived at Sayamashi Station, the nearest station to my house, and got home safely at around 2am.

It was not until I got home that I found out that the north-east of Japan was the worst affected by the earthquake. Late night TV programs showed videos of how coastal towns had been swept away by a massive tsunami. I was at a complete loss for words. Then it suddenly hit me that the Sumida River flowing upstream yesterday evening might not have been an illusion after all.

―――

Shinya Gaku (born November 5th, 1947) is a Japanese author. Born in Tokyo, Mr. Gaku graduated from Keio University and completed graduate studies in sociology there. He made his authorial debut while still in college with travelogues of India, writing guides and essays in 1966. After turning 50, he started to write many historical novels, historical essays and the like. He once served as a visiting professor at the Bunri University of Hospitality and currently works as a lecturer at Housei University.

Acknowledgments

I wish to thank every single person who contributed in any way to this project. *Kizuna: Fiction for Japan* could not have been possible without your invaluable efforts, and I apologize for not being able to thank a single one of you in-person. The following folks have my undying gratitude:

Japanese Translators
Norimitsu Kaiho, Erina Fujita, James A. Smith, Takeo Konno, Kaori Miyake/James Benson, Kazushi Nagayama, Ken Kusuki, Dan Luffey, Yuli K. Bethe, Andy Kitkowski, Orie Hiromachi, Ewen Cluney, Matthew Sanchez, Mamoru Masuda

Japanese Translation and Editorial Coordinator
Kiyoshi Yamagata

Italian Translator
Davide Mana

French Translator
Kirsten Alene

Spanish Translator
David Church Rodríguez

Translation Consultants
Edward Lipsett, Mark Williams, Peter Durfee, Jason Gray, James "ElevenColors", "K"

Proofreaders
Glynn Barrass, Richard Salter, Jason Wuchenich, Lee Pletzers, Ted O'Neill, Oluwatoyin Oluwole, "K", Jenny Silver, Garrett Cook, Jonathan Moon, Andersen Prunty, Curt Seubert, Melissa J White

Cover Design and Related
Christian Krank (front/back cover) @ http://facebook.com/deadearthcomic
Jason Wuchenich (webpage buttons & banners)
David Naughton-Shires (Back/spine design & Facebook icons) [first pages]

Interior Format Design Consultation (Terrific ebook/web design services!)

Melissa J White @ http://www.whitespacecreative.com
The Mad Formatter @ http://www.themadformatter.com

Press Release
Jess Gulbranson and Kid.

Special Thanks to
Michael Maher King @ Smile Kids Japan
"Our Man in Abiko", editor of *2:46: Aftershocks: Stories from the Japan Earthquake* (aka Quakebook)
Kal Masunari

Contact Brent Millis

Kizuna.Charity@gmail.com

Any mistakes contained within this volume are mine, and mine alone.
Brent Millis.

CPSIA information can be obtained at www.ICGtesting.com
Printed in the USA
LVOW101701100613

337847LV00017B/1035/P

9 781466 223172